A Moment on the Lips

Jennifer Faye

Lazy Dazy Press

Copyright © 2015 by Jennifer F. Stroka

All rights reserved.

No portion of this book may be reproduced in any form without written permission from the publisher or author, except as permitted by U.S. copyright law.

This is a work of fiction. All characters and events portrayed in this book are fictional and a product of the author's imagination. Any similarities to real people, living or dead, is purely coincidental and unintentional.

Published by Lazy Dazy Press

Thanks & much appreciation to:

Content Editor: Tessa Shapcott

Copy Editor: Joyce Lamb

Whistlestop Romance series:

Book 1: A Moment to Love

Book 2: A Moment to Dance

Book 3: A Moment on the Lips

Book 4: A Moment to Cherish

Book 5: A Moment at Christmas

Contents

About this book...	v
1. CHAPTER ONE	1
2. CHAPTER TWO	15
3. CHAPTER THREE	27
4. CHAPTER FOUR	37
5. CHAPTER FIVE	51
6. CHAPTER SIX	67
7. CHAPTER SEVEN	78
8. CHAPTER EIGHT	87
9. CHAPTER NINE	101
10. CHAPTER TEN	112
11. CHAPTER ELEVEN	129
12. CHAPTER TWELVE	138
13. CHAPTER THIRTEEN	148
14. CHAPTER FOURTEEN	158
15. CHAPTER FIFTEEN	167
16. CHAPTER SIXTEEN	174

17.	CHAPTER SEVENTEEN	186
18.	CHAPTER EIGHTEEN	193
19.	CHAPTER NINETEEN	204
20.	CHAPTER TWENTY	214
21.	CHAPTER TWENTY-ONE	224
22.	CHAPTER TWENTY-TWO	236
23.	CHAPTER TWENTY-THREE	246
24.	CHAPTER TWENTY-FOUR	258
25.	CHAPTER TWENTY-FIVE	263
26.	CHAPTER TWENTY-SIX	271
27.	CHAPTER TWENTY-SEVEN	276
28.	CHAPTER TWENTY-EIGHT	284
29.	CHAPTER TWENTY-NINE	296
30.	CHAPTER THIRTY	304
	Afterword	310
	About Author	311
	Also By	312

About this book...

A bakery. A coffeeshop. And a sweet dog in need of a new home.

Baker Piper Noble owns the Poppin' Fresh Bakery. With its huge popularity, she's ready to expand into the vacant retail space next door. But when the property is sold before she can make an offer, her grand plans grind to a sudden halt.

Barista Joe Montoya has taken a big risk returning to Whistle Stop with his plans to open Fill-It-Up-Joe. But with his disastrous marriage over, it's time for a fresh start, including opening a coffee shop. Though his neighbor, with her honeyed smile for everyone but him and her curvy goodness, is none too happy about his business moving in next door to hers.

However, when Piper and Joe are elected as co-chairs of Autumn Fest to help the town's revitalization project, they must find a way to work together. In the process, they just might find a new appreciation for each other and perhaps a lot more...

CHAPTER ONE

M*m...*
Piper Noble's tongue tingled with the anticipation of savoring a sweet treat.

"Tell me you aren't going to eat that." The all-too-familiar voice carried with it disgust.

How could anyone find a cupcake offensive?

Piper frowned as her gaze moved from the freshly decorated cupcake in her hand to her mother, who'd just stepped inside Poppin' Fresh Bakery. Lines of disapproval creased her mother's perfectly made-up face.

A frustrated sigh slipped passed Piper's lips as she lowered the treat. "Good morning, Mother."

"That's not the way to have a good morning, with all of those calories. I thought I taught you better."

When would her mother give up trying to control her life? After all, she'd started this bakery all on her own. She'd have thought that, instead of nitpicking, her mother would be proud of her accomplishments. She vowed to never ever meddle in someone's life the way her mother did in hers.

Deciding not to argue and ruin the beautiful day, Piper took a different approach. "It's a new recipe.

Mocha chocolate cherry." Piper waved the culinary decadence in front of her mother, hoping to tempt her into having a bite. "Give it a try it. I promise it's not deadly."

Instead of cracking even the tiniest smile, her mother pursed her lips, and her pencil-perfect brows knit together. "Honestly, Piper, you aren't a young girl anymore. When will you ever show some restraint and act your age?"

A sharp retort teetered on the tip of Piper's tongue. With difficulty, she choked it down. She refused to argue with her mother in her place of business—not that it'd do her any good.

At twenty-six, she thought she'd done well for herself. Now seemed like the time to tell her mother what she'd been holding back, an announcement that was bound to gain her mother's approval.

She glanced toward the tables lining the front of the bakery where Mr. Wilks, an older gentleman, was enjoying his usual breakfast—a blueberry muffin and black coffee—while perusing the morning paper. He glanced up and smiled at her before returning his attention to the paper.

He was such a kind man. His best friend had been his dog until it passed away, leaving him alone with no family and no faithful companion. Her heart went out to him.

Not worried about Mr. Wilks repeating her exchange with her mother, Piper straightened her shoulders. It was time to tell her mother the news. A broad smile pulled at her lips. This was sure to impress her mother.

When she spoke, it was in hushed tones. "You know the business has been doing really well. So well, in fact, that I'm planning to expand into the vacant space next door."

Her mother was quiet for a moment as though digesting the news. *What was there to think about?* It wasn't like she was asking for a loan. For once, she just wanted her mother to be happy for her.

Her mother adjusted the strap of her knock-off designer purse. "Interesting. And I suppose you'll still be selling more of these sweets. I don't know why you couldn't be more like your brother. His investment firm is really taking off."

Actually, it was an accounting firm, but Piper knew better than to argue the detail with her mother. It just wasn't worth the aggravation. "And I'm happy for him, but that isn't what I want to do with my life. I don't like working with numbers."

"You know his upcoming wedding will be the highlight of the town."

"His wedding isn't for months." Her older brother, Mason, was forever her mother's favorite. He could do no wrong. Piper sighed. It wasn't his fault. He was a pretty great guy. She just wished her mother would quit comparing them, because Piper would always come up lacking as far as her mother was concerned.

"And your wedding would have been this month if you hadn't called it off."

"Mother, are you forgetting the pesky detail of me finding David in bed with someone else?"

Her mother's face pinched up into an ugly frown as Piper held back an eye roll. Her mother had a severe case of selective hearing and memory.

"Well, instead of spending all of your time working behind that counter, you should be out finding yourself a husband. You know you aren't getting any younger. Tick. Tock."

"Enough!" Piper didn't know what was up with her mother, but she was certainly on a roll. "This is not Pick on Piper Day."

Piper's gaze moved to the chocolate cupcake in her hand. She longed for the creamy frosting to melt over her tongue. It'd just be one more thing for her mother to hold over her head.

"You're right. I'm sorry." Her mother fidgeted with a ruby ring. "I'm just worried about you. I want you to be happy."

"I am happy. You can stop worrying. Poppin' Fresh Bakery is a success. Someday soon, you'll be amazed at how big I can make this bakery."

A spark of interest gleamed in her mother's eyes. "You really think you can be happy here?" Her hand waved across the top of the display case. "It just seems to me there can't be a big profit margin. You know, it isn't too late for you to go to college—"

"Mom, stop. I'm doing what makes me happy."

Her mother cast her a skeptical glance. "You're sure?"

Piper nodded.

"Well, then, I won't say another word."

They both knew that wasn't true. Her mother would persist—trying to get Piper to do things her way. Not that it'd sway Piper's mind. She already considered herself successful—as a businesswoman. Although, there were other areas of her life where she wasn't so successful. Such as the loathsome twenty-some—erm, closer to thirty—pounds she repeatedly failed to lose.

Her gaze moved to the cupcake. She wouldn't...couldn't eat it. Definitely not in front of her mother.

Wanting to rid herself of the temptation, she held it out to her mother. "Admit it. You're just dying to try one of my creations."

"And ruin my figure?" Her mother smoothed her hand over the black, fitted skirt that covered her trim waist and hips. "I don't think so. I have to think about the future. Who'd want a frumpy, out-of-shape widow?"

"Maybe they'd like you for you and not for what you look like."

"Hardly. And where has that philosophy gotten you? Absolutely nowhere. Remember, dear, a moment on the lips but a lifetime on the hips." Her mother clucked her tongue. "If only you'd show some self-restraint, you'd lose the pounds. You could be so pretty—"

Behind them, a throat cleared.

Piper turned, her gaze landing first on a pair of cowboy boots. A pair of faded jeans and a large silver belt buckle nestled against flat abs. A breath fluttered in her chest. Her gaze rose up over a muscled chest that strained against a navy blue T-shirt. When her gaze reached the man's tanned face, she was surprised to find that she didn't recognize him. These days, Whistle Stop didn't get many visitors—although there were plans in the works to change that sad fact.

So, where in the world had this stranger come from? And why hadn't the bell above the front door chimed upon his arrival? And then a horrid thought struck her—had he overheard her mother's lecture?

The intensity of his warm gaze made her heart thump and her palms grow moist. He might not be one of her regulars, but with his short brown hair, bronze features, and solid build, he was welcome to stop by any time. The more she looked at him, the more she felt as though she should know him. But she couldn't place the face.

At last regaining her ability to speak, she said. "Welcome to Poppin' Fresh. What can I get you?"

"I was hoping I could speak with the owner." He stepped closer to the display case.

"That would be me. I'll be right with you." Piper turned back to her mother.

"By the way, I disagree." The stranger spoke in deep, rich tones.

Confused, Piper faced the man again. "Excuse me?"

"I think you're pretty just the way you are." His voice was noticeably raised—loud enough for her mother to hear.

Heat swirled in her chest and rushed up her neck. She couldn't remember the last time a man had paid her such a compliment. "Thank you. I...I'll be right with you."

The man nodded and moved to get a better view of the freshly stocked display case. Her gaze followed him as he perused the large selection of cookies, pastries, and pies. The man intrigued her, and it went beyond his stunning good looks. Why in the world would he ask to speak with the owner? Anyone could help him pick out some goodies or take a cake order. Had he been here before and she'd somehow missed him? Hard to imagine missing a man as sexy as he was. Her assistant, Hannah, would have said something.

She turned to her mother. "I'm sorry, but I can't talk anymore right now. I've got work to do."

"So I see." Her mother frowned at the man, who smiled back at her.

Piper could almost hear her mother's back teeth grinding. A man who could get to her mother definitely deserved further investigation. She tried her best not to grin as she hurried to the door. She pulled it open, and a warm September breeze rushed in. It swirled around her, sending a few loose strands of her hair tickling her neck.

Her gaze strayed back to the handsome stranger who'd said the sweetest words. She was certain she'd met him before, but where? Then, realizing she was staring, she glanced away. Her mother needed to leave. Now. Before she spoiled everything.

Her mother clutched her black handbag and strode over to the doorway. "I just stopped by to remind you the town meeting is later this week. You don't want to miss it—"

"I won't. I told you before I'd be there."

"Promise?"

Piper resisted the urge to roll her eyes. "I promise."

She didn't need any more reminders. There was no way she'd forget about the monthly town meeting. After all, her mother had somehow talked her into agreeing to volunteer at the meeting to head up the fundraising committee for the town square's revitalization—a project that was long overdue. And one that had hit a few snags with its previous efforts, though the new plan was to have a festival this fall to help raise the money needed.

"I'll see you on Friday," her mother said merrily as she made her way out the door.

Piper gave her head a quick shake, refusing to let the woman's pointed words deflate her day, especially now that it had such promise. She let the door swing shut and turned back to the charming man. A smile returned to her lips, and this time she didn't fight it.

Realizing she was still holding the mocha chocolate cherry cupcake, she rushed behind the counter and set it down. There was no longer any need for comfort food. No need at all.

"I applaud you," the man said.

"For what?" *Not eating the cupcake? Am I that pathetic?*

"You handled that customer with such patience. I'm not sure I would have done so well."

Piper let out a pent-up breath. "Oh, that wasn't any customer." Warmth flared over her face, and her voice lowered. "It was my mother. She has a habit of speaking her mind."

Which made Piper wonder why, in the past four years since she'd opened Poppin' Fresh Bakery, her mother never had complimented her on how successful the business had turned out. Did her mother even notice the new lemon-yellow paint she'd used to cheer up the tired walls? Or the floral wall hangings Piper had handpicked to give the place a breath of fresh air? She selected everything to work with the white garden tables and chairs she'd arranged so her customers wouldn't feel a need to rush off. Every detail, even down to the white eyelet ruffle in the window, had been her doing. And her mini-makeover had turned out even better than she'd imagined.

The man's tanned features paled. "Sorry. I had no idea."

"No problem." Wiping her hands off on her daisy-flowered apron, she hoped to change the subject. She placed a practiced smile on her face. "Hi—"

"You know she's wrong."

Her mother wrong? Piper glanced around to make sure her mother hadn't snuck back in the door. Thank goodness she wasn't in earshot. "And what would she be wrong about?"

"You." He shifted his weight from one foot to the other. "I meant it when I said you're pretty. No, make that beautiful." His gaze slipped to her lips, lingered, and then returned to her eyes. "Any guy would be lucky to have you in his life."

Was this really happening? Did this total stranger say that he found her attractive? Didn't he see all of her embarrassing imperfections? She hadn't even bothered with any makeup that morning. And her long hair, she hadn't done anything special with it. She'd merely pulled it back and pinned it up out of the way—her usual no-fuss hairdo.

He hooked his thumbs in the corners of his pockets. "And you have a great smile. You should do it more often."

A warmth swirled in her chest, easing the festering wound her mother had scratched open. The morning certainly was picking up. Piper hoped this stranger would stick around for a while.

"Thank you." Her shoulders straightened, and her smile broadened. "Now, what can I get you? If you didn't find what you want in the case, let me know. I don't mind special orders." Especially for special people with the most devastating smiles.

"Actually, I'm not here to place an order. I just need a moment of your time."

At this point, he could have more than one moment of her time...heck, he could have the rest of her morning. She gave herself a mental jerk. What was she doing letting herself fall under this stranger's spell? No matter how good he looked, she needed to remember what happened the last time she got involved with a man. She glanced down at her naked ring finger. It hadn't ended well—not well at all.

Piper willed herself to sound professional and not like some schoolgirl with an obvious crush. "What can I do for you?"

"I stopped by to introduce myself." He extended his hand. "My name's Joe Montoya."

Montoya? There were some families by that name around town. In fact, she went to school with some. She studied his handsome face with the chiseled jawline and startlingly blue eyes. There was something vaguely familiar about him.

Her thoughts short-circuited when his long, lean fingers engulfed hers. A zing of energy raced up her arm and warmed a spot in her chest. His hold was firm but not threatening. His skin was rough against her palm, as though he was a man used to hard work.

Upon realizing their handshake had gone on longer than necessary, she grudgingly pulled her hand free. She interlaced her fingers, resisting the urge to run her hand over the goose bumps trailing up her arm.

His gaze probed her, reminding her that it was her turn to introduce herself. "Nice to meet you. I'm Piper Noble, owner of Poppin' Fresh Bakery."

"You still don't know who I am, do you?"

She shook her head, feeling as though she should.

"Seems Whistle Stop's gossip train has slowed down," he said.

"Why should I know you? Is there a wanted poster in the post office with your face on it?"

"Nothing that bad." He rocked back on his heels. "Anyway, I wanted to let you know we're going to be neighbors."

"Neighbors?" She lived above her bakery, which was situated between a street and a vacant shop. Dread settled in her stomach like sour milk. "You bought the old Armijo Mercantile?"

He nodded. "I did."

He'd bought the property next door. Her property. Her future.

The knowledge smacked into her head on, knocking the breath from her lungs. This couldn't be happening. There had to be a way of stopping this stranger from walking away with her dream. He just couldn't move there. Anywhere but the space next door.

She pressed her lips firmly together, not wanting to speak without thinking. After all, it wasn't this guy's fault. He had no idea about her plans to expand the Poppin' Fresh Bakery.

She'd spent night and day, losing sleep, working toward making Poppin' Fresh Bakery a respected name recognized throughout the region. She'd even sacrificed her daily exercising, and had gained back those blasted twenty-odd pounds, to work extra hours, to cater more weddings. And where had it gotten her?

She either expanded her business now or let it stagnate. The muscles in her shoulders tightened. Her lips pursed. She'd earned this opportunity to expand her business and show the town she was more than some pitiful girl who'd failed to get a gold band on her finger. And this guy wasn't going to barge in here and snag it away—no matter how he tried to butter her up or the way his eyes twinkled when he smiled.

Joe eyed her with a speculative gaze. "You look surprised to hear the property sold."

"I...I am." She'd just reached the point of setting aside enough for the down payment. With the place having been on the market for months with no offers, she'd thought she'd have plenty of time to get her finances in order. "When did you buy it?"

"We closed the deal last week. I noticed they haven't bothered to take down the For Sale sign."

"But how can that be?" She scanned her memory. "No one has said a word about a sale."

"It's hard to believe Mrs. Sanchez didn't latch on to the information." Joe's lips spread into a grin, revealing straight, white teeth. "Didn't know it was possible to get anything past her."

"Wait," Piper said, a bit confused. "How do you know her?"

"Until recently, my family owned the Circle M Ranch."

She snapped her fingers as her memory clicked into place. "I remember you now. You were a few years ahead of me in school. You used to wear glasses, and your hair—it was longer."

"You've got a good memory."

He'd also kept his nose buried in a book and didn't socialize much. *My, how things have changed.* The glasses were gone, revealing the most amazing sky-blue eyes. His hair was trimmed short except for a few unruly curls on top. And with that killer smile and smooth voice, he'd obviously brushed up on his social skills.

She took an unsteady breath. *Keep your mind on the task at hand. There isn't time to get distracted. No matter how sexy the distraction.*

Maybe Joe had bought the property as an investment. Something he could hold on to for a bit and then sell at a profit. After all, this town was all abuzz with talk of revitalization. Residents wanted to take Whistle Stop off life support and make it vital again.

"Welcome back," she said, trying her best to keep their relationship friendly. "What made you decide to move back here?"

He shrugged. "Time passes. Circumstances change. People change."

Do they change? Her experiences led her to believe the opposite. People stayed the same—same routines, same habits. Or maybe she'd stayed in the same place for so long that it had colored her view of the world.

Just then the bell above the front door chimed, drawing Piper's attention. Mrs. Noel had arrived to pick up the cake for her husband's seventieth birthday. As proud as Piper was of the decorated sheet cake, she didn't want to be disturbed now. What if Joe slipped away as quietly as he'd arrived? She'd lose her opportunity to try to persuade him to sell the shop. Once he moved ahead with renovations, her window of opportunity would slam shut. Forever.

Piper turned pleading eyes on Joe. "Can you wait a minute while I get Mrs. Noel's order? I have something I need to ask you." The breath hitched in her throat as he consulted his watch.

He glanced back at her. "I only have a few minutes before I have to leave for a meeting."

"I understand. I'll be right back."

It'd give her time to figure out how best to approach persuading him to sell the storefront next door to her. After all, he struck her as a reasonable man. It shouldn't take too much convincing.

She hoped.

Please don't go. Not yet.

CHAPTER TWO

J
oe Montoya's gaze gravitated to the gentle sway of Piper's hips as she walked away. His mouth grew dry. How could he have forgotten how good-looking she was? Then again, back in high school, girls had been the last thing on his mind. He had much bigger issues at home that had taken all of his attention.

And now, he might not be interested in a relationship, but what could a little sightseeing hurt? And what a sight! Piper was a bunch of curvy goodness. So much so that he was surprised to find her ring finger bare.

When her shapely form slipped behind the illuminated display counter, his brain kicked back into gear. He swallowed hard, forcing his gaze away from her. He ended up staring at row upon row of gobs, decorated cupcakes, and miniature tiered cakes, all in rainbow shades. Someone certainly appreciated colors from baby blue to lime green and almost every cheerful shade in between. If only he wasn't watching what he ate, he'd definitely indulge.

This was better. He was thinking clearly again. After all, he was a businessman, and he needed to keep his wits about him. He accepted that certain pleasantries were necessary if he planned to do business in Whistle

Stop, but perhaps he was becoming a bit too friendly with this particular business owner. Perhaps he'd let her contagious smile and warm eyes get to him. He'd have to be more careful with what he said going forward. He'd learned the hard way that he was better off on his own.

Though he did feel sorry for her for having to put up with such an overbearing parent. He knew a thing or two about a parent crossing the line. He and his father never had a close relationship, far from it. But he refused to go there. That part of his life was behind him and best left forgotten. Although, his decision to move back to Whistle Stop might not have been the wisest choice—the memories now surrounded him.

Not wanting to dwell on such matters, he gazed over at Piper as she chatted with Mrs. Noel. He admired the way she put a smile on the woman's face. His new neighbor certainly had customer service down to a fine art. In fact, if he stuck around here too long, he could see himself being swayed into buying an armload of pastries.

In fact, what was he doing still standing here? He started to pace, anxious to get on with his day. He'd done what he'd set out to do—introduced himself. He'd made a point of going through the standard introductions to all of the owners of the shops lining the town square.

First impressions were so important when you were establishing a new business. Getting off on the wrong foot was difficult to erase, if not impossible. In this small town, it'd ruin his business before he put out the Open sign and served his first customer. As it was, he'd sunk everything he had into this new business. It just had to succeed, which meant he had to stay on schedule.

He checked his watch again. It was almost time to meet with his insurance agent. After which, he needed to get settled in the apartment above the vacant shop. He glanced up to wave good-bye to Piper, but she was no longer behind the counter. She must have slipped away to the kitchen.

As a businesswoman, surely she'd understand his need to be timely for his meeting. He started for the door, anxious to get outside and away from his new neighbor with a smile that lit up her green eyes speckled with gold flecks. And her curves were enough of a distraction that he'd forgotten to breathe at one point. His body tensed. He was being a fool letting her get to him. The ink on his messy divorce was barely dry.

He reached for the door handle when a high-pitched voice sounded behind him. "Excuse me. Could you hold the door for me? I don't want to drop this."

He turned to find the customer Piper had been waiting on. The woman with short, silver hair smiled up at him. She held a white cake box that was almost as large as she was.

"Can I take that for you?" he offered.

"No, thanks, sonny. I'm stronger than I look. If you can just get the door, I'll be fine."

He pulled the door wide open and smiled back at her. It earned him a thank-you.

"Joe." Piper came rushing from around the counter. "Sorry about that."

"I really need to go—"

"This won't take long. I promise. I'd like to make an offer to buy the shop from you."

Surely he hadn't heard her correctly. "Excuse me. What did you say?"

"Your store, I'd like to buy it."

He didn't understand. "Why would I sell it when I just bought the place?"

She bit down on her full lower lip. Her forehead creased with worry lines. "I take it you have your heart set on what you plan to do with the space?"

"I'm putting in a coffee shop. Fill-It-Up Joe."

The light in Piper's eyes dimmed. "Oh."

"Listen, I know you're disappointed. But the property had been up for sale for a long time. In fact, it'd been for sale for so long that the owner lowered the price twice to try to draw in a buyer." What she didn't know, and what he wasn't going to share, was that he'd risked every last cent on his plan to make the coffee shop a success. It was a chance to reinvent himself while looking after his aging mother.

A long silence ensued.

"You're...right. This town could use a coffee shop," she offered, but her voice lacked enthusiasm. "And I do like the name. It's catchy."

"Thanks." It was time he made a hasty exit. I'm sure we'll see each other from time to time."

He'd just gripped the door handle when she said, "Wait."

He didn't want to. His gut told him that things were about to get even bumpier between them. Still, he found himself turning around. "I really do have a meeting—"

"Sell me the shop, and I'll help you get a location closer to the interstate. It'd really boost your business."

He shook his head. "I didn't buy the place just to turn around and sell it. And as for the location, I like being in the heart of this town, in the center of the activity."

"What center of activity? You've been away a long time, so you probably don't know that Whistle Stop is dying. People are moving away to look for work. Even the town square is a mess. Does that sound like the kind of place where you want to start a new business?"

He couldn't help but smile at her level of determination. "Do you really think I didn't do my homework before firming up my plans? I know all about Whistle Stop's revitalization project."

Her eyes narrowed as her pink lips pressed into a firm line. So it was possible to leave her speechless. That bit of information he tucked away for future reference.

The disappointment reflected in her eyes told him just how determined she was to buy his property. In a blink, the glint of disappointment turned to desperation. He inwardly groaned. This was not going to end well.

She wasn't a quitter.

As the middle child with an older brother and younger sister, Piper had learned at an early age not to give up. If something was important enough, you had to fight for it.

She eyed up Joe. He struck her as a reasonable person, if not a bit stubborn. His faded jeans and scuffed cowboy boots told her he was conservative—not one to easily part with his hard-earned cash. Perhaps she could make that bit of information work to her advantage.

"Your building needs a lot of repairs and updating." This was the reason she'd waited on making an offer. She'd needed to secure more funds for the renovations. "I know you went to a lot of trouble and expense to buy the place, but you'll soon find out it'll be more bother than it's worth."

His dark brows lifted as his eyes studied her. "Seems to me it'd be the same amount of trouble for you as it will be for me."

She softened her voice. "How about if I sweeten the deal?"

His gaze moved slowly up and down her. "What do you have in mind?"

What exactly was he expecting her to offer? One heated night in exchange for his agreement to sell? The breath stuck in her throat. Was it wrong that for a moment she found the idea tempting? He was definitely quite a package: hot, single, and there was a guarded look in his eyes that made her all the more curious about him.

"I can offer you a bonus. Something to cover your time and trouble."

A look of relief settled over his tired features.

She gave herself a mental shake. Obviously, she'd read way too much into his expression. He wasn't interested in her. She swept aside the ridiculous idea. It wasn't like she was the type to turn men's heads. And she was okay with that.

And though she hated to admit it, her mother had been right about one thing. She was twenty pounds...more like 26.5 pounds overweight. But why be exact? She preferred to round her numbers…downward.

Joe cleared his throat. "If you're so interested in the property, why didn't you bid on it before now?"

How much did she tell him? He was the man she intended to do business with. If she revealed too much to him, it'd hurt her bargaining position. But if she didn't reveal enough, then she wouldn't have a chance to change his mind.

"When the building first went up for sale, I was still working on getting Poppin' Fresh Bakery on solid financial ground."

He crossed his arms. "Are you trying to tell me that it wasn't until today that you were able to come up with the funding?"

This conversation was headed into dangerous territory. She'd have to be careful with what she said, as this man was very astute. And she didn't want him looking at her with sympathy, or something worse. "By the time I had the money, my life plans had changed, and I no longer needed the extra space."

There, she'd said it without going into the messy details of her disastrous engagement. She was rather proud of the way she'd dodged telling the whole truth. There was no reason for him to know that when she'd become engaged, her fiancé had insisted she sell her business, and she'd foolishly given up on her dream to expand the business.

Joe arched a skeptical brow. "Let me guess. Your life plans have changed again?"

She wasn't sure she cared for the sarcasm interlaced in his deep voice. What had happened to the charming stranger who'd paid her lovely compliments? Since he held the key to her future, she let his comment slide. "Yes, my plans have reverted back. That's why I'm willing to pay you more than the selling price. And you won't have to do a thing but sign some papers."

His phone buzzed. "I'm sorry. I have to take this." After a few clipped sentences, he disconnected the call. "Sorry about that."

"Do you have to go?"

"Um, no. My meeting has been rescheduled." He slipped the phone back in his pocket. "If you don't mind me asking, what did you plan to do with the property?"

"I planned to expand the bakery."

"You mean to tell me there's that much need in Whistle Stop for baked goods?"

She resisted the urge to glare at him. "If you'd try them, you'd find out why they're in demand."

The doubt in his eyes said he didn't believe her.

She stifled an exasperated rant. It would only make matters worse. Actions would serve better than words. "Let me get us some coffee."

"That's okay. I don't want to take you away from your work."

"It's no problem." She stepped over to the kitchen door and propped it open. Inside, her assistant, Hannah, stood with her back to Piper while mixing up some purple frosting. "Hannah, I'm going to take a coffee break. Do you need anything first?"

Hannah shook her blond head covered with a hair net. "No. I'm just finishing up this order."

Piper turned back to Joe. "See? Everything is under control. Now why don't you sit down? I'll join you as soon as I get the coffee."

She gestured to the half-dozen white tea garden tables with glass tabletops strategically placed in front of the display cases. She'd searched high and low to find just the right furnishings to evoke a garden atmosphere. Although, when she'd been picking them out with the smallish matching chairs, she hadn't imagined they'd one day be holding someone as large as Joe.

He had to be six-foot-five or -six. His chest was broad. He could definitely be a force to be reckoned with. Not that any of that would intimidate her. Her father had been a big man, and it'd never stopped her from saying her piece.

She rushed behind the counter and retrieved two cups. "Do you take anything in yours?"

After a slight hesitation, he said, "Just black."

A man of simple tastes. She could respect that, even though she preferred to fancy things up. She'd always found that beauty was in the small details, whether it was furnishing a room or decorating a cake.

With two hot coffees in hand, she rounded the counter in record time. She frowned upon finding he hadn't taken a seat. She held out his cup to him. Their fingers brushed, and a shiver trailed over her skin.

Ignoring her body's reaction to him, she moved to a nearby table and pulled out a chair. She sat down, hoping he'd do the same. The blow of the train whistle filled the awkward silence. It gave her a moment to gather her thoughts. She didn't plan to let him out that door until she got him to agree to the sale, or at least agree to give her offer serious consideration.

"So the train still runs through town." He finally sat down across from her.

"It does just like clockwork at six, ten, two, and six. You'll get used to it and hardly notice it."

"I guess it's a good way to keep track of time."

She nodded, no longer wanting to talk about the train. She had more important matters on her mind. "So, about my expansion—"

He held up a hand, stopping her before she launched into her speech. "Why invest in more property? You have much more economical ways to increase your productivity right here."

"There simply isn't enough room for what I have in mind."

He smiled as though he'd just solved the problems of the world. "The answer's simple. Just take out these tables. There's a lot of wasted space here. You could easily expand your kitchen."

Her grip on her cup tightened. "Then where would my customers sit and socialize?"

"This is a bakery, not a restaurant."

Piper sighed in frustration. "I thought that being a businessman, you'd understand the value of connecting with your customers and not rushing them out the door. People like to take their time, read the newspaper, and shoot the breeze. Others order catered tea parties."

He finished off his coffee. "You have parties in here?"

Her shoulders straightened, proud of one of her more successful ventures. "They have to be small, but yes, I cater them. In fact, they've been growing in popularity. Both young and old find them a lot of fun."

His eyes lit up as an impressed look filtered across his face. "I had no idea a bakery could be the hub for so much social interaction."

At last she was beginning to get through to him. "Now do you understand why I plan to expand?"

"The coffee," he said, pushing the empty mug to the center of the table, "it's good. Do you sell a lot of it?"

She nodded.

He frowned. "I should be going." He got to his feet. "I have a lot to do."

He couldn't leave. Not yet. They hadn't ironed out this deal. With it being September, she wanted to get moving on her plans as soon as possible, before the holiday season kicked in. The extra space would allow her to host bigger parties, increase her output, and explore her other idea of offering extreme cake decorating.

Joe moved to the door.

"Will you at least consider selling?" she blurted out.

He drew his shoulders back and turned. "No. I'm sorry, but I have no intention of selling to you or anyone. Not even for twice the asking price."

"But it'd be easy money." Who in the world turned down an easy buck in this tough economy? "And there are other spaces available around town."

As though he was done talking about the possibility of a sale, he changed the subject. "I almost forgot the other reason I stopped by. The workers are going to start the renovations first thing in the morning, and I wanted to apologize in advance for the noise."

Joe was a frustrating mix of manners and stubbornness. There had to be some way to reason with him. But she didn't have a clue where to go from here.

Not that it mattered, because he strode out the door before she could utter another word. Piper knew she'd pressed too hard, but everything was on the line. And she'd blown it.

She needed to think.

She needed a new plan, to show her mother and this town that she was more than the pitiful, overweight girl who couldn't hold on to a guy. Her jaw tightened as anxiety churned within her. It felt as though her world was spinning out of control. She desperately wanted to put things right, but at the moment, she was at a loss for how to accomplish it.

She needed the sweet, creaminess of a frosted cupcake.

And there was one waiting for her behind the counter.

Tomorrow she'd worry about dieting. She needed that cupcake. She'd earned it after her morning.

She picked up the cupcake and peeled back the liner. Her mouth watered. Her lips wrapped around the edge of the little piece of fluff. Her teeth easily glided through the frosting and the velvet cake. A murmur of appreciation swelled in her throat.

Tomorrow would be better.

Tomorrow she'd have everything under control.

CHAPTER THREE

The following day, Joe stood in the service alley behind his soon-to-be coffee shop. He pressed his cell phone to his ear. Only hours into this renovation project, and so far he'd run into one problem after another.

"Just make sure you get the right lumber here this afternoon." Joe spoke into his phone, hoping the salesman understood that he'd escalate this problem further up the chain if he had to. "I don't care if it is lunchtime. I'm not going to pay my guys to stand around and wait for you."

He ended the call and rotated his shoulders, attempting to work the kinks out of his tense muscles. He couldn't believe his lumber order had been completely wrong. How hard was it to read an invoice and load a truck? Now, every minute that passed cost him money, money that was in very short supply.

His ex-wife had walked away from their divorce with the bulk of their investments. Of course, she'd pleaded with the judge, saying that there had been a downturn in business at the three coffee houses they'd owned in Albuquerque. But he knew better. She and his once-upon-a-time friend/manager had quietly moved the funds into some untraceable account. The problem was, he didn't have any way to prove it, or the money to hire a forensic accountant.

Joe gave his head a shake. What was done, was done. Whistle Stop represented his new lease on life. So long as he kept control over everything, he'd be fine. No one could shortchange him or pull a fast one on him again. He'd learned a costly lesson—the only person he could count on was himself.

Wanting to have a quick word with the crew foreman, he stepped inside what had once been a clothing store. Yet, the place was deserted. Where in the world were the men? He'd have thought at least some of them would have hung out here to eat their packed lunches.

He strode through the shop, careful to sidestep the sawhorses and various piles of discarded materials. He yanked open the front door and found the workers' pickups still lining both sides of the sunny street, but no sign of them. They couldn't have gone far on foot.

Joe strolled up the sidewalk. The most delicious aroma of fresh-baked cookies filled the air. He took another sniff. Chocolate chip? It had to be. His mouth watered.

He couldn't resist a glance inside the Poppin' Fresh Bakery. Nothing about the place reminded him of a bakery except the huge display case. It was more like a big garden party with frilly flowers on the yellow walls. And those white, iron tables were far from practical and not the least bit cheap. Now he understood why she'd been delayed in making a bid for what was now his property—the woman had no idea how to handle money.

Someone really should give her some financial advice. But not him. After all, why should he care if she was good or bad with money? She was none of his concern. He should walk away. Quickly.

Except...he did owe her an apology. Their first meeting hadn't ended well. Thinking back to the way she'd pushed him to sell, he knew the dismal encounter certainly hadn't been totally his fault. So why should he swallow his pride and apologize?

Because this was a small town. He hadn't been gone so long that he didn't recall how small towns worked. All it took was one sensationalized bit of news to start up the gossip mill. One person told another person. Another person mentioned it to a group at the diner. And they all told their families, including their second and third cousins.

He should know. His family had been fodder for the gossip mill often enough when he was a kid. The emerging memories caused a foul taste in the back of his mouth. He swallowed hard while shoving away the painful thoughts.

He stepped up to the big display window of the bakery. The big, burly men who were supposed to be working for him were sitting around those dainty white tables, eating large deli sandwiches. What in the world was going on?

If that wasn't enough, Piper was serving them coffee. Joe scanned the counter, noticing the flavored coffee syrups. Those hadn't been there yesterday, had they?

Thoughts of apologizing evaporated. He strode over to the door and yanked it open. The sweet scent of cinnamon and spices rushed up and engulfed him. His empty stomach rumbled, which only succeeded in further souring his already cranky mood.

He glanced up at the price chart. There was no listing for deli sandwiches. What was she up to?

When Piper noticed him, she smiled. Her pink cheeks puffed up. She sashayed up to him. Her rounded hips moved rhythmically, entrancing him and tangling his thoughts. The knowledge that she could get to him so easily only frustrated him all the more.

"What can I get you?" she asked sweetly, before flashing him another of those smiles that made her eyes sparkle.

How could her mother imply Piper was anything but beautiful? She was a knockout. And there was a roomful of eager men who'd back him up. In fact, a few were openly staring at her. Joe's hands clenched. Hadn't their mommas taught them better manners?

"Hey, Joe, you should try one of these turkey sandwiches," called out one of the men.

"The coffee's great, too," another worker added. "Have her add some caramel. Gives it a different twist."

Joe's gaze settled on the woman who'd won over every man in the room, except him. "Do you normally serve lunch? I don't see it on your sign."

"Actually, I don't. But since I knew the guys would be here, I picked up some cold cuts and spread the word."

Joe pressed his hands to his waist. "Just trying to help out?"

Her sugary smile dripped with sweetness. "Of course. Being neighborly, is all. The men all seem happy." The men agreed, and her smile broadened. "Can I get you some coffee? And how about a sandwich?"

Was this her way of pointing out that she could easily sway the whole town into boycotting his coffee shop? A sense of dread came over him. She didn't strike him as the type to do such a thing, but he obviously wasn't a good judge of character. His ex, Denise, was proof of that.

He cleared his throat, hoping to sound friendly. "Would you mind if we talked outside?"

Piper glanced around as though she hadn't realized they were being watched. "Sure. Lead the way."

Once alone on the sidewalk, he turned to her. "Are you so upset I won't sell that you're out to sabotage my business before it even opens?"

"What, by serving sandwiches and coffee?" She let out a hallow laugh. "You're delusional. I'm only trying to be helpful."

"Helpful? By winning over all of my workers?"

Her pencil-thin brows drew together. "If I didn't, they'd have to walk to Benny's Burgers, and that's at least a ten-minute walk one way. This way, they are right next door. They won't be late getting back to work."

Was she being on the level with him? He eyed up the serious expression on the delicate features of her face. "And why would you care?"

She shrugged. "I know those guys. Most of them were in either my class in school or my brother's grade."

Had he totally misjudged her? He wanted to believe her, but after the hell he'd gone through with Denise, he was a lot more reserved and cautious now. "So you did this out of the goodness of your heart?"

"Why do you have such a hard time believing that I'm not out to hurt you?"

Guilt settled on his now drooping shoulders. "I guess I jumped to the wrong conclusion."

"Now you're starting to make some sense. You know, I sold those sandwiches at cost."

She'd forgone making a profit? The concept jarred him back to reality. Had he let himself become so jaded by his ex's antics that he couldn't recognize genuine generosity when it ran up and smacked him across the face? The thought that he'd let himself become that hardened didn't sit well, not well at all.

In Albuquerque, he'd been able to talk to people, to laugh with them. Looking back on those memories was like looking at a stranger. But then again, all of that was before he'd walked into his house with flowers to surprise his wife, only to have the surprise be on him. The flowers had ended up in a heap on the floor as he turned away from the shocking sight of his wife in bed with another man.

He realized that something had died in him on that long-ago day. But had it all happened that day? Even before then, he'd closed off a part of himself—

No, he wasn't going there. Nothing good would come from revisiting the past. Nothing good at all.

Joe struggled to find the right words to undo some of the damage. "I just...I don't know. We didn't exactly get off to a good start yesterday. And when I saw the guys over here, I thought...well, I thought wrong."

Piper crossed her arms and hitched her curvy hip.

He grew uncomfortable beneath her expectant gaze. "What?"

"I'm waiting for an apology."

"Oh." His mouth grew dry, and he struggled to swallow. "I'm sorry that I jumped to the wrong conclusions. I appreciate your generosity. I hope we can start over."

Her brow arched as she seemed to weigh his words. "You know, it seems like you're not going to be a ray of sunshine in the neighborhood. You'll be a lot better off around here if you don't expect the worst from people. I accept your apology, though, and suppose we can give it another go."

Not going to be a ray of sunshine was a polite way of calling him a jerk...a clod...an ass. Joe's shoulders pulled back in a rigid line. He wasn't that bad, was he?

He thought back over their exchange. He smothered a frustrated groan. What was it about this woman that got under his skin and had him acting without thinking? Okay, maybe she had a point. "There's just one thing."

A noticeable pause ensued. "And that would be?"

He started to have second and third thoughts about what he'd been planning to ask her. Maybe it was best left unsaid. Besides, he had no right to ask anything of her. "Uh, never mind."

"Actually, I do mind. I'd like to clear the air between us. So what's on your mind?"

He drew in a deep breath and then blew it out. "It's about the, uh, coffee. Could I persuade you to cut back on selling specialty coffees once I open?"

Surprise flashed in her eyes. "If you want me to quit, you're going to have to give me something."

That was a much better reaction than he'd been expecting. "How about a lifetime supply of your favorite coffee drink, like mocha lattes or caramel macchiatos? I'll even throw in a free mug."

She shook her head, but it was the twinkle in her eyes that told him she already had something in mind. His gut screamed out that whatever it was he wasn't going to like it.

He looped his thumbs through his belt loops. "I take it you already have something in mind. Let's hear it."

"I want you to sell my baked goods in your coffee shop." Her lips lifted into a warm smile.

His gaze dipped to her supple lips. No wonder his men were all smiles. Piper was a stunning woman. He knew it was wrong, but he couldn't help but wonder if her strawberry lips were sweet or tart. If they weren't standing on the sidewalk in the middle of town, he might have risked it and stolen a kiss.

Her pointed stare reminded him that she was waiting for an answer. He cleared his throat. "Why would I do that? All people have to do is walk next door to fill their sweet tooth."

"I've thought of that, and I could offer some different items for your shop."

He'd already contracted with another bakery, one that would supply whole grain and organic items, but it wouldn't hurt to hear Piper out. In fact, at this point, it might be in his best interest. Besides, he was enjoying standing here in the sunshine with the gentle breeze carrying with it the soft floral scent that he guessed was Piper's perfume.

He shifted his weight from one foot to the other. "Such as?"

"The one thing that always goes with a good cup of coffee."

He should know the answer, but right now he was so distracted by her glossy lips that he'd be lucky to remember his own name.

When he didn't respond, she continued. "Doughnuts. I can whip up a special line of them that will be sold only at your place. They'll be fresh each morning. Now that would be a deal worth giving up my coffee sales."

He'd seen the delectable, tempting treats in her display case. They were the exact things his doctor had warned him against at his last checkup—the one right after his father's sudden heart attack. It was the reason Joe had started running each morning and why he'd been selective about what bakery he'd contracted to supply Fill-It-Up Joe. He definitely didn't want to go down the same unhealthy road as his father.

And more than that, Joe didn't want anyone to have any say in his business. And something told him his beautiful neighbor would want a say in what pastries he sold, how he displayed them, and how much he charged. He'd been down this road before. It started with something small but quickly escalated.

Not again.

No way.

But the anticipation reflected in her eyes stifled his words. She reminded him of a kid eagerly awaiting her first puppy—not a good analogy. His gut knotted up. Women and dogs were two touchy subjects for him. They were both best left alone.

He focused his thoughts on Piper and figuring out how best to let her down as gently as possible. So far, everything that had come out of his mouth had only succeeded in upsetting her. Maybe it was best he didn't say anything at all. He settled for shaking his head, and then he braced himself for her response.

The excitement on her face slipped. "But why?"

"I'm sorry, but I've already hired a company to supply all of the baked goods I'm going to need."

"You hired a company from outside the area?" When he nodded, her gaze narrowed. "If you don't want to be neighborly, all you had to do was say so. You didn't have to let me go on about how we could work together."

"That's not it—"

She held up her palm. "Save it. I have customers to attend to. You stay on your side of the wall, and I'll stay on mine."

She stormed off, leaving him alone on the sidewalk. He kicked at a pebble. Why hadn't he explained about his father's death and that his own diagnostic tests regarding heart disease had been borderline?

Because it wasn't her business... Nah, the truth was, he would have explained if she'd have given him a chance. The knowledge didn't ease him. The fact that he wanted to tell this beautiful stranger intimate details about his life scared the hell out of him.

CHAPTER FOUR

Closing time.

And none too soon.

Piper took what comfort she could from her evening routine. Knowing she wouldn't be able to rest, she'd sent her two employees home early. The way she saw it, the more work she had to do, the less she'd dwell on her plans being dashed by the sexy Mr. Montoya.

The chime of the little brass bell over the front door had Piper calling out, "We're closed."

She'd been so distracted that she'd forgotten to flip the lock on the door. She wondered what else she'd forgotten that day. Then again, maybe it was better she didn't know.

"Piper, where are you?"

She immediately recognized Ana's voice. "I'm back here in the kitchen."

She'd been friends with Ana as far back as she could remember. They'd grown up on the same block. Their mothers had been friends. And they'd been in the same grade in school. It was the makings of either a life-long friendship or mortal enemies. Luckily, they'd had enough in common that they quickly became BFFs.

Ana stepped into the kitchen and looked around. "Where is everyone?"

"I sent them home." Piper really didn't want to get into details. The pain of her dream going up in smoke was still too raw for well-meaning words of sympathy.

"How come they got to go home early and yet you're still here working?"

Piper flashed her friend a brief smile. "Because I'm a terrific boss."

"You're also good at avoiding issues when you don't want to talk about them."

Oh no. Ana knew something. Was it Mrs. Noel? Had she overheard something? Or had one of her employees repeated what they'd overheard? Come to think of it, anyone could have told Ana. She sighed. She'd been so caught up in her conversation with Joe that it never dawned on her that they might be overheard. Although, this bit of gossip would barely be a blip on the radar compared to the breakup of her engagement. At least, she hoped it would be.

"Okay. What did you hear?" Piper put the mop in the bucket and rolled it out of the way.

Ana's eyes lit up. "What haven't I heard? You have the gossip lines burning hot."

Piper groaned. "What are they saying?"

"That you and Joe are already an item."

"Fat chance. How do you know Joe?"

Ana shrugged. "We met briefly when he went around introducing himself to the other business owners. He's definitely a hottie."

"If you're into the hard-headed type."

The smile slipped from Ana's lips. "So the rumors aren't true?"

"No, they're not true. Joe and I are definitely not an item." Not that the idea hadn't flitted through her mind once or twice. Even though he had a very long stubborn streak, he was still devastatingly handsome when he smiled. "The part where he bought the vacant shop next door and ruined my chance to really grow my business pretty much killed any chance at romance."

"I'm so sorry. I know how much you were looking forward to expanding."

She wished she hadn't told anyone about her plans until she'd had a signed deal. Now she had to eat her words. Not that her friends, the Bachelorettes of Whistle Stop, as they'd nicknamed themselves, would make her feel bad. In fact, it'd be just the opposite. Ana, Piper, Alexis, and their newest member, Ella, met at least once a week at Ana's restaurant, the Green Chile Cantina. They commiserated, supported, and cheered on each other through good times and bad. Piper would be lost without them.

Piper shrugged. "It's my fault. I was being too cautious. I wanted to make sure everything was perfectly in order before I took the next step."

"Who could blame you? Expanding your business comes with a lot of risks."

Piper moved to the sink and rinsed out a dishcloth. She needed something to do with her hands. "But I waited too long. Is there something wrong with me that I can't just rush blindly ahead, heedless of the risks?"

Ana moved to her side and gave her arm a brief squeeze. "Trust me. There is absolutely nothing wrong with you."

"Then why is Joe already moved in next door and his renovation is well under way? The noise and the hammering goes on all day long."

"How are you getting along with your very cute, very single neighbor?"

"We aren't. Getting along, that is. It isn't that we both haven't tried. It's just that—I don't know—we get on each other's nerves."

"Really?" Ana's eyes lit up. "He gets to you, huh?"

What was Ana implying? That she secretly liked the man? "You're wrong. I would never be interested in such a stubborn man. He's unwilling to listen to reason, and he has no interest in anyone else's opinion."

Ana smiled. "Wow. You do have it bad for him."

"I do not." Did she? She hardly knew the man. Besides, after David, she'd promised herself that she'd keep clear of men. Getting her heart and reputation trampled once was enough for her.

"He is awfully good-looking. And, my, is he tall. You could wear high heels and still have to strain your neck to gaze into his eyes. Did you happen to notice what color they are?"

"Light blue. Like the sky on a sunny day. I've never seen eyes that color. They're very striking."

"I was right. You like him a lot, but you're too stubborn to admit it." Ana wore a smug smile. "Just think of staring into those dreamy eyes every day and night."

Piper started to wipe off the already-clean counter, needing to keep busy. "And yet another reason to stay clear of him. I don't need neck strain to go with my aching feet and sore back from standing around here all day."

"Piper—"

Piper stopped wiping down the counter and turned to her friend. "Drop it. I'm not in the market for romance. And if romance is so great, how come you're still single?"

Ana's gaze lowered to the tiled floor. "Okay. I get your point. Sorry."

Piper sighed. She didn't want to fight with Ana. They'd been friends too long to let any guy come between them, "Don't worry about it. I know you only meant the best. I'm just not ready for a new guy in my life. I don't know if I'll ever be."

"David really screwed up. Just remember, it was his loss and your gain. He never deserved someone as amazing as you."

"You mean someone who gained back all of the weight I lost for the wedding and then some? Trust me, I'm no great catch."

"You're beautiful. And someday you'll find a guy who doesn't want to change you the way David was always trying to do."

Her thoughts spiraled back to her first meeting with Joe. He'd said she was beautiful. Had he said that because he felt sorry for her? Or had he meant it? Not that she cared. They were neighbors, nothing more.

Piper met Ana's worried gaze. "Don't worry. I'll never give someone that much control again. I'm a new woman. I make my own rules."

The worry lines on Ana's pretty face eased. "Go, you!"

"Now if only those darn cupcakes weren't so tempting."

"That's because you make the best in the county, no, make that the state. I should be going. I still have work to do at the restaurant, and the staff probably wonders where I went." Ana started toward the door.

"Hey, you never did say why you dropped by."

"Oh, that. It's nothing." Ana waved away the thought.

Piper sensed that it was definitely something. "Ana, tell me."

"Are you sure?"

She nodded. "If you don't tell me, I'm sure someone else will."

"It's David. He set the date for his wedding. It's in six weeks."

"Six weeks? He sure isn't wasting any time." With her, it'd taken two years to set a date—time for her to *work on things*, such as lose weight and become the perfect society wife.

"I'm sorry. I know it must hurt. Rumor has it that..."

"That what?"

"That his fiancée is pregnant."

"That sure won't look good for a rising politician."

Ana stepped closer. "Would you like me to stay? We can talk some more. Or I can help you close up."

Piper shook her head. "I'm fine. Thanks for telling me before I heard it from someone else. You better go before they send out a search party for you."

After Ana left, Piper clicked the dead bolt into place and switched off the interior lights. The glow from the display case filled the room. There were still a few chocolate cupcakes with chocolate frosting. Her weakness.

Tonight she wasn't even going to try to fight the craving.

Tonight she was just going to enjoy.

A black cloud dogged his steps.

Joe hadn't spoken to Piper since lunch the prior day. The throbbing in his jaw and the shooting pain in his temples had him unclenching his teeth. Not even his morning run, which usually invigorated him, had done a thing to lighten his mood. Nor did the fact his lumber order had been sorted out, and the renovation project was back on schedule. There was something nagging at him, eating at his peace of mind. Not something, make that someone. Piper.

A couple of times he'd considered going next door, but there was nothing he could say that she'd want to hear. He couldn't break his contract with the other bakery without steep penalties that he couldn't afford. And, in truth, he didn't want to. He liked answering to no one. It was best they maintained their distance.

Apparently, his sour mood was obvious, because the workmen kept their distance. Only Bob, the foreman, would have anything to do with him. Joe told himself the less socialization, the more work that got completed. And the faster he'd get the business up and running.

The sound of a circular saw cutting two-by-fours echoed in the enclosed area as the hammering provided a staccato beat. In fact, it was so loud that it made it hard to keep his thoughts straight, which was fine by him. All they did was keep going in circles and coming back to Piper.

He set to work ripping out some rotted wood from the back of the building where he planned to situate his office. His office. He liked the sound of it. He wouldn't have to share the space with anyone. Soon, his dream would come true. He'd have his own business and his own apartment. There would be no one to butt in. If he wanted to leave his dirty socks on the floor, no one could complain. If he wanted to watch a football game and yell at the screen, no one would glare at him for being loud. And, most all, there would be no one to take it all away from him. At last, he'd be happy.

It was then Joe noticed a distinct silence had fallen over the place. He checked the time. It was only half past ten. Definitely not time for his men to hightail it over to Piper's for one of her delicious-looking sandwiches. So if it wasn't lunchtime, what was the problem?

He set aside the crowbar he'd been using to pry off some old paneling. He moved toward the front of the building. He stopped in his tracks when he noticed his mother and Mrs. Sanchez, Whistle Stop's queen of gossip, making pleasantries with his men.

Mrs. Sanchez was anything but dull. His gaze took in the large woman's black dress with fuchsia and orange flowers. Peeping out from below the dress was a pair of bright orange strapped heels, and her toenails were painted the same shade of orange.

Most of her conversations were just as colorful. He never, ever wanted to be the subject of one of her talks. Had she heard about his falling-out with Piper? Having their conversation out on the sidewalk probably hadn't been one of his better ideas. Still, he hadn't anticipated that he'd totally infuriate Piper to the point of her consistently glancing the other way any time they passed each other.

He quickly escorted the ladies outside, letting the crew get back to their jobs. "Mom, is something wrong?"

His mother's face grew pale, and her gaze lowered to the sidewalk. "I...I didn't mean to bother you. I'll go home."

"No. Wait. Don't go." He hated that his father had turned his mother into a timid field mouse. "I'm just surprised to see you here, is all."

"Actually, we were talking about you over coffee," Mrs. Sanchez intervened.

Joe turned to the other woman, at last remembering his manners. "Good morning, Mrs. Sanchez. Should I be worried that I was the topic of conversation?"

His mother spoke up. "Charlotte has a great idea."

His gut churned. He knew that whenever Charlotte Sanchez was involved, it usually wasn't something great. And it usually meant a lot of work for everyone but her.

"What would that be?" he choked out, sensing he was doomed.

Mrs. Sanchez's painted red lips lifted into a wait-until-you-hear-this smile. "We think you should be involved in the town square revitalization project."

His gaze lifted and moved across the street to the dilapidated town square. When he was a little kid, it'd been the hub of community activity. Over the years, time had taken its toll on the place. The grass was mowed and the hedges cut back, but that couldn't hide the signs of age and neglect. White paint peeled off the gazebo. Benches were missing slats. The sidewalk was cracked and chunks of concrete were missing in places. The utter lack of care ate at him. He had fond memories of Sunday picnics in the square with his mother, aunt, and cousins. He didn't have many good memories, but those were some of them.

Someone needed to take charge of restoring the town for future generations, but that someone wasn't going to be him. A job like that would require someone who could boss people around and push them into volunteering their time and supplies. Someone like...Piper. She'd be perfect for the job.

"Ladies, I'm afraid you have the wrong person. I have my hands full getting my coffee shop ready to open on schedule."

His mother moved closer. When she spoke, he strained to hear her whispered tone. "Joe, I don't think you're looking at this right. By helping out with this project, you'd be helping your business. If people hung out in the square, they'd likely stop by your place for coffee."

As much as he didn't want to disappoint his mother, he just couldn't spare the time. He'd find a way to make it up to her. "I don't think—"

"And," Mrs. Sanchez piped in, "people will love the idea of being able to enjoy taking their coffees outside. They can sit on one of the soon-to-be-restored park benches while viewing the new trees and plants."

Before he could make it clear that they should make these plans without his involvement, Piper strolled past. She wore pink capris with a tiny white tee that hugged her curves. On the front was a pink smiley. She looked cheery. Perhaps she was ready to put the hostility behind them. He hoped so.

She greeted his mother and Mrs. Sanchez with a beautiful smile while discreetly avoiding him. His hands clenched. How long was Piper going to give him the cold shoulder? It wasn't like any of it was personal. It was business pure and simple.

He turned as though to go after her. After all, they were neighbors now. They couldn't avoid each other forever. Could they? The thought didn't sit well with him.

He took a step in Piper's direction. The sound of his mother's voice reminded him that he wasn't alone. He stopped. Righting things with Piper would have to wait.

Still, he found himself turning and watching the hypnotic sway of her finely rounded backside. His mouth went dry. Maybe it was a good thing she was being frosty toward him, because every time he looked at her, his blood heated. He didn't know how he'd resist her if, by some slim chance, she were to return his interest. He drew the unsettling thought to a close.

"Joe, did you hear what I said?" His mother wrung her hands.

He jerked his gaze back to the two women standing in front of him. Mrs. Sanchez's eyes gleamed with curiosity. She hadn't missed how Piper had totally distracted him. What had he been thinking to let down his guard in front of this woman? Now the whole town would hear how he had a thing for Piper. He inwardly groaned. He had to do better in the future.

"Of course I heard you, Mom." He lied, trying to save face. "I don't see how this will work. I already have my hands full renovating the coffee shop. I don't have time to rebuild the town square, too."

"That's the thing, dear, you wouldn't be doing the actual work. You'd be organizing the fundraising part. You'd just have to come to the town meeting tomorrow night."

"I'll be working," he insisted.

Mrs. Sanchez stepped closer and lowered her voice. "The thing is, returning home isn't necessarily easy. This could be your way to make inroads with a great many of Whistle Stop's residents. That's always good for business. And I want to see you succeed."

He wasn't stupid. He knew what she meant. People weren't happy about the way he'd sold off the ranch, his father's legacy. He'd been expected to return home and run it. But that was never an option in his mind. And he refused to explain his reasons to anyone. It was no one's business.

His mother's gaze darted around, avoiding him. She was the only one who knew why running that ranch would never have happened. But just like when his father was alive, she didn't say a word. As though, if she didn't get involved, didn't speak up for Joe, none of it would touch her. The knowledge that his mother still wouldn't speak up for him cut deep. But his father had found a way to make sure every problem touched her, including the back of his hand.

A knot in Joe's gut tightened. The unwanted memories filtered through his mind. Like ghosts, they slipped through his grasp, tormenting him.

Mrs. Sanchez patted his shoulder, regaining his attention. "So what do you say? It's in your best interest."

He didn't like being pushed into things, even if the woman was right, which he wasn't willing to admit just yet. "I don't know."

"Piper will be there."

Mrs. Sanchez beamed at him, all too eager to play matchmaker. But she'd made one miscalculation. The knowledge that Piper would be in attendance succeeded only in making him even more determined not to go. He didn't want anyone to get the idea he was interested in her, or any other woman. Not again. He was done with romance and commitment.

He shook his head. "I need to work."

"But you must go. You'll regret it if you don't." Mrs. Sanchez's lips pressed into a firm line.

He glanced to his mother for support, but her gaze was lowered. Why didn't anyone comprehend that all he wanted was to be left alone to start his business?

"You don't understand," he said, giving one last attempt to plead his case. "I already have contracts in place to have supplies delivered in the middle of next month. I have flyers printed up announcing the grand opening. If this renovation falls behind, it'll be a disaster."

Mrs. Sanchez waved away his worries. "All we're asking for is a couple of hours of your time."

He knew it wouldn't end there. They wouldn't give up until he did what they wanted. He'd never headed up a committee before, but he had no doubt it would be a big time suck. And something told him making inroads with the residents of Whistle Stop wouldn't be as easy as Mrs. Sanchez was letting on. People in this town had long memories. The thing was, they didn't know the whole story about why he left town with plans to never look back.

"You know," Mrs. Sanchez said, "this is a small town. People help people. You do want to fit back in, don't you?"

His gaze moved to his mother, who fidgeted with her purse strap. It broke his heart to see her a bundle of nerves and afraid of her own shadow. For her sake, he needed to fit in. She needed him, even if she was unable to say the words.

He sighed, taking a moment to digest everything. There was no way he was going to sway these women into seeing this his way. And what was worse, he was starting to see things from their perspective. During his time away, he'd forgotten just how tight-knit this community was. He'd already messed up when it came to Piper. He didn't need any more mistakes, or he might as well not even bother opening his doors.

He remembered how, after his father's death, his mother had started to get out and about. She had even headed up a bake sale to send care packages to the community's military men and women serving overseas. He'd heard that most everyone in town had taken part, and they respected his mother's efforts. Was that the same case here? Would people sit up and notice his efforts to fit back in?

He didn't know for sure, but he was certain that if he didn't do this, Mrs. Sanchez would make sure everyone knew he'd refused to help the community. He would still be looked upon as the troubled kid who was only looking out for number one. He couldn't let that happen. It'd lead to the ultimate failure of his business, and his future would collapse—he'd lose every last cent.

And if he went to the meeting, he might bump into Piper. Maybe the town square revitalization project could bridge some peace between them. The thought eased his hesitancy. The image of her smiling face filled his mind. Perhaps something good could come of this.

"Okay, you've got yourselves a committee chairperson."

CHAPTER FIVE

WHY HAD SHE LET her mother talk her into this?

Piper strolled across town, along with a large portion of the population. Their destination was the monthly meeting at the town hall. The important topic tonight was the fundraising project to benefit the town square and the train depot. Despite the town's best efforts, their prior attempt had been thwarted by a wildfire. But not this time. There were too many determined residents—including Piper, who missed the beauty and community atmosphere the town square had provided Whistle Stop.

"You came!"

Piper glanced past the array of pickups in colors from black to yellow until her gaze came to rest on her mother, who was rushing across the street. "Mom, I told you I would."

When her mother stopped on the sidewalk, she smoothed a hand down over her three-quarter-length skirt. The white background with large red flowers and deep green leaves was cheery and pretty on her mother, who preferred bold colors. "I know you did, dear, but I know these meetings aren't your favorite."

Piper lowered her voice. "You have to admit that Mayor Ortiz does go on and on. I think sometimes he just likes the sound of his own voice—"

"Piper, hush." Her mother glanced around to make sure she hadn't been overheard. "You just don't understand how these things work."

"You mean repetitive and belabored?"

Her mother glared at her like she was five years old and had been caught stealing a still-warm-from-the oven cookie that was to be sent to her brother at college in one of his numerous care packages.

As a couple of people passed by and said hello, Piper watched as her mother turned all smiles and sunshine. Talk about an abrupt change in attitude. Her mother was all about appearances and sweeping any ugly truths under the rug.

When her mother turned back to her, the smile vanished. "Do you know what you're going to say tonight?"

"Say?" She didn't know she'd be required to say anything at the meeting.

"Yes, you know, a few words about the honor of chairing the fundraising committee."

"You want me to give a thank-you speech?"

Her mother's eyes lit up as she nodded. "You must. And you can tell the folks what ideas you have in mind for the festival that'll help raise the money for the revitalization. You've always been so creative."

Her mother thought she was creative? Really? The compliment helped soothe Piper's irritation. "But I don't have any plans. I don't even know if they'll want me in charge of this project."

"Sure, they will. You're smart and organized. If you can successfully run your own business, you can chair this committee."

"I...I'll come up with something to say." Piper was stunned by her mother's string of compliments.

Before Piper could gather her thoughts, her mother rushed off to meet up with some of her friends. Had her mother really called her smart and organized? A smile tugged at Piper's lips.

Her mother did have her warm and generous moments. And though they were more fleeting than Piper would like, she ended up appreciating them all the more. She may not have been able to expand her business at the moment, but heading up this festival-planning committee was turning out to be a definite Plan B.

The line to get into the town hall was impressive. Not that long ago, only a couple dozen people attended the meetings. But ever since Alexis Greer had gotten the ball rolling with talk of revitalizing the town and by garnering the railroad's interest in transporting tourists to their town, attendance at the meetings had filled the town hall to the point of being standing room only. It was good to see all of the interest in their town. One person could do only so much, but a multitude could breathe new life back into Whistle Stop.

Piper slid into one of the last vacant seats. She ran a hand over her hair, not used to wearing it loose. For tonight's meeting, she'd felt a need to be a little different. So she'd dispensed with her braid and added a touch of makeup. After all, she usually just sat quietly at these get-togethers and listened to all of the happenings around town.

But not tonight.

At her mother's prompting, she was going to step up and really get involved in the community. It would be a new role for her. She knew from past events that people were hesitant to step forward and assume responsibility for these projects. But not this evening. Though she'd been reluctant to admit it to her mother, she did have some ideas about how to raise the necessary money, and she was excited to get officially started.

After all, with her plans to extend her bakery dashed by her stubborn and sexy—in equal parts—neighbor, this was her chance to show this town and her mother that she may not be model pretty, but there was a lot more to her than looks. And she was determined no one would get in her way of putting her mark on the town. This festival would be unforgettable.

Piper glanced around to find her mother hobnobbing with a group of councilmen including Mayor Ortiz, Mr. Greer, Alexis's father and Dr. Baxter, her mother's new dream man.

Cancer had claimed the life of Piper's father more than two years ago, and now her mother had moved past her grieving and launched a manhunt. The thought of her mother batting her eyes and flirting, trying to lasso the widower Baxter, was more than Piper could stomach.

The man was a retired doctor with enough clout to satisfy her mother. If that's what it took to make her mother happy, so be it, but Piper didn't have to be a part of it. It just didn't feel right. It was too soon, but then again, she didn't know if it would ever be long enough to let go of the memories of the family she'd always known.

"Is this seat taken?" a familiar voice asked.

Piper glanced up, finding her younger sister, Katie. A smile pulled at Piper's lips. They barely saw each other since Katie had moved to Albuquerque almost two years ago.

"Hey," Piper said. "What are you doing here?"

"If you let me sit down, I might tell you."

Realizing she'd set her purse on the chair to her right in case her mother wanted to join her, Piper moved it to the floor. "Definitely. Have a seat and tell me what prompted this unexpected visit."

Katie shrugged. "Can't a sister show up just because..."

"You rarely come back to Whistle Stop now that you've moved to the big city. What's the matter? Are you getting lonely? Did you run out of guys to date?" she teased, knowing her little sister was a ten-plus in the looks department.

Katie gave her a dark glare. "It's hard to get away. But I had a little free time, and Mom mentioned you're going to volunteer to spearhead the fundraising committee. So I decided to come check it out."

Piper studied her sister. "Are you okay? You look a little tired."

Katie stared at the floor, her face drawn, as if she were in deep deliberation. "I'm fine. It's just..."

Alarm had her turning in her chair. "What is it?"

"Relax. It's nothing that serious." A pause ensued before Katie continued. "The landlord isn't renewing my lease for KT's Chocolates."

"Oh, honey, that's terrible. Is there anything you can do about it?"

She shook her head. "He's selling it to a development company. I don't know what I'm going to do now."

Piper squeezed her sister's hand. "I know. Move back here to Whistle Stop. We have plenty of vacancies. And the town council is working to bring business back to the area, so the town is starting to grow."

Katie frowned. "You make it sound so easy—"

"It is. I'll help you. And I'm sure Mason will do whatever he can to help—"

"There are things you don't know. Things that will—"

"If it's Mom, I'll handle her. She can definitely be a bit much at times. But now that Mason is engaged, Mom will be thoroughly distracted with wedding plans." And Piper really missed having her sister around. Sure, she had the Bachelorettes, and they were awesome, but her sister understood her on a totally different level.

"I don't know. It'd be a big step—"

"Will you at least think about it?"

Katie paused and then nodded. "But I'll definitely come back for Autumn Fest if you're in charge."

Before Piper could continue their conversation, Mayor Ortiz hammered his gavel and brought the meeting to order. She stared up at the podium as the mayor welcomed everyone to the meeting. He looked so much like his son, David, her ex fiancé. Thankfully they didn't act the same. Whereas David was all about airs and entitlement, his father was more laid back—some might say too laid back when it came to the welfare of Whistle Stop.

At last, Mayor Ortiz announced that it was time for new business and mentioned the revitalization project. "This is very important to every citizen of Whistle Stop. The town square is in shameful disrepair, and it's going to take all of us to bring the place back to its former glory and vitality. We were hoping to have it completed by now, as well as restoring the train station, but the wildfire on Roca Mountain delayed things..."

As the mayor droned on, as he normally did, enjoying his time in the spotlight, Piper's anticipation grew. She glanced over to where her mother was now seated next to Dr. Baxter. If her mother had her way, they'd soon be saying I do. Her mother glanced over with a big, bright smile. Piper wondered if her mother's happiness was about her heading up this committee, or had Dr. Baxter been more receptive than normal to her mother's flirting?

"But before we can do any of that," the mayor continued, "we need one of you fine citizens to step forward and take the lead on this very important project. Do we have any volunteers?"

Piper didn't even hesitate. She stood, eager to get this project under way. This was her chance to redeem herself from the scurrilous gossip after her engagement ended. In the process, she hoped to be successful at bringing life back to the town square. Maybe they could reinstate movie night and band night. It'd be great!

"I'll do it," Piper said loudly enough for all in attendance to hear.

"Thank you, Piper, for stepping forward." The mayor applauded her.

Piper's gaze moved around the town hall, taking in the looks of approval. And then her gaze came to rest on Joe Montoya. His blue gaze met hers, sending her heart skidding into her chest.

He was the absolute last person she'd expected to see at a town meeting. And yet, he was sitting there, continuing to stare at her, as though he had something to say. Was it an apology for being so presumptuous?

The mayor cleared his throat. "Piper, did you hear me? I asked what you have in mind for Autumn Fest."

Heat rushed to her cheeks as she realized she'd been utterly distracted by Joe. His eyes twinkled, as though he was amused by her flustered state. How was it possible this man could get to her every time? She swallowed hard and turned to the mayor. "I don't have anything finalized, but I do have some tentative ideas."

Although, at the moment, she could think of only one thing, erm, person. Joe. What was he doing here?

She'd stolen the words right out of his mouth.

Joe settled back in his seat with a huff. After he'd finally made peace with what his mother and Mrs. Sanchez had told him about taking an active role in the community, he'd come here to do just that. No one had warned him that he might be upstaged.

Did Piper know what he'd been planning? Had she overheard the conversation with his mother and Mrs. Sanchez? Was this her way of getting back at him for not wanting to make any business dealings between them?

His back teeth ground together as he stared at her. As though she could sense him staring, she glanced his way. Was that a look of triumph on her face? She quickly glanced away, but he didn't. He continued openly staring. He noticed that her hair was down. Her long, straight hair flowed over her shoulders and down to the middle of her back. He couldn't miss her hourglass shape, enjoying how her small waist flared out for her shapely hips.

He jerked his thoughts to a stop. The woman was a walking powder keg of problems. Every time he was in the same room with her, something blew up in his face.

He folded his arms and sat there stewing while the mayor gushed over Piper's selfless act of generosity. What was Joe supposed to do now? Jump up and push himself upon these unfamiliar people when they all seemed so happy to have Piper in charge? In actuality, she'd probably done him a favor. He'd find another way to engage Whistle Stop's residents—one that was less of a time suck.

"I think we need to have a vote on it," called out a strong, certain voice.

Joe turned to find Mrs. Sanchez standing on the other side of the room. Her gaze moved to him before returning to the mayor. The gleam in her eyes told him this interruption had to do with him. He inwardly groaned. He had a sinking feeling that Mrs. Sanchez's proposal wouldn't be well received.

"Mrs. Sanchez, I don't see how voting is necessary," the mayor said, looking a bit perplexed. "We only have one person who has kindly volunteered to chair the committee."

"I'd like to nominate someone. That is still permitted, isn't it?"

Mayor Ortiz shrugged. "It's not necessary, but it's permissible. Who do you have in mind?"

"I'd like to nominate Joe Montoya to be chair of the fundraising committee."

"Who?" The mayor's brows drew together as his forehead wrinkled with lines of confusion.

Mrs. Sanchez turned back to the crowd. Her eagle eyes immediately singled him out. "Joe, please stand so everyone can see you."

He didn't want to. But he also didn't want to make a scene in front of his future customers. A tug-of-war ensued within him.

At last, he stood. He could sense Piper's curious gaze on him. What was she thinking? Then again, it was probably best he didn't know. It wouldn't be good—not good at all. He might as well give up trying to strike up a friendship with her. It seemed as though the universe was set on them being adversaries.

"Everyone, this is Joe Montoya." Mrs. Sanchez beamed as though he was a famous movie star. "He is a Whistle Stop native who headed off for the bright lights of the city. After becoming a business success, he eventually figured out that Whistle Stop is where he really wanted to be..."

This was just too much. It sounded to him like Mrs. Sanchez would make a good fiction writer. Him a business success? Well, yes, he had been at one point, before his marriage fell apart. After that, everything had disintegrated. And he hoped to once again be one.

Quietly, he stood by, letting the woman finish adlibbing.

"Joe, we're glad to have you back," the mayor said. "I'm looking forward to having a cup of joe soon." The man chuckled as though he'd been witty with his *cup of joe* reference.

"Thank you, Mayor. I'm glad to be home." Joe took his seat again, anxious to be out of the spotlight.

People started talking amongst themselves. The swell of voices rumbled through the room. Joe had no doubt the main topic was him. They were probably wondering what his story was and what exactly had brought him back to Whistle Stop. None of which he wanted to talk about with them or anyone.

The mayor banged his gavel. "Ladies and gentlemen, this meeting is still under way. We now have two fine candidates to head up this committee. We need to take a vote."

And this is where Joe was certain he would lose. Piper appeared to be the town darling. And, most likely, the honorary title had been well earned. He'd witnessed her with the townspeople and how she'd been so generous with his work crew. She definitely had an amazing way at putting people at ease.

"Would you both stand?" the mayor asked.

Great. When he lost this vote by a landslide, it'd make his humiliation even worse. Still, he didn't have much choice but to do as instructed to avoid making a scene.

When he stood, his gaze met Piper's determined stare. She wanted this nomination. She wanted it a lot. But why? She'd already established her place in Whistle Stop, and from what he could tell, everyone loved her. Why would she want to be bothered with a fundraiser?

It seemed there was a lot more to this beautiful baker than had first met his eye. And he couldn't help wanting to know more about what made her tick.

Mayor Ortiz banged his gavel, quieting the murmur of voices. "Thank you. Now, could we have a show of hands for Joe?"

They were already voting, and he'd been so busy staring at the competition that he hadn't noticed how many residents had voted for his beautiful opponent. But when hands started to rise for him, he was shocked. There weren't just one or two pity votes either. There were quite a few. He might actually have a chance.

"Give us a moment here." The mayor covered the microphone with his hand before turning to talk to the members of the council. A long, tense moment passed. "Folks, it looks like we've got us a tie here."

A woman stood and ran a hand down over her flowered skirt before speaking. It took Joe a moment to place the face. It was Piper's mother. He knew without a doubt whose side she'd be on, and he doubted he wanted to know what she had to say. The woman had a sharp tongue. He could take whatever she threw his way, but he didn't understand how the woman could speak so harshly to her daughter. Which made every muscle in his body tense as he waited for her to speak.

"My daughter volunteered first. Therefore, the position should be hers. After all, the Nobles have always helped the community."

Mrs. Sanchez got to her feet. "I don't see why we have to choose one person over the other. We have two very capable people willing to help this town. I say we accept both of their generous offers. They can share the role and be co-chairs."

What? Joe's gaze darted over to Piper. The surprise lighting up her eyes said that she hadn't seen this coming either. And something told him she wasn't any too thrilled about the idea of working closely together. That made two of them.

They barely coexisted as neighbors, what made anyone think they would make a good pair—um, good coworkers? This was the makings for a disaster. But he refused to concede. He didn't want to leave the impression that when times got tough, he quit. He'd never been a quitter and he wasn't about to start now. No way.

"Think about it." Mrs. Sanchez's voice jarred him from his disturbing memories. "With two of them heading up the committee, things will get done twice as fast. And seeing as they are both very busy entrepreneurs, it'll be less of a strain on each of them."

"I like the idea." The mayor nodded in approval. "Let's take a vote. All those in favor of Piper Noble and Joe Montoya co-chairing the fundraising committee, raise your hand."

A sea of raised hands filled the hall.

"Great. That's what I like to see." The mayor smiled. "By an overwhelming majority, Piper and Joe will lead the endeavor to raise the necessary funds to repair both the town square and the train depot."

A round of applause sealed their fates.

After shaking hands with the mayor and speaking to Mrs. Sanchez, Joe made his way toward the exit. He needed time to think about how to handle this most perplexing situation. Since he already knew he and Piper wouldn't work well together, perhaps they could keep their distance by splitting up the duties.

He'd just reached the sidewalk when he heard his name called out. He stifled a sigh, recognizing Piper's voice. Was it possible she was going to do the sensible thing and back out? He wouldn't hold it against her. It would be best for all concerned. He glanced around until he spotted her making her way through the various clumps of loitering people.

She came to a stop in front of him. "I'm guessing you aren't any more thrilled with this arrangement than I am."

He shrugged, not willing to let on what he really thought. "It could be worse." He wasn't sure how, but he supposed it was possible—somehow. An amusing thought came to him. Deciding to try to smooth out their rocky relationship, he lowered his voice and shared his thought. "I could be working with Mrs. Sanchez."

Piper's eyes lit up, and they both laughed, breaking the tension. "When you put it that way, this arrangement isn't so bad."

"Thanks. I think." He hitched his thumbs in the corners of his pockets. "You know, if you'd like to back out, I'd totally understand—"

"Me, back out?" She shook her head. "That is never going to happen. I thought you'd want out."

"Me? No. I'm not going anywhere." Surely there had to be a way to talk her out of this. Otherwise, they were doomed to fail if their past encounters were any indication. "You know, it's going to take a lot of time, and you've got the bakery to run—"

"I can do both. What about you?" Her green eyes grew darker as she challenged him. "Are you sure you can get your coffee shop launched while helping to plan the festival?"

"Of course."

"Then it looks like we're stuck with each other."

"Guess you're right."

If they had to work together, he needed to do everything he could to make it as non-stressful as possible.

Their gazes caught and held. Did she have any idea how mesmerizing her eyes were? They were captivating. And her long lashes only added to their alluring quality.

He didn't understand how she was still single. Unless, of course, it was by choice. The idea raised a whole bunch of other questions—questions that were none of his business. And yet, he couldn't still his mind.

"You know we only have two more months of warm weather left," she said. "We'll need to start planning immediately. It'll have to be a priority. If you don't have the time to spare, what with your renovations, I'd totally understand. I'd be willing to start on it by myself, and then you could jump in when you have time."

Was she trying to gently push him aside? Or was she trying to be helpful?

He wanted to trust that she was being altruistic, but he'd been down that road before. It hadn't ended well. He thought back to how Denise had taken over the coffeehouses while he dealt with the ranch after his father's sudden death. He'd thought she did it out of the goodness of her heart. He'd been so wrong.

What he hadn't known then was that his ex had been involved with his manager. Her act of kindness had been a veiled effort to skim as much profit from the business as she could in preparation for their divorce. He'd been so blind, so trusting. That wouldn't happen again.

As much as he wanted to believe that Piper meant well, he couldn't. He wouldn't. He had to do what was best for his business, and that was honoring his pledge to the community to raise money to save their town square and make the train depot functional once more.

Joe straightened his shoulders. "Thanks for the offer, but I can handle both projects. In fact, I was planning to jot down some ideas as soon as I get home."

Her eyes rounded with surprise, followed by a smile that tugged at her lush lips. "I'll do the same. We can meet at the bakery tomorrow morning to compare notes. Say, nine o'clock, after the morning business slows down?"

"Sounds like a date...erm, a plan. See you then."

What in the world had he been thinking? A date? Seriously.

If they were going to work together, he had to keep his thoughts centered...and not on her lush lips. This had to be business, pure and simple. But something told him that nothing was simple when it came to Piper. Nothing at all.

CHAPTER SIX

WHY HAD MRS. SANCHEZ suggested they co-chair this project?

And what was up with Joe joking around?

It was the next morning, and Piper still clearly recalled the smile that had eased the stress lines on Joe's face. Her stomach had shivered when their gazes met. What was up with that? She'd never had that sort of reaction to David. He'd been polite and reliable. In hindsight, she realized that everything concerning their relationship had been too blah. He certainly didn't get her blood racing like Joe could with just a look.

What was it about this guy that got to her?

Try as she might, she didn't have any answers. Whatever it was, she had to get past it. They were obviously not compatible, for starters. And secondly, she wasn't interested in putting her tattered heart back on the line, especially not for someone who was so stubborn.

What she needed to do was stay focused on her work. And with the addition of planning the fundraiser, she wouldn't have time to daydream about her new neighbor. It'd be even better if she could figure out a way to get Joe to bow out of co-chairing this event with her.

Now that the morning rush had tapered off, Piper moved around the bakery as though in a daze. Her mind conjured up every conceivable way to take control of the situation, but none would work. Her stomach knotted up. She was stuck running her ideas past a man who could be stubborn and nonsensical.

However, he had tried to make some sort of peace with her the prior evening after the town hall meeting. If he could put on a good front, so could she. It wasn't like she was difficult to get along with. He could ask anyone in town. She always offered a helping hand.

Besides, Whistle Stop had to come before their petty disagreements. The town square and the train depot were both in desperate need of help. The square held fond childhood memories of Easter egg hunts, farmers markets, and meeting up with friends. And the train depot used to bring relatives for the holidays. Oh, how she missed those days.

She wondered about Joe's motivation to help to revitalize the town. Whatever it was, she supposed it didn't matter as long as he didn't intend to upstage her.

Deciding that her sour mood wouldn't help the situation, Piper grabbed a bear claw from the display case. She hadn't had a bite to eat yet today. Adding some caffeine would boost her lagging energy. She grabbed the pot of steaming coffee and filled a mug.

Once she moved to a table, she smothered a moan of pleasure when she bit into the cinnamon pastry. It was so moist and tender. She'd like to think it was this tasty every day, but it seemed especially good today for some reason.

Then she realized that this was the perfect way to butter up Joe. She'd serve him a fresh bear claw and hot coffee. Didn't they say the way to a man's heart was through his stomach? Not that she wanted anything to do with his heart, but making friends would be a good start to this project.

When she spied him through the big storefront window walking in her direction, she glanced down at the remaining big bite of pastry. Not about to waste it, she stuffed it in her mouth, chewed quickly, and swallowed.

After grabbing another bear claw and a coffee for Joe, she met him at one of the tables. "Here. They're on the house."

He smiled, and her stomach somersaulted. "Thanks for the coffee, but I'll pass on the pastry."

She thought he was just trying to be modest or polite or some such thing. "Really, you have to try it." She glanced around to make sure no one was listening. "If you repeat this, I'll deny it, but that batch came out better than normal. I just wish I knew what was different about it."

"I'm certain everything you bake is delicious." He pointed to the glaze. "I'm sorry, but it's too sweet with the maple frosting. I try to watch what I eat." He patted his flat abs.

She frowned. He reminded her of her mother. Not good. Not at all.

Joe picked up the coffee she'd placed in front of him and took a healthy swig. She willed her mouth to remain closed instead of opening it and inserting her size-six foot. Still, his rejection of her pastry hurt. She wasn't sure what to say next.

She liked to think of herself as a lover, not a fighter. She inwardly groaned at her poor choice of words. Luckily for her, Joe couldn't read minds. Still, she found herself taking in his impressive height and trim physique. She realized that using the term *lover* under any circumstances could be a big mistake. Her gaze slipped to his mouth. A very big mistake.

She licked her dry lips and realized that he wasn't paying her any attention as he flipped through a couple of pages on a pad of lined paper. She scooped up the bear claw and headed for the kitchen. If his only complaint was the glaze, she could fix that. She grabbed a knife and scraped the sugary coating into the garbage.

She accepted that he was trying to get their co-chairing duties started on a good note, but she had to wonder why everything with him had to be so difficult. Even a piece of pastry was a bone of contention. Was he truly opposed to the maple frosting? It was so good. She dabbed a finger in the frosting on the knife and licked. Delicious.

Why was she letting his likes and dislikes get to her? He was her neighbor. That was all. Well, thanks to Mrs. Sanchez, he was a little more than a neighbor now. Piper sighed, realizing she was overreacting. When she returned to the table, she'd start by apologizing for the way she'd gone on about having him sell her the storefront next door. She'd do her best to welcome him to Whistle Stop with open arms. Well, maybe she shouldn't go that far.

Piper returned to the table to find a computer printout waiting at her place. He'd really gone home last night and worked on a strategy for the fundraiser. She was quite impressed.

She placed the pastry in front of him, and his brow arched. His question-filled gaze moved to her.

"What?" she sputtered. "You said you didn't like frosting, so I fixed it. Enjoy."

She didn't know if he'd give it a try or not, but standing there waiting and wondering wouldn't get her anywhere. She rushed back behind the counter to grab her own notes for the fundraiser. They weren't on a fancy computer printout, nor did she have an extra copy for him, but they'd have to do.

When she turned around to find Joe sampling her frosting-free pastry, she couldn't help but smile. And when he took a second, even bigger, bite, she grinned. The man might be contrary at times, but he certainly had good taste. Maybe there was hope for them after all—as co-workers, of course.

She took the seat across the table from him. "You know, we should meet every day if we're going to throw this event together in the next month. Why don't we use my bakery as the fundraising headquarters? We can meet here every morning at nine o'clock."

He shook his head. "I don't think so."

She sat back in her chair. "Why not? I have the room, and it's right next door to your worksite. Not to mention, I have coffee and food. It couldn't be more convenient."

A muscle in his tanned cheek flexed. She had him, and he knew it.

"Face it," she continued, to nail home her brilliant idea, "your shop is still under construction, and by working from here, you can manage the fundraising project while supervising the construction. It's a win-win arrangement. Don't you agree?"

He grudgingly nodded. "But don't think this puts you in charge. We're still equals."

"I wouldn't have it any other way. Now let me refill our mugs, and we'll get to work."

He seemed to relax as he finished off the bear claw. Maybe this arrangement wouldn't be so bad. It was a huge job for one person to undertake, but with the two of them splitting the workload, they'd both have time for their respective businesses. After all, she hadn't given up on growing her business. It'd just take a bit more ingenuity.

What exactly had he agreed to?

Joe raked his fingers through his hair. Why had he agreed to work closely with the one woman in this town who one moment reminded him of all he was missing in life and in the next moment drove him up a wall with her stubbornness?

Even though she'd made a really good point about her bakery being an ideal location to organize the fundraiser, he couldn't stop from thinking this was a mistake. A big mistake. But for the life of him, he couldn't put his finger on the exact reason for his reservations.

Piper returned to the table and slid his refilled mug over to him. She took her seat and glanced down at his ideas. "You were thoughtful to type up your ideas and print them out. I'm afraid I didn't think of that. All I have are some notes that I wrote up in bed last night. Why don't you read over them while I go over yours?"

His gaze slipped down to her lips, which were done up with a frosty pink gloss. They looked as sweet as one of those strawberry cupcakes in the display case. Was it possible for a kiss to taste so sweet? He longed to find out.

When her brows arched, and a knowing look reflected in her eyes, the heat of embarrassment steamed up his face. He wasn't here to ogle her. She was trouble. With a capital T. Then again, that should be TROUBLE, in all caps.

Joe accepted the pad of paper she offered him. He was impressed by her easy-to-read handwriting. If his was half as legible as hers, he probably wouldn't have done everything on his laptop.

As his gaze slid down over the long list of ideas for the festival, he was blown away by Piper's extravagance. It would cost a small fortune to bring in carnival rides, including a Ferris wheel, a petting zoo, and clowns. What had she been thinking when she wrote up this list?

Suddenly, he was reminded of Denise. When he'd first had the idea to quit his high-paying yet high-stress job with a mortgage company, she hadn't wanted anything to do with his idea to open a coffeehouse. She told him he was being foolish. When he proceeded to show her the plans for the interior design, hoping to win her over, she'd told him he was being cheap and that nothing he did would stand up to the big-name chains.

He'd reluctantly taken her advice and upgraded his plans. The first shop didn't take off as expected. In fact, he'd almost lost his shirt and shoes as well as everything in between. But when all looked lost, business finally picked up. One coffee shop led to two and then three, spread across the neighborhoods in Albuquerque.

When his ex joined the business full time, the first thing she did was have all three coffeehouses professionally redecorated with extravagant furnishings and trendy art, which necessitated a rise in prices for the customers. Denise bulldozed right over his philosophy to keep it simple and cost efficient. The business started to sink again.

He wouldn't let that happen with this fundraiser. He wouldn't let extravagance prevail. He would get Piper to listen to reason.

Joe tapped his pen on the tablet. "About these things you'd like to have at the festival, they aren't going to be cheap."

"And you think being a penny pincher is the way to go?"

"At least the town will receive most of the proceeds. You won't be handing it out to a bunch of carnies who don't even live here."

Her fine brows scrunched together, and her glossy lips pursed. The urge to chuckle at her puckered face bubbled up inside him, but he resisted, knowing it'd only infuriate her. They had more important things to haggle about at the moment.

He cleared his throat. "The point of this whole thing is to make money for the town square, right?"

The frown on her face didn't ease. She merely nodded.

"Then we have to stick with practical, economical ways to raise the funds we need. If we spend everything we take in, then we won't get ahead."

"While the goal is to raise money for the revitalization, we can't be so focused on the financials that we lose sight of the other purpose of the festival."

He sat back and crossed his arms over his broad chest. "And that would be?"

She smiled. "It's simple. This should be the family event of the year. Your idea of having raffle tickets, bingo, and food isn't going to be enough for a community festival."

"But those items will bring in decent revenues with nominal overhead."

"You're really serious? You think the residents are going to come spend their hard-earned money on raffle tickets and a hot dog?" When he nodded, she continued. "Even if they came out, they wouldn't spend much."

"Why wouldn't they? They'd know it is for a good cause. I thought you'd want to get the most bang for your buck."

Piper shook her head in disbelief. "Haven't you ever heard of having fun?"

He shrugged. "It's overrated."

"If you're planning to run your business like you want to plan the festival, you aren't going to have many customers."

He refused to consider that she had a valid point. His coffee shops in Albuquerque had done okay before his ex's redecorating. "What do people care about the décor of a coffee shop as long as the coffee is the best they've ever tasted?"

She expelled an exasperated sigh. "You know what? Do whatever you want with your business, but when it comes to the festival, we're going to have to compromise."

He didn't like it, but she was right. He had to relinquish control to her—at least some of it. His gut tightened. That was a feeling he hadn't experienced in a couple of years. And it made him extremely uncomfortable to rely on someone else for their input. Even if they were as pretty and generous as Piper.

Since the day more than a year ago when he'd walked in on his ex, Denise, with George, his friend/business manager, Joe had been making all of his own decisions. Even when it came to selling the family ranch, his mother had deferred to him. He didn't want to partner up and have someone question his decisions. He didn't want to rely on anyone but himself. This co-chair position was going to take a lot of getting used to.

"So we'll go over each other's ideas and meet tomorrow to make the final decision on what activities we keep and what we scratch." Piper's pointed gaze met his. "Does that work?"

"Yes, but I think we need some parameters."

"Such as?"

"How many games and activities do you think we should have, you know, to draw in a nice crowd?"

Piper paused as though to give the question due consideration. "I'd say at least thirty—"

"Thirty? Why so many?"

She shrugged. "It would offer everyone something to do, some way to contribute."

"That's an awful lot of planning, not to mention expense. Would you be willing to cut it back to something like twenty activities, not including food?"

Her lips pressed into a firm line. Oh no. So much for the peace they'd established. If she thought she was going to bully him into submission—

"Okay."

What? Had he heard her correctly? "You're okay with that?"

She nodded. "How about you choose ten off my list, and I'll choose ten from your list?"

So she could be reasonable when she wanted to be. Perhaps this compromise thing wouldn't be too painful.

"You've got yourself a deal." He held out his hand to her across the table.

Her gaze moved to his hand, and then hesitantly she slipped her hand into his. He hadn't noticed until then how delicate her hands were next to his. He liked the way her fingers slid across his palm, sending the most stimulating sensation coursing through his veins.

When her gaze rose to meet his, he noticed her eyes appeared to be a different color at different times. It was kind of like the mood rings some of the girls wore back when they were kids. Each color represented a different mood.

Piper's eyes had a bluish-gray tint now. What mood would that be? Had their physical connection roused a need within her? His gaze dipped to her lips. He longed to pull her toward him and claim her mouth with his own. It was torture wondering night after night if her kisses were sweet or spicy. What exactly was Piper like when she let her hair down?

All too soon, she pulled away. "I'll see you tomorrow."

Her words jarred him from his fantasy. He didn't like it, but she was right. It was time he got back to work. "Tomorrow it is."

CHAPTER SEVEN

JOE TOSSED AND TURNED all night.

After he'd gone over Piper's list and made a bunch of notes about the ways they could meld his economical ideas and her excessive ones, he couldn't turn his mind off. Thoughts of Piper plagued him. Knowing she was just on the other side of the wall, since they both lived over their businesses, was quite disconcerting.

In the darkness, his mind had wandered into the dangerous territory of imagining what she might be wearing to bed. An old T-shirt? A frilly nightie? Or was she bold and bare? The torturous thoughts kept him wide awake.

He punched his pillow and flopped over onto his stomach. He assured himself that Piper wasn't what had him so rattled. It was this monk-like existence that he'd exiled himself to that was taking some adjustment. He'd get used to it. Eventually.

When the alarm beeped at five thirty the next morning, Joe pressed the snooze bar not once, not twice but three times before he dragged himself from the bed. Instead of his normal six o'clock run, he headed out at seven. Usually, a few minutes into his run, the adrenaline started to flood his system, and he felt charged up. But today, all he could think about was how to face Piper after he'd fantasized about her the night before. The thought had him groaning and pushing himself faster, harder on his jog around the still-quiet town. The residents who were up and about waved and greeted him. It helped lift his spirits to know some people were willing to give him a second chance.

After a quick shower, Joe pushed open the door to the bakery, not the least bit surprised to find a line of people at the counter picking out pies, cookies, and pastries. He'd only been in town a day or two before he figured out just how popular the Poppin' Fresh Bakery was with the town's residents. And if it wasn't for his father's premature death and the doctor cautioning Joe about his own risk for developing heart disease, he'd love to sample each of Piper's amazing creations. The delightful smell made his mouth water, but he'd refrain. He promised himself. Still, they looked better than any pastry had a right to.

And so did the owner.

Piper glowed as the customers raved about her pumpkin gobs and cinnamon rolls. The smile on her face reached up and made her eyes glitter. A stab of jealousy plunged into him when he realized she never smiled like that for him.

Then he recalled their first meeting, when he'd wanted to replace the wounded look on her face after her mother's insensitive comments. When he hadn't been able to resist complimenting her, she had in fact smiled like that. Her whole face had glowed. Maybe he should do it again. What would it hurt? The reward would be that brilliant smile of hers. It was much better than being at odds with her. Most definitely. When Piper noticed him staring, her smile faded. Ouch! He really had fouled things up with her. He needed to do better. He wanted to show her that he could be a nice guy.

She waved him over to the side, where she handed him a frosting-free bear claw as well as a stiff, black coffee just the way he liked it. A fuzzy, warm feeling grew in his chest. The fact that she'd remembered and taken time to make him a pastry without the frosting touched some part of him that he'd thought had died along with his marriage.

With his treat in hand, he moved to the table next to the window that had *Poppin' Fresh Bakery* in large white letters in the center of the plate glass. The same table he'd shared with her yesterday. Today's meeting was definitely starting on a much better note. He eyed the pastry. When he bit into it, he couldn't stop himself from moaning in delight. The woman was definitely talented. He finished it in a few bites. He licked his lips. Delicious.

As he dusted off his hands, he glanced over to find Piper giving him an expectant look. The warm feeling in his chest wavered and disappeared. He knew that look. He'd been on the receiving end of it many times in the past—back when he was married. Piper hadn't done any of this out of the goodness of her heart. She wanted something...

Several minutes into their meeting, Piper stared down at her handwritten list of events for the fundraiser.

With every item Joe had scratched off, she could feel her blood pressure climbing. The urge to give him a piece of her mind grew with each passing second. He was being utterly unreasonable.

But a logical, reasonable voice told her a fight would only hinder their plans for the fundraiser, and she had too much riding on this event. She was so tired of the pitiful looks about her broken engagement and the well-meaning words about her finding someone else. It was time she gave the people of this town something else to talk about.

"You can't mark off all of the entertainment," she said firmly, doing her best to keep her outrage in check. "What will people do to have fun?"

"Didn't we already have this conversation?"

He was right. They had. There was no point in wasting time. "Okay, there's only one thing we can do. Compromise."

A smile pulled at his lips and eased the stress lines marring his face. "That's the first thing you've said that I totally agree with."

Her insides fluttered. "I think between the two of us we should be able to come up with an event that's fun but cost-efficient. So are you ready to bend a little on the bottom line?"

"A little, but we need as much of the revenue as possible for the town's revitalization. Have you looked around the town square? Really looked around? The place is in shambles. And I was shocked to see the gazebo has rotten wood. It'll have to be taken down to the studs and rebuilt. Then again, with that amount of decay, I don't know if any of it can be saved. They might have to start from scratch."

This is one area where she was ahead of him. "We'll have an estimate soon enough."

"What? But how?"

"While I was feeding your work crew, we were talking. I mentioned the upcoming fundraiser, and the men were interested in helping out. The foreman said he'd give us a quote on the repairs needed. I also called the local nursery to get a quote on the various shrubs and trees that need to be replaced as well as some flowers, just because."

Joe leaned back in his chair. "I had no idea you've been so busy. It would seem that I've been slacking."

"I didn't mind doing it. I know you have a lot on your hands with starting your business and looking after your mother."

"Still, I volunteered for this project. I want to do my part."

"Then let's start negotiating these activities. It seems neither of us was able to come up with the designated ten activities without a lot of notes."

With a clean piece of paper, Piper sat with her pen poised to start listing the not-going-to-happen, the has-potential, and the must-have events. When he pointed out the various costs involved with some of the games, she started to see where he was coming from.

She'd stick with the games they could build themselves and where the materials were inexpensive. Joe acknowledged her effort to cut costs, and soon he was finding ways to make her list of games work.

A couple of hours later, Piper smiled as she glanced over the list of must-haves. "So the Autumn Fest is going to have food, bingo, a cake auction, a gold fish game, a couple of dart games, a couple of pick-the-lucky-number booths, a Ping-Pong ball into the fishbowl game, a basketball toss, a hot-dog-eating contest, a milk-bottle toss, a birthday game, a sack race, tug-of-war, the lucky rubber ducky game where everyone's a winner, and, of course, a live band and dance. Best of all, everything can be created inexpensively and easily, and it'll be lots of fun for all ages."

She took a breather after reading the long list. Her gaze wandered across the table to find Joe grinning at her. Her stomach fluttered again.

"And don't forget that we're kicking off the festival with a 5K run."

She placed an asterisk next to an item on her list. "I'll make sure to move it to the top of the list. In fact, we can get flyers up right away and get the sign-up process started. It'll be a good way to get people talking about the festival."

Joe nodded in agreement. "Looks like when we put our minds to it, we can come up with some good ideas. Don't you think?" When she nodded, he continued. "We still have to line up volunteers and arrange for the supplies."

"But we're still missing something." For the life of her, she couldn't nail down what they'd forgotten. It was just a nagging feeling that wouldn't leave her.

"I don't think so." Joe glanced at the list. "The only thing missing are carnival rides, and we just can't swing that."

"No. Not that." Her lips pursed as she continued to feel as though she'd overlooked something. The thought was lurking just out of her reach. "We need something special, something that will be a big draw."

Joe shook his head. "We can't afford anything else."

She frowned at him. "I haven't even told you what I was thinking."

"Doesn't matter. You know the council didn't allot much money for this venture. As it is, we'll have to see how much people and businesses will be able to donate, especially the lumber for the game booths."

"A dunking booth."

"What?"

"We need a dunking booth. I was at a fair last year where tons of people lined up to listen to the guy in the cage making colorful comments. And they'd roar with laughter when he fell into the water. Men were laying down a lot of cash to dunk the obnoxious guy. And frankly, I couldn't blame them."

Joe paused and gave her an are-you-serious look. "You do know that you'd need to rent a dunking booth, right? And we have no money left in the budget."

She refused to let him rain all over her good idea. This event would be a huge success that people would talk about for a long time. "Fine. I'll rent it with my own money."

"What? But why?"

"Why not? It isn't like I'm going to buy your shop, so I have some extra money."

"And you think this dunking booth is going to be that big of a draw?"

She nodded. "And you can be the first volunteer."

"Whoa there." He held up his hands and shook his head. "Not me. I'd rather face down a scorpion or a rattler than get in my swim trunks and make a fool of myself in front of the whole town."

What was up with this guy? Didn't he ever let his guard down and have some fun? He was far too serious. He needed to loosen up. Besides, she'd love to see him with his shirt off, wearing nothing but some board shorts. What she'd spied of him this morning in his running shorts and sleeveless shirt had left her mind spinning and her screwing up order after order.

He'd be a huge draw for the ladies. Uneasiness churned in her stomach. Suddenly, the idea wasn't quite as appealing. Was it possible she was jealous? No, of course not. She had no vested interest in him. None at all.

"Come on, Joe. It's for a good cause."

He leaned back in his chair and crossed his arms. "It isn't going to happen. I'm not going to shout out ridiculous taunts while sitting over a pool of cold water. I volunteered to help organize this event, and that's as much as I'm willing to do for this town. If you want someone to sit in your dunking booth, you're going to have to look elsewhere."

She refused to give up on him. Whatever had happened to this man had certainly hardened him. What had him living within a protective shell?

She planted her elbows on the table and leaned forward. "And if your name just happened to show up on the list of volunteers for the dunking booth—"

His eyes flared. "Don't you dare."

She couldn't help but smile. "You know life is way too short to be sooo cautious. Sometimes you've just got to learn to laugh at yourself in spite of it all."

Piper made a mental note to add his name to the dunking booth list. She was certain he'd spy it before the festival. It'd be a fun gag. And who knows? Once he spotted it, he might actually change his mind about participating. Stranger things had been known to happen.

She glanced across the table at him as he answered a text message. He wore his serious expression like a badge of honor. What had him tied in so many knots? And what would it take to get him to let down his guard?

CHAPTER EIGHT

Where had the weekend gone?

Monday showed up unceremoniously. And with a large dose of exhaustion.

Piper yawned and stretched. She wanted to convince herself that her inability to sleep soundly had everything to do with the rush to plan the upcoming festival and nothing to do with her sexy co-chair. But even she wasn't that naïve.

Ever since the day he'd shaken her hand and gazed deep into her eyes, something had changed between them. It wasn't something she could put a name to. It was something subtle, yet it was significant. She inwardly groaned. She was so confused.

A glance at the wall clock said it was only a couple of minutes before her daily meeting with Joe. She grabbed the fresh bear claw, minus the maple frosting, put it on a small plate, and poured his black coffee.

Since they'd started meeting to go over things for the festival, she'd continued serving him a bear claw each morning. He'd yet to push one aside. Instead, he practically inhaled the pastry. Surely by now he had to realize he was wrong for not at least considering selling her baked goods in his coffee shop.

She'd just set the coffee on the table when he breezed into the bakery. Faded jeans and a white T-shirt that stretched across his muscular chest left her openly staring. The man was certainly fit. If only she could persuade him to go through with the dunking booth, she'd be first in line. What single female didn't like to check out a fine-looking guy? And the fact he was single was definitely a big bonus.

"Something wrong?" Joe asked.

"Umm... No, I was just thinking." Heat flooded her cheeks. She turned away, hoping he wouldn't notice her embarrassment.

"I'll be right back," she called over her shoulder. "I'm just going to grab a coffee and have a quick word with my assistant."

Hannah was her trusted employee who was almost as good as Piper in the kitchen. She'd be lost without her and Alison, her newest hire. Piper had already gone over the day's agenda with both of them, but she was desperate for an excuse to get away. She needed a few minutes to let the heat in her face fade away.

Hannah glanced up from a batch of cupcakes she was decorating in autumn colors—orange, yellow, and green. "Hey, boss, what do you need?"

"I told you to call me Piper." She couldn't help but eye up the tempting cupcakes. Her mouth watered.

"I know, but when you have that look on your face, you look more like a boss than a friend."

Her gaze moved from the sweet treats to Hannah. "What look on my face?"

"The frown and with your cheeks all rosy—well, never mind."

Alison glanced up from the sink and, without a word, quickly returned to loading the dishwasher.

Was Hannah right? Did she look intimidating? Really? She wasn't angry, more like confused. Right now, everything about Joe had her second-guessing his motives and implications. Maybe the problem was she was doing too much analyzing. Maybe she just needed to relax and see where things led.

"Sorry. I didn't mean to worry you." Piper moved closer to the cupcakes. They looked really good...erm, Hannah was doing a good job decorating them.

Hannah arched a blond brow. "Are you sure everything's okay?"

Piper nodded. "Couldn't be better."

"Really? Then how come you're back here eyeing up the cupcakes instead of out there with that hot cuppa joe?"

Piper broke out in laughter. "Is that the best you could come up with?"

Hannah held up both palms. "Hey, if the name fits."

"He's definitely steamy," Alison piped in.

"Now quit hiding back here." Hannah pointed to the doorway. "Go sit across from him and stare into his dreamy blue eyes."

"You two are terrible."

"We're just sayin' what you're thinking."

The heat rushed back to her cheeks. "Was not."

They both sent her I-don't-believe-you looks. That's okay. Piper didn't believe herself either.

She returned to the dining area without a cupcake—her willpower was hanging in there. Joe, on the other hand, had devoured his pastry. A satisfied smile tugged at her lips. *He likes it. He really likes it.*

She sat down at the table and pulled out a legal pad. "We should talk about prizes."

He shrugged. "Okay. But I don't have much to offer at this point."

She waited for him to acknowledge the pastry, but once again he said nothing. His silence ate at her. He had manners. She'd seen them. So what was up with him?

She struggled to hide her disappointment. "I spent the weekend on the Internet pricing stuffed animals for the game booths and small toys for the lucky rubber ducky game, you know the booth where everyone's a winner. With our limited funds, we'll have to be creative with the prizes."

"You've really put a lot of thought into this. You should have let me know. I would have helped."

She shook her head. "I didn't mind. In fact, if you're too busy I can do the rest of it on my own—"

"Not going to happen." The determination in his voice brought her up short.

"You don't have to be so abrupt about it."

He sighed. "You don't understand. Coming home isn't always easy. People around here refuse to let go of the past. They have their misguided views of what happened with the ranch. They sided with my father, sympathizing with him having to run the ranch all by himself while his son was off sowing his wild oats."

Piper remembered how tongues had wagged over one of Whistle Stop's brightest students skipping out on his family and never looking back. His father had made no secret about it. In fact, at times he'd been quite vocal, garnering sympathy.

The only person who'd never said a word about Joe's abrupt departure was his mother. She'd been totally quiet about it. But, then again, Joe's mother had ventured into town only to do her shopping, and even then she'd always been accompanied by Joe's father. Piper had never met such a quiet woman. She wondered if that was because his father constantly hovered, a frown seeming permanently tattooed on his face.

"Don't let those people get to you. You had your reasons for what you did, and that's all that matters." Piper reached out without thinking and wrapped her fingers around his hand that was holding a pen. "The townspeople will change their minds once they get to know you."

He shook his head. "I don't think so."

"Sure they will." She squeezed his hand in reassurance.

He pulled away from her. "You don't understand. I'm not here to make friends." He hesitated as though there was more to his statement, but then he said, "I moved back here because my marriage was over and my mother needed me nearby. She isn't getting any younger, and she isn't, um, good at speaking up for herself."

Piper could understand his reasoning. It was honorable—being there for his mom. Numerous times she'd thought about moving away like her big brother, Mason, had done when he went off to college. But then their father died, and she couldn't bring herself to leave her mother and little sister, Katie.

After Mason had worked for one of the top accounting firms in the country, he quit and returned home. She thought at last it was her chance to get out of Whistle Stop and find a life for herself, but then her sister had up and disappeared. It'd taken weeks to track her down, and they still didn't know what had happened to her or why she refused to move back to Whistle Stop.

Once again, Piper had had the opportunity to move on, but she didn't. What had stopped her? She wanted to think her reasons were altruistic like Joe's, but in her heart she knew that wasn't so. She hadn't moved away because she liked the security of knowing all of her neighbors. She loved that people milled around in the bakery, including her in their lives. Whistle Stop was one big messy family. And it was never boring. Mrs. Sanchez saw to that.

Piper moved her hand to her lap. "So your effort to fit back in is about making your mother happy?"

Joe shrugged. "Partly. Besides, it'll be hard to build a profitable business if everyone in town hates me."

She wasn't buying it. He wanted more than to make a profit, but he was hesitant to open up, as though he'd been hurt deeply. Her heart went out to him. She could sympathize. Once bitten and she was quite shy when it came to trusting others.

Something told her that Joe hadn't had an abundance of love in his life. Sure, there was his mom, but the woman didn't strike Piper as the emotional type. Someone needed to offer an olive branch to this guy and let him know that he didn't have to be so jaded about life.

She tapped her pen on the pad of paper, wondering about the logic of what she was about to do. "Well, I can guarantee you that not everyone will hate you."

His eyes lit up with interest. "And how can you do that?"

"Because I like you." In that moment, she knew she meant it. He might be contrary at times and a bit miserly, but she genuinely liked him. Not to mention he wasn't so hard on the eyes. And when he smiled, her insides melted.

His gaze met hers and held. There was a warmth to his eyes that hadn't been there before. Perhaps there was far more to this man than she'd ever imagined. She stared into his eyes, wondering what deep, dark secrets he was keeping under wraps. But in a blink, it was as though a wall came down between them. Joe averted his gaze as he slouched back in his chair.

"That's just because you don't know me well enough." His voice held a teasing tone. "Now shouldn't we get back to work? I don't want to be known as a slacker."

Another man who was uncomfortable with emotional moments. Her ex-fiancé had been the same way. He'd rather just ignore things than have to face any uncomfortable emotions. It was just one of the many reasons they hadn't walked down the aisle. But she wasn't going there. Not now. There was work to do.

With the financial part of the fundraiser decided, they made short work of the other items on their agenda. Joe agreed to ask the local lumber company for a donation of wood for some makeshift game booths. They also put together a list of potential volunteers who could build what was needed and also to run the various games. Mrs. Sanchez would be the ideal person to put in charge of the list of volunteers. She loved to be active in the community. And she'd definitely see that people agreed to do their part.

"I'll just get us some more coffee." Piper got to her feet.

"Sounds good. I'll send an e-mail requesting a meeting with the lumber yard to discuss a possible donation of wood. Hopefully, we'll end up with enough for all of the booths." Joe started typing on his laptop.

"Don't forget—" When he paused in his typing to look up at her with those mesmerizing eyes, she almost forgot what she was about to say. "Um...we'll, uh, need material to decorate all of that wood."

"We could slap some paint on it. That wouldn't be too costly. Maybe Wilson's Hardware Store has some old cans they wouldn't mind donating."

"Good idea. But we'll need some bunting."

"For what?" His lips pressed together, his expression perplexed.

"Because this is supposed to look pretty—you know, welcoming. We can wrap bunting around the top of each booth. Or drape it from lamppost to lamppost around the square. Imagine some colorful bunting fluttering in the breeze. It'll draw the eye and attract people."

Joe leaned back in the chair, tilting it back on its rear legs, and crossed his arms. "Sounds too expensive. We can't do it. We don't need it anyway."

"You're wrong about this." She glared at him, refusing to back down.

"I'm watching our bottom line." He leveled the chair he was sitting on and went back to typing. "I need to send out this e-mail."

Piper groaned, not bothering to hide her frustration. Why did he have to be so narrow-minded? If it didn't fit into their very meager budget and it couldn't be donated, he wrote it off as unnecessary and moved on. The man certainly liked to have things his way. At last, she understood why he was single.

She got up and walked away before she said something she'd regret. Thankfully, the bakery was in the midst of the morning lull—the quiet between the morning coffee rush and lunchtime. Though she loved talking with the residents of Whistle Stop, there was something so peaceful and soothing about this time of the day—normally.

As Piper passed the display case, the cupcakes once again called out to her, and her stomach rumbled its complaint. What would one hurt? It wasn't like she didn't deserve it after going head-to-head with Mr. Miserly for most of the morning.

She slid open the case, glanced over to confirm Joe wasn't paying attention, and then snagged a dark chocolate cupcake with chocolate fudge frosting—her favorite. She turned her back to him before peeling off the paper holder. Her mouth watered.

Why did something so delightful have to have so many calories? A hundred and seventy-eight calories, to be exact. She had an app on her phone that was all too eager to let her know just how poorly she was doing on her diet. Was it her fault she was born liking food?

She'd just finished the last morsel when the bell over the door chimed. Hannah came rushing out of the kitchen to wait on the new customer.

Piper waved her off. "I've got it." She turned to find a friendly face. "Ella, what are you doing here?"

"Hey, what kind of greeting is that?"

"Sorry. I'm just surprised to see you back from your honeymoon already. That went by fast."

"You're telling me. And it looks like you've been busy, too." Ella glanced around the bakery, taking in the new paint and frilly curtains. "This place looks great."

Now why couldn't her mother react like that? Shoving aside the troubling thought, Piper said, "Thanks. Glad you like it, but I didn't do much."

"But it works. It's like a summer garden out here. I might need your interior decorating skills soon."

"I'd be happy to do what I can. Hey, shouldn't you be teaching?"

Ella shook her head. "Not until next Monday. We came back a little early to get settled in the new house."

"If you need any help, let me know. I can bring the snacks and a pizza."

"That is very tempting. I just may take you up on the offer. But I heard through the grapevine that you're heading up the Autumn Fest. I also heard that you've got a hunky assistant—"

"Shhh..." Piper glanced over to the side to see if Joe had overheard. She sighed when she found him still engrossed in his computer. The Wi-Fi had definitely earned its fee that day.

Ella lowered her voice. "I take it that's him?"

Piper nodded, resisting the urge to turn and stare. He may well be the most stubborn, irritating man in all of Whistle Stop, but she couldn't deny that he was good-looking—very good-looking. She could stare at him for hours.

"Okay. Now I totally understand the comments—"

"What comments?" Realizing she'd raised her voice, she felt the heat of embarrassment warm her face. Making sure to soften her voice, she asked, "What are people saying?"

"That Joe really gets to you—"

"Of course he does," Piper whispered. "He always has to be right. And he actually has an aversion to my cupcakes. I mean, who besides my mother could pass them up?"

Ella's lips spread into a big smile before she broke out in a laugh. "Boy, you do have it bad."

"For him?" She shook her head. "No way. We're working together. That's all."

Ella nodded, but the twinkle of amusement in her eyes said she wasn't convinced. "If you say so."

Piper crossed her arms. "I do."

"I won't keep you. I just stopped in for a half dozen of your giant blueberry muffins. I've been missing those the whole time I was out of town. You have me spoiled."

"I try." Piper washed up her hands and then grabbed a white pastry box from behind the counter. "Do you need anything else?"

Ella's gaze scanned the display case. "Could you add a half, no, make that a full dozen of chocolate-chip cookies for my new nephew?"

Piper was impressed with the way Ella had been willing to take on a ready-made family. Her new husband was in the process of adopting his orphaned nephew. It was proof that something good could come of a tragedy. "Are things going well with Johnny?"

"I think that escapade on Roca Mountain scared him straight. Other than skipping a couple of homework assignments, he's been really good."

Piper finished packaging the treats. "I'm so glad everything is working out for all of you."

After they squared up the bill, Ella leaned over the counter. "Maybe lighten up on your partner. He's probably just nervous." Without any further explanation, Ella strolled out the door.

Nervous? What did he have to be nervous about? It wasn't like this was some sort of date. Far from it. Still, Ella might have a point. Maybe if she lightened up on the details for the festival, he might follow her lead.

And she did have an idea for the bunting, but he'd shot her idea down so quickly that she hadn't had a chance to share it with him.

She refilled their coffee mugs and moved back to the table. "Sorry about that. Ella just got back from her honeymoon."

Without bothering to look up from his laptop, he said, "Ah, that explains the giggling."

Giggling? Really? Well, if that's all he'd heard, then she'd count her blessings. "You know, I was thinking some more about that bunting—"

"We already settled this." His voice held a note of finality.

"No, we didn't." She struggled to keep the irritation out of her voice. "You shot down the idea without hearing me out."

He paused from typing on his laptop and glanced at her. "Okay, I'm listening."

"I'm going to ask the quilting circle to make the bunting. My mother's a member, so it shouldn't be too hard to get them to volunteer."

Joe arched a dark brow. "And what are you going to do for materials?"

She hadn't considered that, so she uttered the first thing that came to mind. "I'm going to buy them with my own money."

His eyes widened. "You're sure about this."

She nodded. "It'll be my donation."

"In addition to the dunking booth?"

She shrugged. "I guess. It's not like the materials can cost that much."

He wasn't so sure about that, but she'd know more about crafts than he would. "While you were getting the coffee, I was thinking that maybe you're right—you know, about decorating."

Had he just admitted that she was right? Well, he hadn't exactly *admitted* it. He'd made sure to include a *maybe* in there. Still, it was progress. Perhaps there was hope for him after all.

"Tell you what"—his deep voice drew her from her thoughts—"let me know how much the materials for the bunting come to, and I'll split it with you—"

"But you don't have to."

"I want to."

She couldn't help but smile at his generosity. Sometimes he surprised her with his kindness. He had a way of keeping her guessing.

Once they'd concluded everything on their agenda for the day, Joe gathered his papers. "I've got to go. I've got some calls to make."

"Where exactly do you work since you don't have an office yet? And it'd be far too noisy to do any work in your apartment with all of that hammering and sawing going on."

The corner of his mouth lifted. "Lately I've been making my phone calls back in the alley. And I've been checking my e-mail via my phone."

If he could be generous today, so could she. "I have an idea. Since we've already claimed this table, why don't you stay here and work? As you know, I have Wi-Fi, so you'd have Internet service."

"I don't know." He glanced around at the empty dining area. "Are you sure I wouldn't be in the way?"

"You'll be fine here. And I've got unlimited coffee. Just let your foreman know you'll be over here if he needs anything. That way you'll be able to get some work done and still be close at hand for any questions your men might have for you."

"You don't have to be nice to me just because, well, because we're co-chairing this project. And I don't want to sit out here and chase away your customers. You've got quite a successful business going here."

She liked that he respected her as a businesswoman. Warmth started in her chest, swirled around and rushed upward, bringing a smile to her face. "Thanks for being so thoughtful. But you don't have to worry. The customers are super nice. No one will notice you're working here."

With that, she walked away, realizing that wasn't quite accurate. *She* would notice. She wondered how in the world she would get any work done when there was a hunky man sitting in the front part of her bakery.

And when that bit of news made the rounds, every single female would be filing into the Poppin' Fresh Bakery. They'd place an order for cookies and pastries that most likely wouldn't fit into their diets just so they could flirt with Joe.

The thought had Piper frowning. Maybe this wasn't such a good idea after all. She glanced back at Joe getting settled. It was too late to change her mind.

CHAPTER NINE

"NEED MORE?"

Joe, totally lost in thought about the final plans for the coffee shop, glanced up. "What did you say?"

Piper held a coffee pot. "Do you want a refill?"

"Uh, sure." Before he could move the cup, she was leaning over his shoulder to pour the steaming brew.

For a week now, he'd been making himself at home in the Poppin' Fresh Bakery. He even had his own unofficial table that substituted for a desk. He was surprised by just how much business Piper got all morning long.

And the patrons were nice—real nice—to him. To say he was surprised was an understatement. Apparently, he should have listened to Piper. She knew what she was talking about. Some of the young ladies had even left him their number. He said he'd call when he started interviewing for positions at the coffee shop. That made them smile before Piper ushered them out the door.

"Sorry about that. I hope they weren't bothering you."

"No. Apparently, the word's out that I'll be interviewing soon." He held up numerous strips of paper. "They keep leaving me their numbers."

Piper rolled her eyes. "Please tell me you know better than that."

Joe's gaze moved from her to the papers and back to her again. *Oh no!* "You mean they're interested in me?"

Piper smiled. "Now you're catching on."

"In that case, here." He shoved the pieces of paper to the end of the table. "I'm not even sure they're all out of school." He shuddered. "Thanks for the save."

"No problem." Piper topped off his mug and straightened. "Are those your drawings for the coffeehouse?"

"Yes." He didn't like anyone looking at them except for the crew. He wanted to keep it under wraps...for now. He wanted to pique the residents' curiosity and draw them in for a look. Still, it might help to know what Piper thought of his layout. He'd done the interior design all by himself. In his mind's eye, he could envision Fill-It-Up Joe down to the tiniest detail.

"Looks like you...um, spent a lot of time on the drawings." Her voice was stilted.

That certainly wasn't the ringing endorsement he'd expected. Anxious to hear what had her so hesitant, he asked, "So what do you really think?"

He craned his neck so he could see her face. Color infused her cheeks, making him wonder if it was their closeness that had put the roses in her cheeks or if it had something to do with his drawings. He was hoping it was his presence that had her worked up.

"The layout...it's, um, great if you're going for a very simplistic look."

"You act like there's something wrong with a simple approach."

She shook her head. "No. Not wrong. But..."

"Spit it out. What's wrong with my shop?"

"It doesn't exactly say, *Come on in, get comfortable, and enjoy your latte.*"

"You mean it isn't anything like your bakery with these cutesy tables and frilly curtains." Hurt flashed in her eyes, and he immediately regretted his thoughtless words. "Sorry. Your place is really nice. It's just a little more feminine than what I want."

The lines bracketing her lips and eyes smoothed. She looked around at her own creation, and pride reflected in her eyes. "I can see where you'd think that. And I wouldn't expect you to do the same. But that doesn't mean you have to make your décor stark and cold."

Stark and cold. Ouch! He looked at the sketches again. He thought they were sleek and functional. Was Piper right? Was his vision wrong? His gut churned. Every bit of his savings was riding on him getting this right.

Piper pulled out a chair and sat down. "If you want some ideas of how to warm things up, I could help. After all, I did the bakery all by myself."

While he hesitated, figuring out what to do, she leaped into action. She pulled the sketches across the table so she could look over them. She hemmed and hawed. He didn't have a clue how to interpret any of the sounds she made.

"You might consider adding a couch here." Piper pointed to a spot on the drawing. "And a comfy chair there."

Joe recalled how his ex-wife had initially scoffed at his plans for the coffeehouses. She thought for sure he'd lose his shirt. But as the business garnered her attention, she'd made a little change here and a bigger change there until there was nothing about the business that resembled his original dream. Right before his eyes, it had morphed into something unrecognizable—from the décor to the menu. He wasn't about to let Piper do the same, whether her suggestions were well-intended or not.

Joe cleared his throat. "Thanks, but the drawings are exactly how I want them. I'm not planning to have people camp out at the tables. That's one of the reasons I agreed to help revitalize the park. People can take their coffee and mill around over there."

"What do you have against people hanging out in your coffeehouse? Your customers will be expecting to have space to read the paper or browse the Internet while enjoying their coffee before needing a refill. You don't want to just shove them out the door, do you?"

He frowned. She had valid points, and he didn't like it. But he needed to think this through—on his own. But he didn't know how to gently push aside her help without angering her.

"What sort of business experience do you have?" Piper asked, her gaze narrowing in on him as he focused on the pen in his hand. "Running another coffee shop?"

He bobbed his head, not trusting himself to open his mouth. He still had so many emotions tangled up with what had happened with Denise and George. Not only had they both cheated on him and stolen his money, but most of all they'd stolen his dream. And what was a person without their dreams?

"What happened to your other coffee shop?"

His body tensed. No way was he going down that road—not with her. Not with anyone. He didn't want Piper to look at him differently. In that moment, he recalled how his father had looked at him, as though he was weak and gullible.

The breath caught in Joe's lungs. He hadn't recalled those painful memories in ages. He thought he'd at last succeeded in banishing them. He'd been wrong.

His burning lungs insisted on air, no matter how uncomfortable it was for him. He let out the breath. All the while, he could feel Piper's steady gaze studying him. Why did she have to be so inquisitive?

He couldn't stomach having Piper look at him like his father had. This was his new beginning. He couldn't mess it up. The past need not be revisited—none of it.

"I need to go have a word with the crew." Joe got to his feet. "I'll see you later."

He didn't wait for her to say anything as he scrounged up his stuff and headed for the door. Outside, with the sun on his face and a light breeze blowing, he was at last able to breathe in a full breath of air into his tightened chest.

He needed to be more careful around Piper. He wasn't going to let her get too close, no matter how much she pleaded with those mysterious jade eyes. Nothing good would come of it.

The bell above the door chimed.

"I'll be right with you," Piper called from the back of the bakery.

This was Hannah's day off, and Alison had called in sick. Piper was left rushing back and forth covering the front counter, the kitchen, and the phone. Business had picked up so much that she could afford to hire a third person, but first she had to find time to write up the job description to run in the *Whistle Stop Telegraph*.

As the phone rang—again—she reconsidered her plan. She'd hire two more people. With the additional help, she could do what she really loved—designer cakes.

After taking an order for two dozen blue cupcakes decorated with a red, white, and blue superhero theme for little Billy Sanders to take to school the next day for his birthday, Piper rushed to the front counter. "Sorry about that, I'm short-handed today. I—" The words caught in the back of her mouth when she realized the identity of her customer.

"Hello, Piper." The young woman lifted a pair of sunglasses and rested them atop her head. A friendly smile lifted her red lips. "I thought we should talk."

Piper blinked, not quite believing her eyes. The woman who'd broken up her engagement was standing in her shop. *Oh no.* What was she supposed to do now? *Breathe in. Breathe out. Act normal.* After all, it was all in the past. She'd moved on. "Hello, Laney."

"I've never been in your shop before." She glanced around. "It's truly lovely. I see now why people rave about it."

Piper hoped they raved about her assorted baked goods and not the décor. But she wasn't one to brush off a compliment. "Thank you." The best thing she could do for her peace of mind was to hurry Laney on her way. "What can I get for you?"

The smile faded from the young woman's face as her gaze lowered to the yellow and white skirt of her dress. "I want to apologize. You know, for all of the nastiness that happened—"

"You mean your affair with David?"

Pink stained the other woman's cheeks. "Yes, that. It all just ballooned out of control. I'm so sorry you found out the way you did. Well, I guess we both found out about each other that night."

What? Had she missed something? "Are you saying you didn't know David was engaged?"

"I had no idea. If I had, it never would have happened. I swear."

Piper didn't want to believe her. It was so much easier to think of Laney as a lying, cheating, conniving hussy. But Laney wasn't from Whistle Stop. She lived farther north, on the outskirts of Albuquerque. It was quite possible David had duped both of them—quite possible indeed.

So where did that leave them?

Piper clearly recalled walking into David's apartment and finding him in bed with Laney. The woman had looked at her in surprise before demanding to know who she was, but at the time Piper hadn't thought anything of it.

It'd been quite an uncomfortable moment for all of them. The worst part being that Piper had never seen it coming. She'd been so wrapped up in keeping her bakery running while trying to find someone to buy it, as well as making elaborate wedding plans fit for the son of the mayor, that she'd never had any downtime in which to wonder why David had never been around anymore.

She'd spent all of her time turning herself inside out trying to be the perfect bride for him. And while she'd been starving herself to fit into a size-five wedding gown and sacrificing the business she'd built from the ground up, he'd been off doing who knew what with whomever. The dredged-up memories left a bitter taste in the back of her mouth.

Piper cleared her throat. "That's all in the past."

Laney's gaze met hers. "Do you mean it? You forgive me?"

"Yes." Piper wanted to believe in Laney's innocence and let it go. Her ex, on the other hand, was a totally different story. "Now, what can I do for you?"

A timid smile pulled at Laney's lips. "You are amazing. No wonder David speaks so highly of you—"

"He does?" Piper bit down on her lower lip, hating that she'd let her surprise get the best of her.

Laney nodded. "He's always saying how much he admires you."

Piper just couldn't imagine David saying any such thing. She had the sinking feeling Laney was buttering her up, but to what end? Surely the woman didn't want to be her friend.

"Laney, what are you doing here?"

"Sorry. I was getting to it." She clutched her designer handbag. "You know how David and I are getting married soon?"

Talk about smiling while sinking the knife in and giving it a little twist. "What does that have to be with me?"

"We've decided to have the wedding here in Whistle Stop."

"And what? You want to invite me?"

"Heavens, no." Laney pressed a hand to her chest, showing off the enormous rock on her left hand. "I'd never want to rub our wedding in your face. I know how hard it's been on you, what with losing such a great guy"

Really? A great guy? Somehow, that isn't the definition she'd use in reference to David. "Okay. I give up. Why are you here?"

"I'd like to try to make things up to you. Maybe we could start over since we'll soon be living in the same small town."

Piper crossed her arms. Something told her this was going to be quite interesting. "And how do you plan to do that?"

Laney leveled her thin shoulders and lifted her pointy chin. "I'd like you to create our wedding cake."

If there had been the slightest breeze, it would have blown Piper over. Not quite sure she'd heard correctly, she asked, "You want me to decorate your wedding cake?"

Laney's blue eyes lit up as she vigorously nodded. "I thought it'd be perfect."

For whom? Certainly not for her. She wanted to be as far from that wedding as humanly possible. As it was, she still caught people giving her pitying looks and shaking their heads. No doubt they'd already written her off as an old maid, especially since her social life was nonexistent.

"I'm glad to see you're at least thinking over the idea. Just before I came in here, I was worried you'd reject the offer without even considering what it'd mean to you."

"What it'd mean to me?" She wasn't following Laney's line of thought. Was this some twisted way of rubbing it in Piper's face that she was a loser? Wasn't it enough that Laney had stolen away her fiancé? Was she spiteful enough to want Piper to suffer more?

Laney's expression wasn't anything but friendly. "With my father having one of the largest chains of car dealerships in the Southwest, there will be people from all over coming to the wedding."

"And?"

"Don't you see? It's going to be the wedding of the season. Your cake will be seen, and tasted, by hundreds of people. It'll most likely end up in various society columns. This would help your business."

It would. A splashy affair like Laney described would definitely get the word-of-mouth advertising started. The thought of being able to immerse herself in extreme cake decorating was so tempting.

"Why would you do this for me?" There had to be a catch.

"Because you took the high road even after what David and I did to you. I really admire you. I don't think I could have taken it so well."

Piper may not have publicly displayed her broken heart, but that didn't mean the breakup hadn't taken its toll on her. She had other ways of dealing with the pain, starting with pints of chocolate ice cream followed by a large supreme pizza with extra cheese. And then there were the cupcakes—they were always there to help drown the pain.

"No one should ever go through what I did." Piper met her gaze head on.

Laney flinched. "You're right. Please let me make it up to you."

Free advertising in exchange for a fiancé and her reputation? Somehow, they didn't seem to equate.

And yet, there was a pleading look in Laney's eyes that had Piper believing what the woman was saying. Did that make Piper foolish? Naïve? Gullible?

Or would it once and for all prove to the citizens of Whistle Stop that she was past the broken engagement? Would the pitying looks finally cease? And would the event really help her business?

"So, will you do it?" Laney clasped her hands together. "Pretty please."

Piper really wanted to dislike Laney, but she just couldn't muster up the emotion. The truth was, they'd never be friends, but Piper could do business with her. She'd show David and the whole town just how strong she really was.

"I'll do it. Why don't you have a seat over by the window and I'll bring you some cake samples to choose from? And we can go over your ideas for the design."

Laney smiled and nodded. "I knew this would work out."

Piper sure hoped she was right.

CHAPTER TEN

Joe couldn't believe an entire week had flown by so quickly. Piper had laid off the personal questions, and life had taken on an easy routine. After his morning run, he showered and showed up at the Poppin' Fresh Bakery with the papers for his business and those pertaining to the fundraiser in hand. Only this morning, there was someone sitting at his corner table.

A frown pulled at his face. He'd staked a mental claim on that table. For now, it was his only office. He knew the thought was ridiculous. It was a table. But from that corner seat, he had a clear view of the entire dining area plus the counter. When Piper was out and about, he could soak up her beauty. He could admire the way she put people at ease with her charm and how she made them smile. If there was ever a natural saleswoman, it was her.

Piper glanced up from the cash register, making eye contact with him. He couldn't just stand there and wait for the man to finish perusing the sports page and eating his pastry. Joe took a seat on the other side of the room, but he didn't like it. It took him a moment to realize why. His view of Piper was restricted.

Just his luck, his crew was doing work on the shared wall between his shop and Piper's. The banging of hammers and the drone of power tools from the renovation echoed through the bakery to the point of distraction. Joe shook his head, amazed Piper wasn't throwing a royal hissy fit. If the roles had been reversed, he was certain he'd be at the end of his tether by now.

Piper was quite the standup lady. Not to mention the way she had a warm pastry and coffee waiting for him each morning. But he knew there was more to her gesture than just kindness. He could feel her eyes on him each morning as he devoured the still-warm bear claw. He knew what she wanted—an order for his coffee shop. But no matter how tasty her baking was, he was going to run his business exactly the way he wanted. He refused to be railroaded by a guilt trip. Why couldn't she understand his need to do things his own way?

He only had so much willpower. It was so bad these days that by the end of his run, he was already envisioning the melt-in-his-mouth pastry waiting for him. At this rate, if he was around the bakery much longer, he'd gain at least twenty pounds. His doctor would give him a stern lecture, warning him about the risk factors for heart disease and his already borderline blood pressure. They had to finish up renovations on the coffee shop. And soon.

"Thanks for stopping by." Piper's sweet voice rang out. "I'll be looking forward to those dance recital pictures."

The bell above the door chimed as the customer left.

Now, Piper would be heading his way. She'd be armed with a bear claw. This time, he'd resist. He'd tell her that he'd appreciate it if she'd quit serving them to him every morning. He'd be nice and apologetic, but he'd set up some boundaries.

He'd just pulled his stack of papers from his attaché case when Piper rounded the corner with the expected bear claw minus the frosting and steaming hot coffee. The coffee was okay. It was black. No cream or anything bad for his diet.

As for the pastry, he'd politely push it away. He was ready. He could do this.

"Good morning." Piper set the pastry in front of him along with the caffeine. "Beautiful day for a run."

The smell of cinnamon rose up and filled the air. His stomach rumbled. He should have eaten before he came over. It would have made this so much easier.

"It was a great morning. Nice and cool." He stared down at the bear claw.

His mouth watered. What would it hurt to eat just this one? Tomorrow he could tell her that he didn't want any more of her mouthwatering creations. Yeah, that was it. He'd do it tomorrow.

He picked up the bear claw and took a healthy bite.

Piper interlaced her fingers and stared at him as though waiting for him to say something. She wanted him to admit he was wrong about them not jumping into business together. Suddenly, the pastry didn't taste quite so good. He returned the half-eaten bear claw to the napkin.

"Don't you have anything to say?" Her voice lacked patience.

"About what?"

"The pastry I serve you every morning just the way you like without frosting."

His shoulders grew rigid. He should have known this moment would come sooner or later. His taste buds had been hoping for later. "Thank you."

She stood there wearing a frown, her arms crossed and her right hip jutted out to the side. She obviously wasn't going to let the subject rest. "And?"

Certain he wouldn't say what she wanted to hear, he decided to play dumb. "What else do you want me to say?"

"How about mentioning that you like my baking. And don't deny it. You practically inhale those bear claws."

That's what she wanted? A compliment? He felt like a total dunderhead. How could he have totally forgotten his manners? His mother had taught him better than that. Seemed like every time he was around Piper, his mind short-circuited. Well, this was one problem he could and would fix. Easily.

"I'm sorry. I've totally forgotten my manners. The bear claws are quite delicious. Thank you for going to so much trouble to have one waiting for me each morning. Worrying about the coffee shop opening on time has me totally distracted." It sure wasn't the only thing distracting him—not by a long shot.

"You're that worried about it?" She eyed him up as though trying to decide if he were leveling with her or not.

"I am. I have flyers ordered, and I took an ad out in the local paper." And this was where the conversation would get difficult for him. This was the best opportunity to say what must be said. "As for the pastry, you really shouldn't go to such trouble. The coffee is more than enough. Speaking of which"—he reached for his wallet—"this is for you." He held out what he hoped was enough to cover the food and coffee that he'd consumed, but Piper stepped back, refusing to take the cash. "If it's not enough, I have more."

Her brows scrunched together into a formidable line. "What is it with you? Can't you accept that I like to do things for people without expecting to make a buck?"

He'd insulted her. Again. His lips pressed together in a firm line. It was all his fault. For so long, he'd argued and fought over money with Denise and her attorney that it seemed he'd let everything come down to dollars and cents. He'd forgotten there were other, more important things in life. Piper was giving him a wake-up call.

"I'm sorry. I didn't mean—"

"Save it. You meant everything you said." Disappointment reflected in her eyes, causing guilt to stab at him. "I've got work to do."

"What about the plans for the fundraiser—"

"It can wait."

Piper strode away. He could practically see the steam pouring from her ears. He slouched back in the chair. When would he ever learn how to deal with women? He'd been so certain that she'd been out to trap him into letting her sell her products in his shop that he hadn't even stopped to realize he'd never complimented or thanked her for the pastry and coffee.

His forehead landed on his palm as he realized how insulting it must have been for her when he'd waved money in her face. If he wanted to deal with the public on a daily basis, he was going to have to do better than this.

As he gathered his stuff, he realized he couldn't just leave things like this. There had to be a way to make this up to Piper, but how?

The bell chimed above the door. He glanced up to see Piper's mother walk in. Her nose had an upward tilt, as though allowing her to look down on the rest of the world. Or was it just her daughter whom she looked down on?

Every muscle in his body tensed.

Joe didn't even know Piper's mother. He hadn't so much as spoken one word directly to her, and yet he didn't like her. Not at all.

From the little he'd observed, she was all about appearances, from her short platinum blond hair stylishly cut and combed until every strand was just so, to her perfectly manicured nails, to her finely pressed clothes. Everything about her screamed perfectionist.

Joe couldn't turn away, much less leave. After witnessing the rudeness of the woman the last time she was in the bakery, he hoped she'd be friendlier this visit, but he wouldn't so much as wager his coffee on it. He'd be worthless the rest of the morning without a dose of caffeine.

Joe shifted his seat to the side and opened his laptop. The vantage point from this table didn't allow him to see Piper behind the counter, but he could see her mother. Not wanting to openly stare, he pretended to compare the list of volunteers Mrs. Sanchez had drafted into duty to a spreadsheet on his computer. In truth, his full concentration was on the conversation between mother and daughter.

"Piper, tell me it isn't true. Please. It just can't be."

"Slow down, Mother. I don't have a clue what you're talking about."

"The rumor. It's all over town."

Piper shook her head. "You should know better than to listen to gossip—"

"But this is different. It's about you."

"Me?" Piper's voice lowered. "What are they saying?"

"That you agreed to bake the cake for David's wedding."

"Oh. That. It's not a rumor. It's the truth."

Piper's mother gasped.

"Mother, relax. It's all going to be fine. Laney and I talked."

"You talked?"

Piper smiled. "Don't look so horrified. I thought you'd be happy."

"Happy? Are you kidding?"

This was the most entertainment Joe had experienced since moving to Whistle Stop. He fought back a smile at the way Piper had turned the conversation around on her mother and had taken charge.

"Mother, is that all you wanted?"

"What? Um…no. I came here to tell you what a great job you're doing planning the festival. I heard about the wedding cake at the same time they were buzzing about how much fun Autumn Fest will be."

"Don't forget," Piper said, "I'm not planning it alone. Joe is doing his part, too."

"Oh, you don't need some outsider—"

"He's not an outsider. He's from Whistle Stop. You know that. You're in the quilting circle with his mother."

"*Hmpf*. From what I hear, he bailed on his family. He left his poor father to work himself to death on that ranch—"

Joe's spine grew rigid. That's what people thought? That his father died because of him? Why hadn't his mother spoken up and clarified things? Then again, his mother never spoke up—ever. His hands clenched. Wait. That wasn't right. There was one time—one tenuous time.

"Mother, enough!" Piper lowered her voice. "Joe's life is none of your business, and I'd prefer if you didn't spread unfounded gossip."

"It's not gossip. It's the truth—"

"Mother."

"Fine." Her mother sighed. "But all I'm saying is you can do this fundraiser on your own and take all of the credit. It'd really get you noticed. You never know, maybe you could end up with a date or two from some of the eligible bachelors."

"I'm not looking for a date."

"You had one very promising prospect, and what did you do? Toss him aside. And now what are you doing? Baking his wedding cake. That should be your wedding cake, not that little blonde's—"

"Mom, I have work to do."

"How could you agree to bake their wedding cake? Do you have any idea what people will think?"

Joe strained to hear every word. His curiosity was piqued. It seemed he wasn't the only one who'd been unlucky in love. But it was none of his business, even if he pitied Piper for being reminded about it by her tactless mother.

"Oh, before I go," Mrs. Noble said, "I saw these and thought they might help you." Something about the woman's singsong voice had him raising his head. The woman's manicured fingers were wrapped around a bottle she held out to Piper. "This is an herbal supplement that's supposed to help with weight loss. Hopefully, it'll help you with your problem."

He may not be able to see Piper's face, but he could only imagine the pain passing over her beautiful face. And the timing couldn't be worse. He'd just hurt Piper with his offer of money in return for her friendly gesture. He started to get to his feet to interrupt this spiraling conversation when he heard Piper speak up.

"I...I really don't need them."

"Sure you do." Her mother moved her hand with the bottle out of sight, but Joe assumed it was to place it in Piper's hand. "Just follow the directions. And quit eating those sweets."

"Thanks, Mom." Piper's deflated voice dug at him.

How could a mother make her daughter feel so bad about herself? But wasn't he guilty, too? Only, his comments had had nothing to do with Piper's looks. He thought she was the most beautiful woman he'd ever laid eyes on, which only added to his discomfort when he was around her.

Piper needed to tell her mother to back off. He knew it wasn't easy to stand up to your own parents. If only he'd done it sooner, maybe his dog, Fudge, wouldn't have had to pay such a steep price.

An old, gut-wrenching pain came over him, turning his stomach. He should have known coming back to his hometown would dredge up these unwanted memories—things that were better off left buried. He should get up and leave. It'd be so much better than sitting here, letting the torturous memories wash over him.

Deep in thought, he'd lost track of what was happening between Piper and her mother. He glanced up to find mother and daughter gone. He breathed out a sigh of relief. At least the conversation hadn't ended in a shouting match, or worse, tears. At least, he didn't think any tears had been shed. He decided he should check on Piper.

He gulped down the remainder of his coffee before walking up to the counter. He waited a couple of minutes before Piper returned with a tray of frosted cinnamon rolls. His mouth watered, but he willed himself to stick to his diet. "Piper?"

For a moment, she didn't move. When at last she turned, she blinked repeatedly, but her eyes were still red and shiny. His gut reaction was to vault over the counter and pull her into his arms, but he couldn't do that. He'd only end up making things worse, not better. Because not now, not ever, could he play her knight in shining armor. He was too damaged on the inside. He'd just end up hurting her even more.

So instead of offering his arms to Piper, he stood there, feeling awkward.

Her gaze rose, but didn't quite meet his. "Do you need something?"

Then he remembered his feeble excuse for bothering her. "Could I get some more coffee?"

Her surprised gaze met his. It was as though she'd been waiting for him to pity her over her mother's callous words. But he wasn't going to do that. He knew what it was like to be on the receiving end of those callous words, and he hadn't wanted pity either. It would have only made him feel worse. He wanted Piper to know that she wasn't alone. She had a friend.

"You know, I was going over our plans for the festival, and I noticed that so far not many people have signed up for the 5K Fun Run." He paused, not sure that in her current frame of mind she'd be receptive to discussing the festival.

She returned to the counter with half a pot of coffee. "I thought it was a great idea when you came up with it. I'm surprised more people aren't signing up."

"Maybe if we talked it up some more."

"You think?"

He nodded. "Word of mouth is the best form of advertising."

The hurt in her eyes faded as she focused on their common goal. She was such a strong person. It was such a shame that her mother zeroed in on Piper's insecurity and exploited it.

She filled his mug. "I can put a sign-up sheet here, next to the register. And I can mention it to the people I think might participate. Have you considered expanding the event?"

He hadn't thought of that, but he was intrigued. "Expand? How?" His mind started to race. "If we make it a marathon, we'll lose more participants."

"Not that way. We could make it a Fun Run and Walk. Then no one would have an excuse to miss out on the event."

"I like that idea. And one more thing..." Now that he had her attention, he needed to reel her in.

"What else could there be?"

"You."

"Me?" She pointed to herself as worry lines creased her forehead.

"As the co-chairs, you and I need to get out there and participate. Run the 5K with me?"

She shook her head. "Oh no. Not me. I've got work to do."

"It's important you set a good example. People will notice you every morning, getting out there and training for the event."

"You want me to run with you?"

He smiled and nodded. With a little more coaxing, he'd have her. And the thought of starting his day off with her smiling face was just too tempting for him to give up.

But instead of her returning his smile, her face creased with a blatant frown. "This is about my mother's visit, isn't it? You want me to run every day so I'll lose weight."

Damn. He hadn't thought she might misconstrue his motives. Nothing could be further from the truth. As it was, she filled his fantasies at night. But he couldn't tell her that bit of information. It would only succeed in scaring her off.

"This has nothing to do with that woman." He failed to keep the disdain from his voice. "I don't agree with her. I think you're beautiful as is. You don't have to change for me."

Piper's brows arched. "Are you serious? You really think I'm beautiful?"

He shifted his weight from one cowboy boot to the other. This conversation had taken an unexpected turn, and he wasn't the least bit comfortable with the new direction. Somehow, he had to get them back on their original track.

"Yes, I do think you're beautiful." There, he'd said it. And he'd meant it. But he couldn't let it go to her head. "So about the 5K run, how about you join me tomorrow morning, and we'll see how you do?"

A dopey smile eased the stress on her face, and the twinkle was back in her eyes. That right there made his admission worth it. Just so long as she didn't think his compliment meant he was interested in her or anything...even if there was a part of him that wished their circumstances were different.

"You've got yourself a date," Piper said. "Now I've got to get back to work before the lunch crew comes in."

A date? Joe staggered away from the counter. He'd never said anything about it being a date. They were co-chairs, plain and simple.

However, deep inside he felt the lines were starting to blur. They were more than co-chairs, but what did that make them? Friends? Yes, friends. That sounded good, less worrisome. Yet, somehow, it didn't seem like enough. But he refused to accept there could ever be more than that.

Worst of all, every time he thought of meeting up with her in the morning and seeing her in running shorts and a tight tank top that showed off her voluptuous curves, his breath caught in his throat and his palms grew damp. He shouldn't have been so eager to have her join him, but then again, this small-town girl had deep roots in this town, with no signs of going anywhere. Maybe it was possible this venture could be beneficial to both of them.

If only he could keep his mind from straying...

Had she made the right choice?

Later that afternoon, Piper was still debating the logic of her decisions. Luckily, there'd been a steady stream of customers to keep her occupied. Still, the thought of meeting Joe every morning for a run wouldn't help her to keep her interest in him at bay.

"Did you hear the news?" Ana burst through the doorway of the bakery, nearly colliding with Mrs. Webster, who was carrying her grandson's birthday cake. "Oops! Sorry."

"That's okay, dear. It's good to see you looking so excited."

"It's good to see you, too. You and your husband will have to stop by the Cantina soon. We miss having you."

"My husband hasn't felt well lately. As soon as he's up and about, we'll stop by. I promise."

"I hope he feels better soon."

"Thank you. I'll tell him you asked about him."

Piper kept glancing toward the door as she filled another order. She wondered what had Ana so worked up. Of all her friends, Ana was the most laid-back, so whatever the news was that she'd heard must be big.

After Mrs. Webster departed, Ana rushed to the counter. Piper held up a finger for her to wait a moment while she rung out the current customer.

At last, everyone had been tended to and she hurried over to where Ana was texting on her phone. "What happened?"

"You didn't hear?"

"Ana, a lot has happened today. You'll have to clue me in."

"The wedding—"

"Wow. That didn't take long to make the rounds. Listen, if you're here to talk me out of it, you're too late."

Ana's forehead wrinkled. "Talk you out of it?"

Piper nodded. "As soon as my mother heard the news, she made a beeline over here. She was horrified that I'd agreed to make the cake for David's wedding—"

"You what?" Ana's eyes grew round as lines on her forehead became even more pronounced.

"Isn't that what you're here to discuss?" Maybe she'd spoken too quickly.

Ana shook her head. "I wanted to tell you that Cord popped the question to Alexis and she accepted."

"Oh. Wow!" Piper quickly shifted gears from being defensive to being ecstatic for her friend. "I was starting to wonder if they'd ever make it official."

"Looks like next year is going to be a busy year, what with your brother and Bella getting married, and now Cord and Alexis are tying the knot, too. Next thing you know, we'll be planning baby showers."

"Really? You think?"

Ana nodded. "It won't be long until you and I are the only bachelorettes in Whistle Stop."

"It sure seems that way. But I'm sure you'll find Mr. Right soon."

"That would imply I'm looking."

Piper studied her friend for a moment. "You're really okay with not having a significant other?"

"I have enough on my hands what with my father being ill, running the restaurant, and dealing with my brother when he makes one of his surprise appearances. I don't need anything else to contend with." Ana arched a brow. "I don't mind being the last bachelorette."

"The last one? Why would you say that?"

"Oh, I don't know. Just because you have a really hot guy making himself at home in your bakery every morning."

"That's business."

Ana sent her an I-don't-believe-you look. "Uh-huh. Then how do you explain the way he stares at you?"

"He does not." Boy, was it getting warm in here?

"Oh yes, he does. And I'm not the only one who's noticed."

Piper's mouth opened, but nothing came out. She didn't know what to say. She was still stuck on the fact that Joe was interested in her. Was that really possible?

"Well, I should get back to the restaurant. But before I go, you have some explaining to do."

"I do?"

"Yes. What were you thinking by agreeing to do the cake for David's wedding? Did you fall and hit your head?"

Piper sighed. Why did everyone make it sound so bad? Had she miscalculated the benefit over the cost when she'd agreed to Laney's plan?

She gave Ana the highlights of her conversation with Laney. "So you see, this is a chance to get the residents of Whistle Stop to stop pitying me because what happened will all be ancient history. And I could gain some new clients, maybe some big accounts. Now doesn't it make sense?"

Ana didn't say anything as she just stood there staring at her.

Piper couldn't stand the silence. "Well, say something."

"Fine. Do you want my honest opinion?"

Piper nodded. Ana's opinion meant a lot to her.

"I think you made a huge mistake. I think you're so worried about what everyone thinks that you aren't taking into account your own feelings."

After Ana left, Piper brushed off her friend's concerns. Ana just didn't understand. It was important as a small-business owner to gain the town's respect. After all, look how hard Joe was working to fit back in.

Ana was just too cautious.

This would all work out.

CHAPTER ELEVEN

Five sunrises.

Five sunsets.

Five days of torture.

Piper stopped in front of Sam's Hitchin' Post to catch her breath. Her entire body screamed out in exhaustion. She hadn't known it was possible to have so many aches and pains all at once.

"Come on. You can do it." Joe jogged in place, waiting for her to catch up.

She didn't feel like she could do it. In fact, pulling up a piece of sidewalk and collapsing on it sounded heavenly. But she refused to give in and admit defeat. She started to move again. Mind over matter. Wasn't that what people said?

Step by agonizing step, they covered one block—then another. Piper moved slower and slower. Whatever made her think this was a good idea?

"Don't give up now," Joe said, barely winded. "We're almost done. All you have to do is make it to the town square."

"I'm done," she gasped. "I can't go any further."

Joe jogged back to her, looking all peppy and ready for another trip around town. "You aren't telling me you're a quitter, are you?"

Even though she glanced up to see his teasing smile, the question pricked her ego. She may have her share of shortcomings, especially in the weight department, but she didn't want to add quitter to that list.

From somewhere, she dredged up a modicum of energy. An inchworm could have outpaced her, but at least she was moving. That had to count for something. Right?

But would it be enough to get her down the last block to the town square, to her finish line? Each step was a challenge. Her gaze latched on to Joe's backside—his very fine backside—and it was like he was pulling her along.

After five days of running together, Piper had to revise her initial impression of Joe. If she were to be honest with herself, he was actually interesting and engaging. When the running got tough for her, he slowed down and never complained. He was a great sport.

At last, the town square came into sight. She made it! And if she weren't so tired, she'd point out that she wasn't a quitter. But she was just too plain exhausted to waste her breath.

Joe patted her on the back. "Don't worry. With a little more training, we'll bring up your time."

Her time? She sucked in a breath, her lungs burning. She'd made it to the end, and she was still breathing—that was all the accomplishment she needed.

Joe stretched. "Looks like this is going to be a great Hump Day."

Piper didn't think it was possible for her overheated face to grow even warmer, but her cheeks felt like they were on fire. How could this man make an innocent enough comment and yet her mind twisted it into something steamy and tempting? And worst of all, Joe starred in her fantasy. Her imagination needed a cold shower—icy cold.

She bent over, bracing her palms on her knees.

"Are you okay?" Joe peered at her, his handsome face creasing with concern.

She nodded. "Winded."

At this particular moment, it wasn't the run that was getting to her—it was him. Maybe her mother was right. She should take a look around and find herself a date. Because if she was finding herself attracted to Mr. Things-Must-Be-My-Way, she must be getting desperate. He was far too irritating to be likable, wasn't he?

"Come join me," Joe said, taking a seat on one of the weathered benches in the town square.

She shouldn't. It wasn't advisable, especially with the errant thoughts running rampant through her mind. And with Joe in running shorts that showed off his lean, toned legs, he was making it all the harder to keep her thoughts from drifting to the idea of giving in to her desires and finding out just how attractive Joe found her.

"I have to get back to work."

"Hannah has it under control." Joe patted the seat next to him. "You need a couple of minutes to rest. And we need to talk."

Talk? About what? Was it something serious? She hoped not. With it still being early, the town was quiet. Even the bakery wasn't open to the public yet, although the work had begun hours ago. Running her own business, Piper quickly had learned that it was early to bed and early to rise.

She supposed if he needed to talk, it was probably something to do with the fundraiser—a problem that would have to be solved ASAP. She sat down next to him, making sure to leave a modest space between them.

"Hey, look at that." Joe pointed to the sky.

Piper turned her head, catching sight of a couple of hot air balloons. One was red, white, and blue. The other was pink and purple. They made such a pretty picture against the clear azure sky.

"That gives me an idea." Her mind started churning with excitement.

"Are you planning to share?"

She glanced over at Joe, finding curiosity reflected in his eyes. "What if we got some hot air balloons to float by during the festival?" Joe's mouth opened, but before he could speak, she got an even better idea. "What if we got someone to do balloon rides? Wouldn't that be fantastic?" When he didn't respond, she asked, "Why aren't you saying anything? Do you think it's a silly idea?"

He shook his head. "I'm just wondering if it's my turn to talk."

"Sorry. I got excited."

"So I noticed. What I was about to tell you is that I know someone with a hot air balloon—"

"You do? That's awesome. There's an open spot in the center of the town square. Do you think it'd be big enough to tether the balloon?"

"Whoa, slow down. I don't even know if he's available that weekend. Or if he'd be willing to help us out."

"But you'll call him, won't you?" She loved the idea so much that she wasn't above begging. "Pleeease."

"Who knew that all it took was a balloon to turn your head?"

She playfully swiped at his arm. "Quit teasing me. Will you call your friend?"

"I suppose if it's that important to you—"

"It is." She grinned. Autumn Fest was going to be a smashing success. She could feel it in her bones. "Well, I should go shower so I can get back to work."

"Not so fast. Just because you got what you wanted doesn't mean you can just go running off. Stay and talk with me a bit."

She hadn't meant to come across as rude. "What did you want to talk about?"

"You. Tell me about yourself," Joe prodded.

"What?" She didn't even bother to hide her shock. "I thought you wanted to talk some more about the festival."

"We talk about that every day. I'm curious about you and why you stay here in Whistle Stop when you could be a baking sensation anywhere in the world."

Sensation? Really? She fanned herself, hoping he'd assume her discomfort was due to the run and had nothing to do with the flattery he'd just presented her. *Sensation*. The word rolled back and forth through her mind like a shiny marble tantalizing her.

"Whistle Stop is my home. I thought of moving away after high school, but the opportunity never presented itself. I hadn't thought about it since...until...until recently."

She was so tired of the gossip about her breakup with David. Oh, and she couldn't forget the part about her gaining back all of her weight. Certain people wouldn't let her forget that part after she'd lost twenty-five pounds for the wedding. The clucking tongues and rolling eyes were about to drive her crazy. It had to change, or she just might very well pack up and head on outta here.

His brows shot up. "So this town is starting to feel a bit too small for you? A little too claustrophobic?"

"I...I didn't say that." She was stunned that he'd nailed down her feelings exactly.

"You didn't have to. Your face said it all. If my mother was outspoken like yours, I'd hightail it out of town, too."

"It's not all about my mother. There are other things—"

She paused. She hadn't meant to get into any of this—not with him. Her past wasn't something she wanted to make light conversation about while sitting sat around in a park. It wasn't that she was still in love with David. She was surprised how fast she'd gotten over him. It was the mortification of finding out how easily she'd let herself be coaxed into becoming someone she didn't recognize.

But the expectant look in Joe's eyes told her that she'd already said too much. She'd opened Pandora's box, and now he stood in the way of her closing it again.

"You aren't going to just let this drop, are you?" she asked vainly.

"Not a chance. The gossip mill has kept you up on my life. It's only fair that I know something about yours. So what's your story? What happened to make you want to run away from this place? What made Whistle Stop too small for you?"

She glared at him. "I wasn't going to run away. Whistle Stop may not be a thriving metropolis or a resort destination, but it's got character. It's got history. And best of all, it has a closeness to it—friends helping friends. You can't find that just anywhere."

He held up his palms. "Okay. You don't have to sell me on the place. Remember, I'm the one who moved back. You're the one pondering leaving. So what gives?"

More traffic started to move through the streets. One by one, people were getting out and about. She needed to return to work. But she knew Joe well enough by now to know that he wasn't going to let the subject drop. And the last thing she wanted was for him to bring up the subject at the bakery, where there would be far too many eager ears.

"Here's the abridged version. I was engaged to the mayor's son. Long story short, I ended up giving up more of myself than I could live with... I almost sold the bakery. I lost a ton of weight so that I could wear the perfect wedding gown to marry the perfect guy and be the perfect wife."

"Let me guess. You figured out you didn't fit into that perfect mold?"

"Not by a long shot. The problem was, I wasn't willing to admit the truth to myself or anyone else. I was lightheaded and a bit nauseous from the crash diet I was on. I would never have made David happy if I was miserable. But in the end, he made my choice to end things easy for me."

"Just be glad you figured it out in time." Joe squeezed her hand. "Some of us don't."

"I tried to be exactly what David wanted. The devoted fiancée. I dressed in the right clothes. I went to all of the boring lunches with his mother. And I even agreed to sell the bakery." She drew in an unsteady breath. "But in the end, I was miserable. And, apparently, he was too because...because he found someone else."

A muscle in Joe's jaw tensed. "It's his loss, not yours."

"But maybe if I'd tried harder..."

Joe placed a finger beneath her chin, prodding her to look at him. "You didn't fail. You succeeded in being true to yourself. And that's the most important thing."

His direct gaze held hers. The breath trapped in her lungs began to burn. When his gaze dipped to her lips, the pounding of her heart echoed in her ears. Was he going to...would he...kiss her?

In the next second, his head lowered, and her eyes fluttered shut. She wanted this. She needed this. Just this once, she needed to know what it would be like to be wanted for herself and not for who she might be someday.

Her heart pounded in her ears. This had to be a dream. There was no other reasonable explanation. Sexy Joe Montoya, who could have his pick of the single ladies, was going to kiss her. And he was going to do it in broad daylight, right here in the middle of town where anyone could see them.

His lips brushed over hers, soft as a gentle, warm autumn breeze. This was definitely no dream. The feathery touch only escalated her desire. She longed for more of his kisses. Her hand moved to his whisker-roughened cheek.

As though her touch had shocked him, he jerked away. Her eyes sprang open in time to find him alighting from the bench and walking away. A bereft feeling swamped her. For a moment, she'd let down her guard. She'd tossed caution to the wind only to be rejected. How could that be?

He'd been the one to initiate it. He'd wanted her. She was certain of it. She needed to know where it'd gone wrong. Yet she couldn't bring herself to go after him to demand an answer.

What is wrong with me?

Then a moment of clarity came to her. The kiss had been a pity kiss.

She didn't need anyone's pity. She could lose weight. She could be beautiful...if she tried. Maybe it was time she gave the fitness and dieting some serious effort.

She'd show Joe that she didn't need his pity.

CHAPTER TWELVE

WHAT HAD HE BEEN thinking?

The kiss, though days ago, still played in Joe's mind like a skipping record, constantly repeating the most delicious sensation of his life. But how could that be?

He hadn't meant anything by the kiss other than to let Piper know he found her beautiful, inside and out. It'd been meant as a confidence boost. Nothing more.

Somehow, it'd backfired on him. The memory of her warm, soft lips pressed to his even kept him up at night. Worse, he'd noticed that things between him and Piper had grown tense as they continued working on the plans for the festival and meeting for their morning runs. And the awkwardness between them was only intensifying.

He'd been the one to kiss her, so it was up to him to fix things. But he certainly wasn't going to do it in the bakery, where they were always under scrutiny by either customers or Piper's employees. No, this had to be done in private—at least where no one would overhear.

While out on their morning run, Joe knew this was the best time to clear the air between them.

Piper was a few steps behind him, so he slowed down, letting her catch up. He had no idea how to begin this conversation, but he couldn't deal with the one-syllable answers and the long periods of strained silence anymore.

"Piper—"

The blare of the train whistle interrupted him. It was easier to wait until it passed than to try to shout over it. At last, there was silence once more.

"Piper, I need to apologize for the other day."

She stopped running. With her hands on her waist, she turned to him. Her chest heaved as she gulped down one breath after the other. "It's...fine."

"No, it isn't. You barely speak to me anymore."

He really did miss her chattering, even if it was to insert her unsolicited opinions about the coffee shop. There had to be a way to get their friendship back. Other than Holden Wainwright, who'd purchased Joe's family ranch, Piper was his closest friend in town. Any childhood friendships he'd had evaporated years ago. Not that he'd had many of them. But those people he'd known had either moved away or now gave him leery looks, as though he'd been a traitor for leaving town. Maybe if they knew the raw, unvarnished truth, they wouldn't look at him like he'd committed an unpardonable sin. But he wasn't that lonely—nothing would get him to share those horrific memories.

"What do you want me to say?" Piper's questioning stare searched his face.

"The kiss, it didn't mean anything. I...I just wanted you to know that you are beautiful. And that jerk who wanted you to change, well, he doesn't know what he's talking about."

Instead of relief sweeping across her face, the lines between her brows and bracketing her mouth deepened. "So you were just proving a point?"

Joe nodded. "Exactly." He sighed. "Now you understand?"

Once Piper realized he wasn't pressuring her into starting anything with him, she'd relax. They could go back to their playful verbal sparring, and he could enjoy her beautiful smiles that warmed him from the inside out. Something that had been lacking since he'd lost his head and kissed her. If he could do it all over again, he'd take back the kiss... Wouldn't he?

The indecision left him feeling off-kilter.

And so did the frown that touched her eyes, making them sad.

It didn't seem like he was saying anything right. He had to give it one more shot. He cleared his throat. "Piper, I'm sorry. Honest. Can we just forget the kiss ever happened?"

She blinked. "Sure. I understand. It meant nothing. We're fine."

The pressure on his chest eased. "You're sure?"

She nodded, but her gaze didn't meet his. "Of course. Sorry if I made you think I read more into the kiss than there was. I...I knew it was just a pity kiss—"

"Whoa. Wait. It wasn't a pity kiss."

"So if it wasn't a pity kiss, then what was it?"

He raked his fingers through his hair, not caring if he messed it up. This woman could be so frustrating. It seemed that no matter what he said, it was bound to be wrong. "Fine. I kissed you because I like you."

She cocked her head and smiled. "That sounds like the smartest thing you've said today. Now how about we get on with this run? I have work to do."

Well, he'd certainly bungled that conversation. And now she had him admitting that he liked her. Before he could clarify his statement, she took off running. His gaze latched on to the sway of her hips.

He was in trouble—big trouble.

With effort, he lowered his gaze to the pavement. Things between them would be all right, he assured himself. He'd straighten everything out. Somehow...

He liked her.

A week had passed and Piper couldn't stop smiling. She'd been all wrong about him. That kiss hadn't been out of pity after all. Not that she was ready to get involved with him. But as they continued to work on the details for the festival, there'd been less discord and a lot more harmony. Maybe running at the crack of dawn did have its benefits.

She was still thinking of Joe when her mother strolled into the bakery. Piper didn't want her mother to stomp all over her good mood. But Piper was cleaning the front of the display case, leaving her no chance of getting away unnoticed.

"Hi, Mom. What has you out and about this morning?" Piper straightened, smoothing her white apron over the dark jeans she'd found in the back of her closet.

Her pants were a size smaller than she'd been wearing. They were snug but not uncomfortable. It felt so good to be in something that didn't make her feel dowdy or dressed like a wallflower. Still, even though she was down a size, she automatically sucked in her gut, like she'd been doing for years when in her mother's presence.

"I wanted to talk to you about the cake auction." Her mother paused and gave her a discerning once-over. "Have you lost weight?"

Piper tightened her stomach a little more. "Uh, maybe. I hadn't really noticed."

"I knew those supplements I picked up for you would do the trick," her mother said smugly.

"I don't know about that." Piper's pride stung after her mother's attempt to steal the credit for her shrinking figure. The truth was, she'd forgotten about the pills and hadn't taken any of them.

After running for a couple of weeks, she'd gotten the drive to push herself harder to run more and more and to cut back on what she ate, hoping to make that scale fall faster. She'd never admit it to her mother, but the scale had barely budged. Piper assured herself that it was because muscle weighed more than fat. She'd started to wonder if she was truly making any progress, but her mother's comment was all the proof she needed. Her mother wouldn't lie about her weight loss, not even to make Piper feel better.

Maybe at last things were starting to go her way. If she just didn't give up, if she kept pushing a little harder, maybe that blasted scale would start to move.

Her mother gave her that all-knowing smile. "Trust me, dear. I'm your mother. I know what's good for you. And I just happen to have picked up another bottle for you."

Her mother retrieved the white bottle from her green and aqua quilted purse. "This is the largest bottle they had. Just let me know when you need more, and I'll pick them up for you."

As Piper accepted the bottle, Joe strolled through the door. He was right on time for them to go over the organization of the game and food booths in the street surrounding the town square. He waved before making his way to their usual table in front of the window.

He didn't even pause to notice she wasn't in her usual faded, baggy jeans. Even her mother had noticed the change in her. What was his problem? Frustration bubbled up inside her.

Instead of Joe thinking of her as the cupcake girl who served him coffee each morning before they got down to work, she wanted him to really notice her—as a woman—like he had the day he'd kissed her.

She just had to make some more adjustments to her exercise and diet was all. Her gaze moved to the bottle in her hand. And maybe these supplements would help her push her weight downward. At this point, she was willing to give it a shot if it meant turning Joe's head and having him see her as a desirable woman and not some pathetic waitress.

"Thanks for the herbal supplement, Mom. They'll come in handy," she said, having made up her mind to take them. What could they hurt?

Her mother beamed. "Glad I could help."

"Now," her mother said as she moved closer to the display case, "I want to place an order for the cake auction. Since I don't bake, I was hoping you could do up something special for me to hand in at the festival."

Piper wanted to laugh, but she refrained. Her mother, who was always going on about how bad baked goods were for her, was asking Piper to whip up something special. It was kinda ironic, but pointing this out to her mother would only succeed in ruining this surprisingly pleasant visit. And Piper was in no mood to get in a squabble with her mother. She had other things on her mind today—like making Joe notice her slenderizing jeans.

"Sure, Mom. I'll make sure you have a cake that you can be proud of."

"And you won't tell anyone." Her mother gawked around the bakery to make sure there weren't any witnesses to their exchange. When her gaze landed on Joe, she asked, "You don't suppose he heard us, do you?"

Piper shook her head. "I doubt it. And if he did, he won't say anything. You can trust him."

Her mother worried the inside of her painted red lip. "If you're sure. I wouldn't want anyone to know...well, that you helped me."

"Of course, Mom. No one will know. I'll drop it by the house the night before the auction."

Her mother's mouth lifted into a satisfied smile. "I knew I could count on you. Thanks. Now I've got to run. I have a little shopping to do before I meet Mrs. Sanchez for lunch."

Her mother rushed out the door as Piper turned to Joe, who still wasn't paying any attention to her. Well, she'd just have to do something to change that. "I'll be right with you." She held up her rag. "I just want to finish cleaning this glass."

His gaze met hers, and her heart jumped in her chest. He shouldn't have that effect on her. She didn't want to be attracted to him. She just wanted to prove a point—that kissing her hadn't been a mistake.

"Take your time."

And she would, too. She bent over and went back to cleaning, going over glass that she had already cleaned just to make sure she got all of the fingerprints. A display case could never be too clean.

For the first time, the colorful cupcakes lined up on the tiered shelves didn't tempt her after a visit from her mother. She stared at a red devil's food one with an extra big dollop of butter cream frosting and a maraschino cherry on top. Usually, it would make her mouth water, but not today.

Today, she had something…erm, someone else distracting her. Piper resisted glancing over her shoulder. She was dying to know if he'd noticed her figure-flattering outfit, but she'd know soon enough when she joined him to go over the plans for the fundraiser.

Not wanting to linger too long, she straightened. Once her cleaning supplies were put away, she grabbed his coffee and headed to the table. "Ready to figure out the layout for this shindig?"

He smiled at her. "Sure. All I've got so far is a scaled drawing of the town square and the surrounding street. I thought we'd want to do this with actual dimensions to make sure we can fit every booth and stand."

"Sounds good to me." She leaned forward to look at the graph paper, admiring his neat handwriting and straight lines. "Did we already figure out the dimensions of the game booths?"

"I have it written down somewhere." He flipped through the legal pad where they'd listed various items for the fundraiser. "Here it is. Most are the same size, but there are a few that require a different configuration."

The bell over the door chimed. Automatically, Piper's head lifted. A tall cowboy strolled through the door.

She didn't recall ever seeing him before. The man's gaze darted around the room before settling on Joe.

Piper stood and approached the man. "Welcome to Poppin' Fresh Bakery. If you're looking for a sweet treat, you came to the right place."

When the cowboy's gaze took her in, he removed his hat and held out his hand. "Howdy. I'm Holden Wainwright. I'm new to town."

"Welcome. I'm Piper Noble. And this is Joe—"

"I know."

Her gaze darted between the two men, and then his name rang a bell in her memory. "Oh, you're the one who bought the Montoya ranch?"

The man nodded. "That would be me. I was hoping I could talk Joe into giving me a hand."

"Did you run into some problems with that well?" Joe set aside his pen and turned in his chair, giving the man his full attention.

"Yep, was hoping you might have some time to give me your take on things."

Joe's gaze slipped to Piper. "Well, we were working on finalizing some plans for the Autumn Fest—"

"Go ahead and go." Piper knew he was itching to run off and do guy stuff. Besides, he hadn't even once acknowledged her different clothes. "We can work on this tomorrow."

"Are you sure?"

"Of course."

He grabbed his hat and pointed to his attaché case. "Mind if I leave this stuff here?"

"I'll put everything behind the counter. You can pick it up later."

"Thanks." And that was it. He rushed out the door.

Her grip on the pencil tightened. Luckily, it wasn't a lead pencil, or it would have snapped. She'd never seen a man so eager to make an exit. If she worked harder at her weight loss, maybe he'd no longer feel sorry for her. And then perhaps he wouldn't mind spending more time with her.

CHAPTER THIRTEEN

EARLY THE NEXT MORNING, Joe, as usual, was the first to show up at the town square for their morning run. Piper may be a baker, but it was obvious the early mornings didn't come natural to her. She was forever running a few minutes behind. He hoped she wore her usual baggy sweat shorts and not something that hugged her rounded backside like those jeans she'd had on at the bakery yesterday.

He thought for sure she was going to catch him ogling her as she'd bent over to clean the display case. Damn. He ran a hand over the tightened muscles in his neck. He felt like some hormonal high schooler again. Gawking at Piper like he'd never seen a beautiful woman before. But he'd never seen her dress like that, in clothes that enhanced her body.

Those new dark jeans had fit her like a second skin. He'd thought his eyes were going to pop out, and it was all he could do to keep from drooling. She usually wore lose, nondescript things that didn't provoke his very active imagination.

He'd already made the mistake of kissing her. He couldn't repeat that mistake. Or worse, admit that he couldn't think about anything but pulling her into his arms and letting his lips do the talking.

When Holden had made his surprise appearance, it'd been like divine intervention. Joe hadn't cared at that moment what Holden needed. Joe would have volunteered for just about anything in order to keep himself from doing or saying something to embarrass himself. And the wide-open range and fresh air had been the prescription he'd needed to screw his head on straight. He was in control now.

Thankfully, when Piper finally exited the bakery, she was wearing nothing fancy or clingy. Still, the image of her in those snug jeans and fitted top was tattooed upon his mind.

She rushed across the street to join him in the town square. "Good morning. Sorry I'm a little late. I was helping Hannah with a special order."

"You were working?"

Her fine brows scrunched together. "Yes. Just like every morning before we go running. You surely didn't think I just rolled out of bed, did you?"

Um, yes. He'd never really given it much thought. Now he felt a bit foolish. "No. Of course not. Do you need to stay and help her?"

"We got most of today's orders done before I left. She should be good until I get back."

"Boy, you really do work long hours, don't you?"

She nodded. "Twelve hours a day. Six days a week. But I won't be the only one working from sunup till sundown. Once your shop is open, you'll be pulling down long hours, too."

He nodded. At least he would in the beginning, until he could afford to hire additional help. "We better get started. Sounds like you have a big day ahead of you."

As she moved through her warm-up routine, he'd occasionally catch glimpses of how her T-shirt strained across her chest. His heart rate accelerated, and it had absolutely nothing to do with exercising. This was all her fault. He'd never had problems like this until she'd strutted around the bakery all done up like she was going on a date.

"Ready?" she asked, just like it was any other morning—like she hadn't taunted him yesterday.

He cleared his throat. "Sure."

And they set off. Joe needed the release that jogging provided him. His feet pounded the pavement. Faster. Faster. He welcomed the exertion, wanting to clear the tormenting thoughts of Piper from his mind. After all, he had to continue to work with her. He couldn't just walk away and dump the festival in her lap. She was counting on his help.

He assured himself that his reaction to her was a purely physical response after too many long, lonely nights. Only, Piper wasn't the type of woman to scratch his itch and walk away. She'd want more. And he didn't do relationships—not anymore.

They were about halfway around town when he realized that in his efforts to outrun these unwanted feelings for Piper, he'd totally left her in the dust. He felt awful. After all, he was the one who'd come up with the idea of running together to get her in shape for the 5K Fun Run.

He stopped to give her a chance to catch up. While standing there, he noticed a beautiful chocolate Lab nosing his way up the other side of the road. Joe glanced around but he didn't see the owner anywhere in sight.

When he focused back on the dog, it stopped and turned to him, as if he sensed he was being watched. Joe's throat constricted. In that instant, the years were peeled away and he was a kid again. He stood motionless on the side of the deserted street. He continued to stare, and the dog mirrored him.

This couldn't be right. The rational part of his mind said this couldn't be Fudge, no matter how much the dog resembled his beloved dog. Fudge was long gone, except for the loving memories he'd left in Joe's heart.

Neither of them moved. Joe hadn't allowed himself to delve into those heart-wrenching memories in a very long time. Some things were best left untouched. But now a distinct reminder of his unwanted past was standing there looking at him as if the pup were in need of help.

Joe wanted to turn around and leave, pretend he'd never seen the dog. This was just too much to ask of him. The wounds ran much too deep. But the dog didn't move. And with no owner in sight, he needed help.

"Hey, what's up with you?" Piper panted. "You ran like the devil was on your heels."

He continued to stare at the dog. Anguished memories and tormenting thoughts collided. He rubbed his throbbing temples.

"You okay?" she asked, drawing him back to the present.

"I'm fine. That dog—he seems lost. Do you recognize him?"

Piper raised a hand to shield her eyes and glanced across the street. "Nope. Can't say as I've ever seen him before."

"He must belong around here somewhere."

"I'm sure he'll find his way home. Whistle Stop isn't that big. Come on. Let's keep going."

His feet felt like they'd been planted in cement. "We can't just leave him. He looks like he needs help."

Piper turned back to the unmoving dog. "He looks healthy to me. No ribs sticking out. And look, there's a collar on him." She pulled on Joe's arm. "Let's go before I start to cool down. You know, I'm down a couple of pounds this week. I'd like to see if I can eke out one more."

"Hey, boy," Joe called out, checking both ways before crossing the road. "Come here."

The dog took a hesitant step forward, but then paused. He didn't blame the dog. You couldn't be too safe these days. But if he was going to help the dog, he would have to be willing. If he started to run, Joe knew he'd never be able to catch up, especially with the lengthy gap between them.

"Come on, boy. It's okay."

The dog stood at the curb and cocked his head, as though trying to decide if Joe was telling him the truth. An independent thinker, so much like his faithful friend Fudge had been. The thought made Joe's heart clench with a crush of memories.

"He obviously isn't interested in your help." Piper jogged in place. "We really need to keep going."

"Go ahead if you want. I'm staying here."

She stopped moving. "What's the deal with the dog?"

He couldn't tell her. He'd never told anyone. Not even his ex-wife. He didn't think he could ever form the words. They'd clog up in his throat and choke him.

Not going there. Just concentrate on the dog.

"Come on, Fudge..."

"How do you know the dog's name?"

He didn't. "I...I guessed."

He could feel Piper's puzzled stare boring into his skull. He'd have to be careful what he said, or he'd end up starting a conversation he never intended to have with her, or anyone.

The dog took a hesitant step toward him. A wave of relief washed over Joe. He didn't like the thought of this dog roaming the streets, even if this road was a quiet one.

"You're serious, aren't you?" Piper asked. "You're not going to move until the dog is taken care of. Who'd have ever guessed you're a dog person? What else don't I know about you?"

Plenty. But nothing worth mentioning.

He didn't bother to answer her as the dog lumbered across the street. The animal's movements were slow and cautious. When the dog reached him, Joe held out his fist and let the dog take in his scent. Within seconds, the dog licked his hand.

Joe's vision blurred, causing him to blink repeatedly. He remembered how Fudge used to look at him with a slight tilt of his head just like this dog. He couldn't resist running his hand over the dog's smooth head. Piper was right. This dog wasn't a stray. In fact, someone took great care of him...until today when he got loose.

"Hey, boy. Let's see where you belong." Joe didn't make any fast motions, not wanting to startle the dog.

The red collar had all of the appropriate tags, including one with his name.

"Well?" Piper prompted. "What did you learn?"

"His name is Java."

"Really? That's so interesting. Almost like your paths were supposed to cross."

No, that couldn't be. Even fate couldn't be twisted enough to throw his painful past in his face. Not after he'd worked so damn hard to move past the nightmares that had haunted him for years.

Joe ran his hand down the dog's back. "Don't worry, boy. We'll get you home."

"And how are we going to do that?" Piper asked, kneeling down to pet the very lovable dog. "Is there an address or phone number?"

"No. But, like you said, this is a small town. Surely someone will know something." Joe tucked his fingers around the collar and said, "Come on, boy. We'll get you home."

"Wait. Where are you going?"

What didn't she understand? The dog was lost, and Joe was going to find his home. A dog needed to be taken care of, because there were people out there who weren't so nice. People who were callous and cruel. People who would hurt a dog like this—and worse.

He turned to Piper to explain, but when he opened his mouth, the words wouldn't come. The words lodged in the back of his throat as he recalled Fudge and how much he wished someone had been there to save him.

Her eyes opened wide with concern. "Joe, what's the matter? Your hand is shaking, and you're pale as a ghost."

He truly felt as though he had seen a ghost. He glanced down at his hand that was clutching the dog's red collar. There indeed was a noticeable tremble. And he was powerless to stop it.

"Come. Sit down for a moment." Piper's fingers wrapped snuggly around his forearm before she gave him a solid tug.

He glanced around. With it being so early in the morning, not many people were up and about yet. He let her guide him over to a tree along a sidewalk in front of the elementary school. The dog willingly followed.

It was like they were one big happy family. Nothing could be further from the truth. At best, Piper was his friend without benefits. And Java... Well, as much as he'd love to take the pup home, the dog already had one. They just had to figure out where he belonged.

"What are we doing?" he asked. "I need to get this guy home."

"First, you can't just run off. You don't even know where this fellow lives. And, secondly, you look like...well, like a ghost crossed your path."

He wished she'd quit talking about ghosts. It was very unnerving, especially with the close resemblance between Java and Fudge. Joe scrubbed a hand over his face.

"What is it about this dog that has you so unnerved?" Piper stared at him expectantly.

Was he that easy to read? And here he'd thought he'd mastered the art of keeping his feelings locked deep inside, hidden away from prying eyes. He never wanted to let on that he could be wounded and bleed like everyone else. It was a protective mechanism he'd learned as a kid.

"You can talk to me." Piper sank down on the grass and patted a spot next to her. "Because we're not going anywhere until I know what's up with you."

He didn't like where this was leading. Even though they were in the wide open, this moment felt too cozy for his comfort. He should take the dog and keep walking. That's what the logical, self-preserving side of his brain told him to do.

But there was this other part of him that was dying to lay open his dark secrets. For so long, he'd been lugging around the nightmares and guilt. Over the years, the load had become heavy and cumbersome.

And though he'd shoved the memories into the dark recesses of his mind, they were still there and popped up at the most inopportune times. Like now. He just wanted to let them go. But they clung to him like leeches draining away his happiness.

And yet he found himself sitting down next to her. Then Java lay down between them. Joe couldn't resist running his hand over the dog's head.

"We shouldn't be sitting here doing nothing," Joe grumbled, resisting the urge to tell her about Fudge. Just thinking his name made Joe's insides churn with a familiar raw pain.

He glanced down at the ghost dog. All of those buried nightmares were threatening to break through his carefully laid defenses. And that couldn't happen. He started to get to his feet.

Piper placed a calming hand on his arm. "Slow down. Did you ever think that the owner is hunting for Java? And that if we stay still, they'll catch up to us?"

Couldn't she sense how much he wanted to leave, to avoid rehashing the past? She continued staring at him with an expectant look. He wasn't going to open up. He glanced away.

He'd thought when he left Whistle Stop all of those years ago that he could at last put his past behind him. But what he'd learned since then had proved him wrong. The past wasn't just a series of events to be relished, or in his case, forgotten. The past was like fibers woven into the fabric of his life.

For better or worse, the past had made him the man he was today.

CHAPTER FOURTEEN

JOE EASED BACK TO the ground. There would be no escape for him. All he could now was make the best of things and avoid the dreaded questions.

Java rested his head on Joe's leg. He couldn't resist scratching behind the dog's ear, which only had Java snuggling closer.

"He likes you." Surprise laced Piper's words.

"And that's so shocking?" He'd always been good with animals. In fact, he'd always thought he'd be a cowboy the rest of his life... But, unable to remain at the ranch, he'd had to make another choice for himself.

"That's right. I almost forgot that you grew up on a ranch." She plucked at a blade of grass and twirled it between her fingers. "I always wondered what happened to you. You disappeared after the last day of school. You never even showed up for graduation."

Years of avoidance started to peel away. His jaw tightened, his back teeth aching from the mounting tension. He hadn't gone to the graduation ceremony because he'd skipped town. The fact he'd stuck it out until the last day of class in order to graduate and receive his college scholarship was no small feat.

Nothing and no one could have made him stay at the ranch or in this small town a minute longer.

Joe shrugged. "I was never into ceremonies."

"But where did you go? Why did you leave so abruptly? It couldn't have been easy for your family—"

"My family! You've got to be joking."

Java lifted his head, his eyes and ears on full alert. Piper had a similar startled look.

"Sorry." Joe regained his composure and soothed the dog. "You don't need to feel sorry for my family. They knew I was leaving. I shouldn't have stuck around as long as I did."

Piper's gaze softened as she searched his face as though trying to understand where his burst of emotion had come from. "I had no idea there were problems. Your mother never said a word. And your father, well, he never talked much."

"You're lucky he didn't talk to you." Harsh strains of his father's voice echoed in Joe's head. "The only time that man spoke was to curse when he was angry, which was often. Or to bellow when something he thought should have been done wasn't completed. Or if it wasn't done to his satisfaction."

Piper's eyes opened wide. "I...I wondered."

Her soft admission gained Joe's full attention. "You did?"

She hesitantly nodded. "Your...your mom never came to town alone. Your father always lurked about." Piper's hesitant gaze caught his, as though she wondered if it was all right if she continued. When he didn't say a word, she said, "Your mother always seemed nervous, and she never talked with the other women. It was... Well, it was like she was afraid."

"She was." The bold confirmation startled even him. He never ever talked about this part of his life with anyone. Not his ex-wife. Not his former best friend. He reasoned if he didn't talk about it and no one knew, then he could go through life like it'd never happened. It wasn't until now that he realized he'd been fooling himself. As dreadful as those memories were, he couldn't ignore them forever. They'd impacted him in ways he was only now starting to understand.

Here he was on this early morning, the September sun warming his neck while he sat next to this beautiful woman, about to dredge up the darkest memories of his life. And as much as he wanted to tamp them back down and stuff them in the box, he wasn't strong enough. The images flickered in his mind like those from an old black and white projector.

Java moved closer, putting both paws across Joe's legs. He'd heard it said that animals could sense their owner's emotions, but how could that be possible with Java? They'd just met. Still, Joe ran a hand over the dog's dark brown fur, taking comfort in the act.

When Joe spoke, his voice was deeper than normal. "My father was not an easy man, and his temper was lightning fast. And it burned red hot. Nothing could cool him down until he'd taken his fury out on those closest to him."

Piper's mouth gaped until she noticed he was staring. She pressed her lips together and glanced away. "That must have been rough. How did you manage?"

"I didn't know any other way of life, not until I became a teenager. Then I couldn't wait to get out of there." Maybe this conversation was for the best. He was tired of the townsfolk thinking he'd been a bad son who'd abandoned his family. "It's why I spent every single minute with my nose in a book."

"Oh, I thought you just liked to read."

"Nope. I was desperate to get a full scholarship to anywhere…anywhere but here." The old feeling of oppression and desperation rained down, shrouding him in the grayness of his past.

"That's why you were so quiet in school."

He shrugged. "It was easier to keep to myself. It was tough enough being an awkward teenager. I didn't need people asking a bunch of questions that I couldn't—wouldn't—answer."

"So you made up your mind that you'd had enough of your father's temper and packed your bags? It must have been scary leaving home for good."

"It was better than staying there." Joe shook his head, willing away the wave of emotions that rose up in his throat as he recalled those last days.

"Wasn't your father proud of you for receiving a scholarship?"

Every muscle in Joe's body tensed. How did this woman know exactly which razor-sharp questions to ask? In that moment, the years of scar tissue peeled back, and his past gaped open in his mind.

Java pulled back and stared at him. Guarded and waiting.

Piper didn't move, but her steady gaze prodded him, begging him not to shut down.

Joe lowered his gaze to the freshly mowed grass. He didn't want to go where she was leading him, but he couldn't stop the crush of memories. He needed to purge them. And he trusted Piper. He knew she was a good person, inside and out. She would keep his secret, but was it fair to burden her with it?

"You don't want to hear this." His throat ached from the tension in his neck. In fact, his whole body was in revolt over dredging up this nightmare.

Piper reached over and squeezed his hand. "I want to hear whatever you're willing to share. I'd like to understand why you left."

Joe lifted his head and met her warm gaze. What he found there surprised him. He felt secure in their friendship and found strength in her compassion. Two things he hadn't realized he'd been longing for until now.

Joe squeezed her hand. "My father was a hard man who wanted things done on his command and to his specifications. There were no such things as excuses. Ever."

"That must have been hard, especially being a kid and wanting to hang out with your friends."

Joe shook his head. "There was no time for friends. He didn't believe in wasting money on hiring ranch hands when he had a perfectly capable son to do the work."

"When did you have time to study?"

"I didn't."

Piper's eye grew round as she connected the dots. "So you were always studying at school because that was the only time you had."

Joe nodded. "If my old man had had it his way, I'd have dropped out of school to do more work. He thought school was a waste of time."

"But what about your grades? Surely they had to impress him."

The past washed over Joe like a dense, dank fog, swallowing him into its darkness. "He didn't know about my grades. He didn't want to know. All he cared about was how much I did around the ranch."

"That's horrible. What about your mother?"

"She had her own problems with my father and couldn't risk angering him further by making a big deal out of my academics. My father would have blown a gasket. He did that enough without prodding."

Piper's head lowered, and her voice came out soft as a whisper. "And here I thought I had issues with my mother and her constant need to change me, to perfect who I am."

"Your mother hasn't done you any favors either."

"I'm surprised he let you go away to college."

"He tried to stop me..." Joe's voice faded as those very vivid memories played in his mind like a motion picture. "In fact, one of the happiest days of my life turned out to be the beginning of a horrible nightmare."

Piper threaded her fingers through his and squeezed. No words were necessary. He knew she was there for him. And now that he'd started down this dark, lonely road, he welcomed her warmth.

"The day the mailman delivered a big white envelope with my name on it—the one I knew just had to be my college acceptance—my father got to it first. He ripped it up and told me I'd never go." Joe's breath grew shallow as his heart clenched with old, familiar pain. "I had to tape the pieces together to see what it said."

"What about your mother?"

"She stood off to the side, not saying a word. She'd learned early on, after losing a couple of teeth, not to question my father. He held her firmly under his thumb."

"That's awful. I'm so sorry. No wonder you left."

Joe pulled away from her. He needed to get through this last part on his own. To prove to himself that he could do it. "That isn't it. That isn't why I left. I knew the way he was. I didn't expect anything different."

Piper's eyes shimmered with sympathy. "No child should ever have a parent treat them like that."

"It got worse the closer it came to my graduation."

Piper worried her bottom lip. "If this is too difficult, you don't have to finish—"

"Yes, I do."

The firmness of his words caused a flash of surprise to flicker across her delicate features. It surprised him as well. For so long, he'd done everything in his power to keep his past exactly where it was, in the past. But now, sitting here with Piper, who was the most understanding person he'd ever met, and running his hand over Java's smooth coat, he felt strangely at ease. It was as though airing out the ghosts that still haunted him would at last free him.

The thought of at last finding peace spurred him on.

"No matter what my father said or did, I wasn't going to give up on college. It was my ticket out of there, and I wouldn't be stopped."

His chest tightened as he thought of his old pal Fudge, so much like Java in looks and demeanor. They could have been siblings. He scratched beneath the dog's ear, just like Fudge had liked. His dog had been his best friend. Fudge had made the miseries bearable.

When Fudge had come to Joe's defense during one of his father's tirades, his father had threatened to get rid of the dog. Joe had quickly learned to keep Fudge locked up in the tack room when his father was around. There had been no love lost between those two.

Joe glanced over at Piper. How much of this should he tell her? Did he dare open up about all of it?

"I had a dog. His...his name was Fudge. He looked a lot like Java. So much so that, for a moment this morning, I'd thought I stumbled across a ghost."

"What happened to Fudge?"

"It was right before graduation when my father found out that I'd accepted the scholarship to college against his wishes. He went ballistic. When he was coherent again, he gave me an ultimatum. Either I stayed there and one day took over the ranch like a son ought to, or I left with nothing but the clothes on my back and never came back."

"Oh my." Piper clamped a hand over her mouth.

Joe turned away. The anger and pain churned in his gut. He didn't want Piper to witness all of those awful emotions on his face. It even scared him a little by the depth of anger he felt for his father after all of these years.

"I told him there wasn't anything on that ranch I'd miss." His voice cracked as he realized how wrong he'd been to utter those words.

"I can't imagine—"

Joe held out his hand to silence her consoling words. If he was going to do this, if he was going to let her understand why, he needed to stay in control. If he stopped now, he'd never get it out.

His hands clenched as he tried to stem the wave of agony. "The next day I came home from school. Fudge always met me down at the road, but...but that day he wasn't there."

Every muscle in his body tensed as those very real, very horrid memories assaulted him. He struggled to keep his emotions in check. His throat ached with unleashed sobs, and his eyes burned with threatening tears. But he refused to give in.

His voice was hoarse when he spoke again. "I knew then and there that something was wrong. I ran to the house, but there was no Fudge anywhere. When I asked my mother where Fudge was, she became flustered. 'Gone,' was all she'd say before locking herself in her bedroom."

Joe pulled his arm away from Piper and got to his feet. Java sat straight up and sent him a puzzled gaze. Joe didn't dare make eye contact with Piper, not sure he could maintain his composure beneath her sympathetic gaze.

Right then, the pain was so overwhelming that he just needed to move. He needed a moment to suck down some of the turmoil so he could finish this nightmare. He forced a deep breath into his tightened chest, followed by an unsteady sigh. He could do this. He could get it out, and then maybe at last he'd be at peace.

"I knew something awful had happened. My mother only ran and hid in her bedroom when she was scared. And if she was scared, I knew it had something to do with my father. Something bad had happened...something real bad."

CHAPTER FIFTEEN

Trapped in a nightmare.

And the only exit was the truth.

Joe drew in another unsteady breath. With his back to Piper, he stared off into the distance. But he wasn't seeing Whistle Stop. In his mind, he was back at the ranch.

"I pounded on my mother's bedroom door, begging and pleading for her to talk to me, to tell me where I could find Fudge. All I heard was the occasional anguished sob. I knew something was wrong, but I had no idea just how bad things were about to get."

Java moved to his side. The dog sat down and nosed his hand. It was such a sweet gesture, so like Fudge.

Joe's nerve started to fail him. He didn't know if he could get through this last part. It was unimaginable, so monstrous. His stomach lurched nauseatingly as saliva pooled in his mouth. He swallowed hard.

"I...I don't know what gave me the idea, but I walked into the living room and glanced up at the fireplace. My father's shotgun was gone."

"Oh no! He didn't..."

Joe swiped a hand over his face, surprised to find it damp. "I ran outside. I'd never been so scared in my life. I was running toward the barn when there was..." He drew in a breath in his tight chest as his eyes burned. "There was a shotgun blast. How could he do it? How could he kill..."

In the next instant, Piper was there, wrapping her arms around him. No words were needed. He drew strength from her caring touch. He didn't know how long they stood there, wrapped in each other's arms.

When he'd drawn himself together, he pulled back. His voice came out raspy. "He took away the only thing I truly loved."

"No one at school or in town knew."

"They weren't supposed to. I didn't want anyone to know what my life was like, to feel sorry for me."

"But surely someone could have helped."

Joe shook his head. "When I found Fudge in the barn, my father told me he didn't need some lazy dog to take care of since I'd be gone." His voice cracked. "He...tossed a shovel at me."

The last words came out as a strangled whisper. Piper took his hands in hers. The warmth in her touch thawed his icy veins. Her tenderness and caring buoyed him to the present.

"After I ...um, took care of Fudge, I left, and I never looked back."

"But where did you go? What did you do?"

"I had no particular destination in mind. I just had to get away from my father, from the pain. I ran as far and as hard as I could."

"And that's why you weren't at graduation."

He nodded. "Finals were done."

"I'm so, so sorry. No one had any idea. I knew your father was...was a tough man, but I had no idea he could be so cruel."

Joe scrubbed his face with his palm. "Now do you understand why the people of Whistle Stop have everything about my life all mixed up and backwards? My father doesn't deserve their pity—"

"And you don't deserve their condemnation. Why haven't you ever told anyone?"

"Don't you dare repeat what I've told you. It was for your ears only. Just leave the past where it is."

"But—"

He pressed a finger to her mouth. Her lips were soft and smooth. He was tempted to kiss away her rebuttal, but he couldn't let himself do that. He couldn't give in to his desires. He'd done it once, and it had been for her sake, but this time...this time it'd be for him and all about what he needed. And he couldn't let himself need Piper. It'd only lead to another painful loss in his life.

"Just leave it be," he said. "You know, and that's all that matters."

Her shoulders slumped as though the argument went out of her. Java took the moment to move closer and again nudge Joe's hand with his wet nose. For just a second, Joe had a glimpse of what life could be like surrounded by those who cared—but it would never happen for him. His heart was too damaged, too scarred.

Joe heard a vehicle off in the distance, but he was too caught up in staring into Piper's eyes to pay it much attention. "Thank you for listening to me."

"Thank you for sharing."

The open honesty in her eyes tugged at him. Maybe just this once...maybe he could give in to his desires. After all, a kiss was just a kiss, wasn't it?

"You know I'm not looking for anything serious?" he asked, wanting to set the playing field before he moved to first base.

"I know."

She didn't look disappointed or mad or even hurt, and she didn't pull away from him either. Instead, her gaze dipped to his mouth. That was all of the invitation he needed.

Joe's head lowered. His eyes had drifted closed when someone's shouting halted his advance.

"Hey! Java!"

Piper jumped back as though she'd come to her senses, something he wished he could do. An older man lumbered toward them with the aid of a cane. "Java. Here, boy."

The dog barked as his tail swished back and forth.

"Hello, Mr. Wilks." Piper approached the man. "I didn't know you got another dog."

The man's bony shoulders rose and fell. "When you get my age, the days get empty and lonely. I don't have any family, so I figured that Java and I could keep each other company. It's just, with him not being much more than a puppy, he has a lot more energy than me."

As the two continued to chat, Joe's mind strayed. He couldn't shove aside his disappointment at not being able to steal a kiss. It wasn't until then that he realized just how much he'd needed that intimate connection. There was something very special about Piper, and it went far beyond the magic she created in the kitchen.

"Isn't that right, Joe?" Piper looked at him expectantly.

He had no idea what had been said. But he refused to show her just how distracted he'd been by the near-miss kiss. He nodded. "Right."

The amusement dancing in Piper's eyes and the smile lifting her lips told him that she knew he hadn't been paying attention. It was as though they now shared some sort of special bond. Was that possible? Or was it all a product of his imagination?

"Don't know what got into Java today," the man said, a bit winded. "Guess he wanted his morning walk, and I just wasn't up to it."

The dog moved to Mr. Wilks's side immediately, looking thrilled to see him.

"We're just glad you caught up to him," Joe said. "Java looks anxious to go home."

"Probably wants his breakfast. He was so excited to go exploring that he didn't wait to eat. Silly pup." A deep and abiding love was evident in the man's voice. "Ready to go home, Java?"

"Thank you, both," the man said. "I'd be lost without Java."

"We're just happy we could help." Joe gave Fudge...erm, Java one last pat on the head. As the man and dog walked away, a deep sadness came over Joe. He assured himself that it was just the lingering emotions over the story he'd told Piper. Besides, he didn't have time in his life for a dog. He was starting up a new business, and that's where his sole focus needed to be.

"You should consider getting yourself another dog," Piper said, as though reading his thoughts.

"I don't think so."

"But why? You obviously love dogs, and if Java is any indication, they love you, too."

"I can't."

"I don't understand. What's stopping you?"

"Isn't it obvious?" When she shook her head, he added, "Every time I let myself care about something or someone, it costs me. I've lost the things that have meant the most to me." He drew in an unsteady breath. "My father...he took away the most loyal and loving dog. The man I considered my best friend slept with my ex. And Denise, well, she took away the coffeehouse business that I started. I just can't afford to lose anymore."

Piper reached out and squeezed his arm. "You can't give up on life. You have to go after the important things."

His gaze met hers. In her eyes, he found strength and determination. He used to have both of those in spades...didn't he? He thought so. When had he let the bad stuff start outweighing the good stuff?

Piper definitely fit in the good-stuff column. She was opening his eyes to all the things he'd closed himself off to in life. And he wanted to live a full life—he just had to learn to let down his guard.

And he would start now. His gaze zeroed in on her tempting lips. He longed to taste her sweetness, to feel connected with her on a deeper level.

His head dipped, and his lips claimed hers. She didn't move at first, as though he'd startled her. Was this not what she'd meant by going after the important things in life?

But then her mouth moved beneath his, and her fingers tentatively touched his cheek. That small touch heated his blood and sent his heart racing. Thank goodness they were in public, because his need for her thrummed in his veins.

And just as quickly as the kiss started, Piper pulled away. Her eyes were dilated, and her breathing was rapid. The rosy hue in her cheeks made her even more adorable.

He didn't want her to go, not yet. When he went to kiss her again, she pulled back.

"I...I have to get to work." She headed for the bakery.

Great job, Joe.

She was trying to help him, trying to be his friend, and he'd read it all wrong. But if it was so wrong, why did it feel so right?

CHAPTER SIXTEEN

ALMOST THERE. JUST A little farther.

Piper's legs screamed in exhaustion, and her lungs burned. Still, she just had a few more steps, and she'd make it to her destination—the town square.

She could do it. She wasn't a quitter. It'd been three weeks since Joe coaxed her to go running. Three long, hard weeks. But she'd been consistent and shown up six days a week. Friday was her day of rest. And when she stepped on the scale the next morning, she'd thank herself for pushing herself to the limit. She hoped.

As soon as her foot hit the concrete abutment, her forward motion screeched to a halt. Maybe she hadn't made it to the bench, but she'd said the town square, and this was definitely the edge of it. She didn't care if she was rationalizing her tiny bit of cheating. She couldn't run another step today if she tried.

Her stomach ached, and her head hurt. Maybe she should have had a little more to eat today than just a can of soup. But she wasn't going to get that contrary scale to move if she didn't keep pushing herself, restricting herself. She could do this. She'd done it once before for her now-defunct wedding.

Laney was now the bride-to-be, and a beautiful one she'd be with her willowy figure. Wedding gowns were made for people like Laney, not for someone like herself with a much fuller figure.

Who had she been kidding? The wedding was tomorrow. Piper had told herself that she'd be fine with it, and she had been until today. It wasn't jealousy—far from it. It was more that she didn't want people talking behind her back and sending her pitying looks because she hadn't been able to hold on to her man.

Then again, if she delivered the cake early enough, she should be able to avoid most everyone. Speaking of the cake, she was a tad behind on it—

"You're running again?"

The familiar male voice caused her to jump. With the town square in desperate need of repair work, not many people ventured into it. And with it being the dinner hour, most people were home with their families.

"Joe, you startled me." She eyed up the bench he occupied. It looked so inviting.

With the hand he was holding half of an uneaten sandwich, he waved her over. "Have a seat. There's plenty of room."

He didn't have to invite her twice. Her steps were slow, but she made it to the bench. She thumped down on the rough wood and leaned back. Her muscles practically hummed in relief. In an instant, any bit of energy she'd had fled her system, making her limbs heavy.

"What's the matter? Didn't you get enough running in this morning?" The smile that touched his eyes and softened his handsome face let her know that he was teasing.

She didn't return his smile. She just wasn't in the mood. In fact, she realized she hadn't been in that great of a mood all day. She'd been hoping the run would improve her spirits, but all it'd done was make her tired and ravenous. But Joe didn't need to know any of that.

"After the bakery closed, I just felt like some fresh air." When he gave her a pointed stare, she added, "I thought I'd work on my time for the 5K."

"And to think in the beginning I practically had to drag you out for a run. Now look at you, the overachiever."

She wasn't about to admit that the scale had stalled out on her that week. In fact, it'd crept up slightly. She was desperate to make it go back down. But she wasn't about to share that bit of embarrassment with Joe or anyone.

He took a bite of his sandwich, and her stomach rumbled. She jerked her gaze away, concentrating on the gazebo that had yellow warning tape wrapped around it to keep people from getting hurt on the rotted wood. That was one of the reasons for the Autumn Fest. The gazebo and the rest of the town square would get much-needed makeovers. Once again, the square would be such a lovely place to hang out.

"Would you like some?" Joe held out the other half of his sandwich.

"No," she lied. Her stomach cramped from hunger. "I'm good."

"Doesn't sound like it. I can hear your stomach rumbling from over here."

The heat of embarrassment ignited in her chest and flamed up over her face. "Sorry. I'm going to grab something after I get a shower."

"Here." He again held out the food. "You need to eat now."

She wasn't going to accept it, but when she saw what it was, she couldn't help but laugh. "You're eating a PB&B sandwich?"

"Something wrong with peanut butter and banana?"

It was the first time she'd laughed that day, and it sure felt good. "Nope. Nothing wrong with it at all. In fact, I haven't had one in years."

Her hand had a slight tremor as she reached out to accept the food. Maybe she had been pushing herself a little too hard. She didn't waste any time taking a bite. She moaned in approval. Crunchy peanut butter, too. A man with good taste.

He leaned closer. "If I'd known I could make you moan so easily, I'd have made you dinner sooner."

Her already warm cheeks blazed with more heat. She refused to give in to her embarrassment. Instead, she decided to play along. "It'd take a lot more than food to get me to moan."

"Are you daring me?" His voice grew deep and husky.

"Maybe." Her gaze met his darkening eyes.

She should turn away. Change the subject. Or walk away. But she sat motionless. She was drawn into this game like a honeybee drawn to a bright red zinnia. However, when Joe didn't respond, disappointment sliced through her. Granted, she wasn't experienced in the art of flirting, but she hadn't thought she'd said anything wrong, had she?

She glanced his way, but his gaze didn't meet hers. Perhaps it was best to just let the subject rest as she felt totally out of her depth. She munched on the sandwich half, making short work of it.

Once finished, she brushed the lingering crumbs from her fingers. "I should go."

When she went to stand, he placed a hand on her thigh. She hesitated, not sure what he wanted from her. Not sure if she should care or not.

She was tired. Tired of being hungry. Tired of the headache that plagued her. And tired of playing games with him. All she wanted was a cold shower, some watermelon, and her television remote.

"Please don't go." His voice was deep and rich like the rum cakes she makes for the holidays.

"Why?" she asked, her agitation bubbling up and giving her the courage to speak her mind. "You can't even bring yourself to flirt with me."

His head lifted, and his gaze met hers. A shocked look reflected in his eyes. "Is that what you think?"

Her indignation refused to let her walk away. "Listen, I know I'm overweight. My mother makes it impossible for me not to pretend otherwise—"

His eyes opened wide. "You think this has to do with those awful things your mother says? You think I agree with her?"

Piper would have crossed her arms, but they were too tired. "Don't you?"

"Of course not."

"Then what's up with you? Ever since you told me about Fudge, you hardly look at me, much less speak to me. It's because you're afraid of becoming attracted to a fat chick, isn't it?"

It all came tumbling out. The hurt. The embarrassment. The anger. All gates were down, and she stared directly at him, waiting for him to try to deny what she already knew.

"You've got it all wrong—"

"No, I don't." She wasn't about to let him soft-pedal her. "I know what men think of me." She got to her feet. She wasn't going to just sit there and swallow his lies. "I've got to go."

He jumped up in front of her, blocking her. "You have to believe me when I say you are the most beautiful woman I've ever known. And your beauty, it's not just on the surface. You've got a big, generous heart."

"Really?" She didn't know whether to be utterly flattered and rush into his arms or to be upset with him for sending out mixed signals. She was so confused. "Then why do you act like I have the plague?"

"Because...because you affect me more than I ever expected. And I don't know what to do about it or how to act around you."

His words made her heart go pitter-patter. But could she trust him? Was he just saying what he thought she wanted to hear? She laced her fingers together. "Why should I believe you?"

His jaw firmed, and his intense gaze held hers. "Because all I've wanted to do since our first kiss was repeat it."

The pitter-patter of her heart became a loud *thump thump*. She licked her dry lips. "It...I mean, you have?"

He nodded.

His gaze lowered to her lips. He really wanted to kiss her? Her heart leapt into her throat. She couldn't breathe. She was stuck in a perpetual state of anticipation. Did he have any idea how much she wanted him to kiss her again?

She didn't have to wonder any longer as he leaned toward her. His smooth lips brushed over hers. A moan swelled in her throat. She'd never wanted something so much in her life.

She stepped closer to him. His arms wrapped around her waist, pulling her the rest of the way until they were chest-to-chest. Could he feel the rapid pounding of her heart?

With one hand around her waist and the other on the back of her neck, he claimed her lips. This was so much better than her memories. Attraction and anticipation combined to create a heady combination. Why exactly hadn't they been doing this all along?

Letting down her defenses and going with the moment, she savored the way his lips moved over hers and his tongue danced with hers. The moan in her throat grew with intensity as his kiss picked up its intensity. She hungered for him like a person who hadn't tasted something so sweet and intoxicating in years.

Lifting onto her tiptoes, she trailed her fingers through his hair, enjoying the silky strands as they slipped between her fingers. She simply couldn't get enough of him.

A gust of wind rippled over her skin, reminding her that they were out in the open, in the middle of town. Definitely not the place to get carried away.

She grudgingly pulled back, slowly. Her hands were still wrapped around his neck. A question reflected in his eyes.

"Not here," she answered, hoping he'd want to take this back to her apartment.

Before she could utter the invitation, her cell phone buzzed. The temptation to ignore it outweighed her business sense. She didn't want anything or anyone to ruin this moment. Her need for Joe with his amazing hands and arousing kisses thrummed through her veins.

A frown filtered across his face as he stepped back. She could feel the moment slipping away, and she didn't want that to happen.

"Wait. I'll turn it off." She reached for where she had clipped the phone to her waistband. However, when she saw the caller ID, everything changed. "Um...I really need to get this."

Joe sighed. "Don't let me stop you."

"It'll just take a second."

That may be true of the phone conversation, but she knew it was the end of their romantic interlude. She answered the call, finding an anxious bride on the other end.

"I can't believe tomorrow's the wedding. Can I see the cake?" Laney asked, nervous tension lacing each syllable.

See the cake? Not a chance. She should have been working on it instead of going out for a second run that day and then sharing a PB&B, as well as a kiss that was the sweetest treat ever.

"Well, um...you see, it isn't done yet." Honesty without details. Because there was no way she was admitting that the cake layers were bare.

"Not done! The ceremony is in fifteen hours and thirty-nine minutes. It has to be done." Nervous tension took a sudden turn into flat-out panic.

"It will be. In fact, it's mostly done." Liar. But it was only a little white lie, and it was for a good cause. The bride was already on the edge of a meltdown the night before her wedding. And if that happened because of the cake, the entire town would blame Piper.

"Mostly done?" Laney's shrill voice shook.

Piper made eye contact with Joe. His eyes were alight with curiosity. Piper turned her back to him. Even though he couldn't hear the other end of the conversation, it was extremely uncomfortable spinning a white lie in front of a witness. She definitely wasn't an accomplished liar.

"It's just that I'm a perfectionist." That part was not a lie. "And I don't like people to see my work until I have every detail worked out. Trust me. You'll love it."

"I will?" There was a long sigh, as though Laney had been holding her breath, waiting for Piper's reassurance. "You had me worried. I mean, what's a wedding with no cake?"

"It'll be everything you imagined and more. I'll deliver the cake first thing in the morning."

"Great!" The bride sounded chipper now. "I knew you wouldn't let me down."

Piper's stomach knotted as she thought of the naked four-tier cake waiting to be dressed in a cloak of smooth off-white fondant and royal icing string art in snow white. The finishing touch would be a bouquet of violet fondant flowers.

"You don't have a thing to worry about." It was a promise she intended to keep, even if she had to stay up all night. If nothing else, her word had to mean something to people.

She rushed off the phone, knowing that every minute counted now. How could she have let herself get so distracted that she forgot about her priority—her business?

"I take it from the frown on your face that there's a problem with the cake?" Joe asked.

She turned to him. "Problem? Oh yeah. A big one. I'll be up all night in order to get it done for the morning wedding."

"Can't you take some shortcuts?"

She shook her head. "No way. This cake has to be perfect."

His head tilted to the side as he studied her. "What's so important about this cake?"

"You mean, besides my entire professional reputation being at stake?" When he nodded, she decided to tell him the rest. It wasn't like it was a secret or anything. "I don't want anyone to think I'm still hung up on my ex. Nothing could be further from the truth."

"Wait. I don't understand. What does this have to do with your ex?"

"It's his wedding."

A look of dawning filled Joe's face. "And you agreed to do the cake? Why?"

He wasn't the first one to pose the question. "The truth is, in the beginning I was totally opposed to the idea, but then his bride-to-be stopped by the bakery. She was nice. And...and she apologized. That's more than David ever did."

"Apologized for what?"

Oops. She'd skipped over that part of the story. "I caught her in bed with my then fiancé."

"And now you like her?" Disbelief reflected in Joe's eyes. "No one can be that nice. Not even you."

"David can be quite charming and manipulative when he wants to be. He's an attorney with his eye on a political future. And Laney swears she didn't know about me when they got together."

"Did you ever stop to consider this woman might be lying to you?"

Piper glared at him. "Of course I did. But I heard her out, and what she said made sense. Besides, it's best this way."

Joe shrugged. "If you say so, but I could never do it."

"Maybe you could—"

"I can promise you that the day I found Denise in our bed with someone I'd foolishly considered a close friend was the last time I spoke to that friend. I have no room in my life for either of them."

At last they had something in common, but why did it have to be this? No one should ever be betrayed like that. "I'm sorry that happened to you."

Joe's lips settled into a frown. "There's still no reason to put yourself through the trouble of making a cake for your ex's wedding. It can't be easy for you."

Piper shrugged. "I'm long over David. The fact that I tried to make myself into something I'm not bothers me more than him moving on."

Her last statement struck her. She was doing it again with all of the dieting, exercising, and agreeing to bake this wedding cake. She was trying to transform herself into what she thought other people wanted her to be. In the process, she was losing focus on her own dream.

Her thoughts strayed to the bare cake layers waiting for her. Instead of doing her job, she'd been out running for the second time that day. She had a chance to gain some free press coverage, and she was about to blow it. After all, this wedding was a chance to make a name for herself and the bakery.

If only she wouldn't lose her focus by trying to make herself into the sort of woman who would interest Joe.

She'd tried doing that with David, and it'd blown up in her face. She needed to do things differently this time around.

"This thing between us, it shouldn't have happened," she said, knowing she could never fit his image of the perfect woman. "I'm sorry. I've got to go."

"Will I see you in the morning for a run?"

This was where she had a choice to make: continue trying to impress the people of Whistle Stop and a man who wouldn't loosen up enough to make room for her in his life. Or break her Joe addiction and concentrate on the one thing in her life that had never judged her or made her feel not quite good enough—Poppin' Fresh. Her heart said one thing, but her mind said another.

She'd followed her heart once before, and it had gotten her in the worst sort of trouble. This time she'd go with her mind, with the only answer that made sense. After all, they'd shared only a couple of kisses...a couple of soul-stirring, toe-curling kisses—

No, she wasn't going to change her mind.

She pressed her hands to her hips. "I'm done running. I need more time to focus on my business."

"But, Piper, you can't spend all of your time working."

"I've made up my mind." Had she truly given up on running? She wasn't so sure, but in her moment of frustration, saying it eased her stress a bit.

She turned away, unable to meet his gaze before she rushed off across the town square. She sensed Joe's gaze burning a hole in the back of her head, but she resisted the urge to turn around. She knew if she did, she'd crumble. And that couldn't happen.

CHAPTER SEVENTEEN

Joe had no idea what had just happened. One minute they were sharing the most arousing kiss on the planet, and the next, Piper was walking away from him. The determination in her steps told him that she wasn't going to come back. But why?

He'd swear she wanted that kiss as much as he had. There had to be something he was missing, but for the life of him, he couldn't figure out what. Women remained an utter mystery to him.

He turned back to the bench and started to collect the remnants of his meal—if you could call it that. He'd been lazy when he threw together the PB&B. He really hated cooking for one.

As it was, he was still hungry. He smiled, recalling how Piper had made short work of the other half of his sandwich. Then a thought struck him. With all of her exercise, she was probably hungry. Maybe that accounted for her mood change.

Certain he was on to something, he rushed off to his apartment.

Not even a refreshing shower lifted Piper's sinking spirits. She didn't know who she was more upset with. Joe for toying with her when he obviously didn't want to start anything serious with her, or herself for letting her defenses down with him.

The more she thought about Joe, the more she slammed the items she needed to decorate the cake onto the counter. The good news was the cake was baked and cooled. And the fondant was rolled. There was still a lot to do before it fulfilled the vision the bride had in mind. The intricate string design would take all of her concentration, which was good. She wouldn't have time to think about anything else.

The back door squeaked open. Who in the world could that be? She wasn't expecting anyone. However, this was a small town, and people had a habit of dropping by without an invitation, which, on any other occasion, would have been fine. Tonight was a totally different story. She should have locked the door. She didn't have time for socializing.

Before she had a chance to move, Joe stepped into the brightly lit kitchen. His hair was a bit scattered, but it was the uncertainty in his eyes that held her attention. She didn't think in all of the time she'd known him that he'd been uncertain of anything. The man wore ego like a second skin. So what had changed?

"Joe, I really don't have time to talk. I have work to do." She pointed to the chocolate cake layers with raspberry ganache filling that she was just about to cover with a smooth layer of white fondant. "I've got a long night of work ahead of me."

"Then let me help."

He was offering to help her? She inwardly groaned. Barely over an hour into her resolution to keep him at arm's length in order to focus on her work and here he was putting a serious chink in her armor.

She knew she should tell him to buzz off, but what came out of her mouth was totally different. "What do you have in mind?"

"For starters, have dinner with me."

Oh no. She wasn't falling for that line...no matter how tempting she found the invitation. She had to stick with her priorities. "I can't go anywhere. I have to get this cake decorated."

Joe moved his hands from behind his back and revealed two wrapped dinner dishes. "I came prepared. I knew you wouldn't be able to get away. I hope you like steak and a potato."

The refusal caught on the back of her tongue. Her stomach rumbled. That PB&B hadn't gone far.

He moved past her and put the plates on the counter as though he knew she wouldn't be able to resist his invitation. And what bothered her most was that he was right.

Without saying a word, she grabbed some utensils, and they each pulled up a stool at the counter. Piper's mouth watered. The aroma was divine. The meat was tender, and the spices brought her palate to life. The man was wasting his time with a coffee shop. He should have his own restaurant.

"Did you make this?" she asked, just to be sure.

He nodded and swallowed. "Why? Are you surprised I know my way around a kitchen?"

"When I've been running in the evening, I've noticed you spend a lot of time at Benny's Burger Joint or the local café."

His fork paused on the way to his mouth. He sent her a guilty smile. "So I'm busted, huh?"

"Pretty much."

He lowered the still-full fork to his plate and smiled. Her insides shivered with excitement. No man had ever affected her with a mere smile.

"I had to wait until the wiring had been replaced and the stove was delivered before I could fend for myself. So I sampled the local cuisine."

"Find anything you like?"

His eyes lit up as he stared into her eyes before his gaze lowered to her lips. "Definitely. Something I wouldn't mind having thirds and fourths of."

Her stomach fluttered like she'd just hit a big dip on a roller coaster. She swallowed hard and tried to pretend that the implication of his words hadn't just rocked her world.

"This...this steak is really tasty." She failed to keep the slight tremor of awareness out of her voice. "What did you use on it?"

"A little of this and a little of that." He took a bite of his potato, while his eyes remained trained on her.

Suddenly, her appetite fled. But she couldn't let him see that he was getting to her—again. She scooped up some baked potato and took a bite, no longer tasting the food. All she could think about was Joe, here, alone with her, feeding her, staring at her.

Silence enveloped them as they worked their way through the meal. When they finished eating, Piper patted her stomach. "I think I ate too much. But thank you. It was delicious."

"You're quite welcome. Now what can I do to help?"

"You just did it. That meal will keep me going all night."

He shook his head. "I want to give you a hand with the cake. I know I can't decorate or anything, but I can help with cleanup. I might even be able to mix up frosting or whatever it is you need."

He was serious? She searched his face, finding a perfectly sober expression on his face. Maybe she'd jumped the gun with him. Maybe he was willing to let down his guard and let her in. Her heart thumped at the thought.

She calmed herself. She was rushing ahead. It was best to take this thing between them one step at a time. She assured herself that letting him stay didn't constitute anything serious. After all, she could use the help. She had more work ahead of her than she cared to think about, and she couldn't remember the last time she'd had to pull an all-nighter.

"You're sure about this?" she asked, giving him an out. "You won't mind getting dishpan hands?"

He rolled up the sleeves of his chambray shirt. "I think I'm up for the challenge."

"The good news is, I have a dishwasher, but everything will be caked with sugar that'll need to be cleaned off before being placed in the dishwasher. There's already a heap in the sink."

"Say no more. I'll get to work."

And that was it. He set to work. She tried to pretend he wasn't in the room as she mixed together a batch of white royal icing to begin the string lace. The bride loved the detailed decoration, and Piper had to admit that she enjoyed the challenge of creating an edible work of art.

She'd worked out a plan of attack ahead of time. And considering the lateness of the hour, she referred to her handwritten notes regularly, not wanting to forget anything. As she got absorbed by the art, she forgot about the man who was lending her a hand.

She had no idea how much time had passed when she heard approaching footsteps. She finished anchoring the arrangement of handmade fondant flowers to the top tier and turned to Joe.

"Are you done already?"

He pointed at the now-empty sink. "I've been done for a while now. I was just watching you work. You're an artist."

"Thanks. What time is it?"

He glanced at his watch. "It's after midnight. Just tell me what else I can do to help so that you can get some sleep tonight."

"Thanks, but I have to do the rest. I have more flowers to make. They'll cascade down the sides."

"Are you sure there's nothing I can do?"

She nodded. "But thank you for dinner and the help. I owe you big-time."

He waved away her words. "Don't worry about it."

She had to pay him back. It wasn't in her nature to be indebted to someone. "You know, I had some thoughts about how to do the sitting area in your coffeehouse. I could come over to your place tomorrow, and we could—"

"No. I don't need your help."

His short, harsh words were like a slap in the face. They shattered the illusion that he was letting down his wall and letting her in. Why in the world had she let herself think it could be any different between them?

Because she was a romantic fool. Well, she wasn't about to be anyone's fool again. "You should go now."

He didn't say a word. The only sound was that of the back door drifting shut. There was a finality to the sound.

Suddenly, Piper felt isolated, miserable, and, most of all, frustrated for overacting. As much as she wanted to go after him and soothe things over, maybe it was best to put a little distance between them.

Because every time he was around, she had the strongest urge to continue that kiss where they'd left off. And that was a very bad idea. She couldn't afford to get rejected again. The scars on her heart hadn't fully faded.

CHAPTER EIGHTEEN

Piper dressed for a night out on the town.

She'd delivered the wedding cake that morning and the bride readily approved of it. It wasn't until then that Piper realized how tense she'd been about getting the cake just right. She took numerous photos to add to her bakery website, which had been woefully neglected lately, and quietly slipped out the back door before the guests arrived.

Thankfully, she had dinner plans for the evening. Alexis had texted the Bachelorettes of Whistle Stop to meet at the Green Chile Cantina. Most likely, it was to celebrate her engagement. Piper was so happy for her and Cord. For tonight, Piper would forget her own problems and be happy for her friends. Dressed in her slimmer-sized jeans, a tiny pink tee with a sparkly smiley on the front, and her cowboy boots, Piper let herself down the back steps of her building. She'd just stepped into the alley when she glanced around, finding Joe headed in her direction.

She quickly turned away, needing a moment to gather herself. And though she never bothered to lock her doors, because it didn't get any safer than Whistle Stop where the biggest crime was a bar fight at Cactus

Mike's Saloon on Saturday night, she nonetheless made the pretense of locking her door.

She knew she was being ridiculous. She took a calming breath. *Just act normal. Everything will be fine.*

She settled her purse strap on her shoulder and turned toward him. What should she say? Should she apologize again? Her hands grew clammy. Or should she pretend the whole fiasco had never happened?

Then she realized he wasn't alone. He had a dog with him. Interesting. For a moment, she wondered if at last he'd let go of the ghosts of his past and adopted a furbaby. But upon closer inspection, she realized it was Java.

When they were within a few feet of each other, he finally met her gaze. Not good with awkward silences, she said, "Hi. Beautiful evening, isn't it?"

He nodded as he kept coming closer. "I hope you have a good evening out."

She slowed to a stop. "Thanks. I hope to. I see that Java has been out for another jaunt. I bet Mr. Wilks is worried."

"I'm just about to call him and then run Java home."

"Can I do anything?"

"Thanks. I've got it."

He kept walking—past her. She glanced over her shoulder to see him and Java heading for his door. Their buildings shared a wall. Their apartments shared a wall. But the most noticeable wall was the one between them. She knew she was partly responsible for putting it there... But for the life of her, she didn't have a clue how to get around it.

Not about to let him catch her standing there gawking, she continued walking. She wondered what he'd do if she were to get him a puppy. She could just see him getting lathered in puppy kisses. It'd be absolutely adorable. The puppy would have Joe wrapped around its paw in no time.

But the reality was that Joe had a wall up between himself and the rest of the world. And though he had every right to a protective barrier after all he'd lived through, it still frustrated her. What would it take to show him that he could trust her?

If she were to get him that puppy, she worried that he'd refuse it. Though how anyone could turn away a sweet, loving furbaby was beyond her. Perhaps it was best if she left that idea alone.

"Hey, Piper."

She glanced up to find Alexis waiting for her outside the Green Chile Cantina. Piper waved and picked up her pace.

She'd been so caught up in her thoughts of Joe that she hadn't even noticed her walk much less anyone she'd passed along the way. Not good. She had to put Joe out of her mind before her friends noticed and started questioning her.

Piper crossed the road and stepped up on the sidewalk where Alexis was waiting for her.

"I'm surprised you wanted to be out and about, what with just getting engaged."

"Ah, but you're forgetting that my fiancé is a cowboy. So he's camping out on the range tonight. They're moving the cattle to a different pasture."

Piper nodded as though she were actually familiar with cowboying. She wasn't. "Well, his loss is our gain."

"I just hope everyone is able to show up." Alexis pulled open the door of the Green Chile Cantina.

Golden oldies music greeted them. It played on the local radio station only on Saturday evenings. And right now, her favorite song, "Rockin' Robin," started to play. The best part was that the whole staff sang along. It never failed to put a smile on her face, and tonight was no exception. Her head started bopping, and she started singing the fun tune.

That's what she loved about the Cantina. It was full of character, from the music to the red and white décor and the colorful Southwestern decorations. Her favorite part of all the artwork were the paintings displayed there on consignment by local artists. They had a Southwest motif, from canvases of colorful pottery to the majesty of the Rocky Mountains. It seemed like every time she stepped through the door, something new was on the walls.

This place was what had given her the ambition to give her bakery a makeover. Sure, her bakery wasn't as lively as the Cantina, but she hoped the cross she'd made between a café and a spring garden was welcoming to people.

Ana was already seated in the big, curved corner booth, and she wasn't alone. Ella Granger, Whistle Stop's newest newlywed, still had a golden glow from her time in Hawaii with her very own cowboy. It seemed her friends were finding their happily-ever-afters. So what was wrong with her?

Piper followed Alexis as they made their way through the crowded dining room where almost every cherry-red, ladder-back chair was occupied. At last they made it to the booth.

"You've got a great crowd tonight." Alexis took the words out of Piper's mouth.

"If you think this is something, you should have been here earlier." Ana shook her head. "It was a zoo. This is the first time I've had a chance to sit down. As my mother would have said, my dogs are barking."

"I totally understand." Piper knew what it was like to be on her feet all day.

A couple of baskets of fresh-made tortilla chips and bowls of homemade salsa were delivered to the table. Piper eyed the food. Her mouth watered. She knew she shouldn't indulge. But since when had that ever stopped her?

They all munched on chips while catching up on each other's lives. They used to get together regularly, but lately everyone was too busy. Piper didn't even want to think about when all of her friends started having children. There'd never be time to get together.

"How's Autumn Fest coming?" Ella asked while dunking a chip in one of the bowls of salsa. "It's all the kids at school are talking about."

"That's good. I'm relieved to hear someone's getting excited about it. We're even trying to line up a hot air balloon for the event."

"You mean as in rides?" Ella reached for another chip. When Piper nodded, Ella added, "Just wait until the kids find out. They'll be raiding their piggy banks."

"Is there anything you need us to do?" Alexis asked.

Piper thought of the bunting she had to finish. The quilting circle had declined to help, as they'd had a prior commitment. Piper couldn't bring herself to pawn it off on her friends. They were all so busy. Ana had the Cantina and was caring for her ill father. Alexis was handling the ranch solo. And Ella was settling into a new home, as well as adjusting to being a parent to a nine-year-old.

"Thanks for the offer, but I've got everything under control." Liar. Liar. Piper couldn't quite meet their gazes. "As long as you all show up to man your booths, we should be in good shape."

Once their entrees were served, Alexis spoke up. "While you are busy enjoying all of that delicious food, I thought I'd tell you why I called you together. I want all of you to be in my wedding. Will you be my bridesmaids?"

A loud round of yeses made Alexis smile.

After being a bridesmaid in Ella's wedding, Piper had the feeling she was to always be a bridesmaid and never a bride. Not that she wasn't happy for her friends—truly, she was very happy for them. But being single sometimes got lonely with no one to share with at the end of the day.

Piper used her fork to move around the cheese enchilada smothered in green chili sauce. "When's the big day?"

Alexis set aside her chicken taco. "We don't want to wait too long, but I want some time to plan something very special, so we settled on April."

Everyone started chattering at once about locations for the ceremony and the reception.

Piper got caught up in the conversation. Alexis and Cord were going to make a perfect bride and groom.

"Whatever you need me to do, just let me know," Piper offered, fully expecting a request for a cake.

"Thanks. I'm sure I'm going to need lots of help." Pink tinged Alexis's face. "I want this wedding to be unique."

"Well, I'm intrigued," Ella said. "I can't wait to hear what you come up with."

Ana grabbed a chip. "We all have experience with weddings. Some to a lesser extent, like me. But I've been in a couple now. So I'll volunteer to do the hard part—the bachelorette party."

A roar of laughter went up.

"In all seriousness," Alexis said, still smiling, "if any of you have some time to help me with the details, I'd be eternally grateful. Cord's absolutely no help with this. He'd be just as happy to get married in the middle of the paddock with nothing but the horses for witnesses. So if any of you want to visit me at the ranch, let me know. We can make it a girls' night."

Piper glanced around at the smiling crowd, eagerly devouring their delicious entrees. She couldn't blame them. This was hands-down her favorite restaurant. Ana had definitely turned things around since taking over the restaurant after her father became ill.

Piper spotted a strawberry blonde moving toward the counter. It had to be Bella, her soon-to-be sister-in-law. "Hey, Bella." The cacophony of voices in the restaurant was too loud for her to be heard without yelling. "Bella!"

That did it. Bella turned, searching the crowd for who'd called out her name. When her gaze made it to Piper's table, Piper waved her over.

"Hi." Bella's gaze moved around the large table. A hesitant smile lit up her face. "I just stopped by to pick up a to-go-order."

"A late night at Miss Mabel's?" It was Whistle Stop's only remaining dress shop.

Bella nodded. "We just got in a new shipment of winter clothes, and Miss Mabel wants the remaining summer inventory marked for a clearance sale."

"Well, join us for a bit." Piper slid over, making room for her. "We're glad to see you."

Everyone chimed in with their agreement.

"Okay, but I can't stay long."

"I'm sure you're anxious to get home to Mason," Alexis chimed in.

The smile slipped from Bella's face. "He probably isn't there. He's been working a lot of overtime lately."

"He's probably just eager to get things in order for the wedding," Piper said, hoping to reassure her. Her brother loved Bella. That was evident any time he looked Bella's way.

"We were just talking about weddings." Ana snatched up another chip. "It seems next year, we're going to have lots of weddings."

"And soon it'll be baby showers," Piper tossed out.

Alexis shook her head. "I don't think so. I'm just getting my Internet business launched. Between that and Cord, I have my hands full."

All heads turned to Bella, whose face filled with color. "I...I'm not having kids."

This was news to Piper. She wondered if her brother knew. Well, of course Mason knew. After all, they were getting married in a matter of months. To each his own, but Bella didn't look at ease about the decision. It was more like the thought of kids made her scared. But why? She'd be a great mom. Maybe someday she'd change her mind.

"Enough about weddings and babies," Ana said. "What I want to know is how things are going with Joe?" Her eyes twinkled with interest as she stared at Piper.

He was the last person she wanted to discuss, but everyone was staring at her, waiting for a response. Piper inwardly groaned. "He's been a lot of help with the festival—"

"Oh no, we're not talking about the festival. I think his interest in spending time with you is far more personal." Ana stared at her as though she knew something, something scandalous.

Oh no. What does she know?

"Well, tell us." Ella leaned forward, resting her elbows on the table.

Alexis frowned. "Obviously, I've been spending far too much time at the ranch. Okay, Piper, we want all of the juicy details."

"Yeah," Ella chimed in. "And don't leave out any of the good parts."

Piper willed herself not to blush. It'd just give all the more credence to whatever Ana thought she had on her. But that didn't stop the heat from swirling in her chest and rushing up to her cheeks. Now she must really look guilty of the unspoken charge.

"Don't look at me." Piper pointed at Ana. "Ask her. I don't know what she's talking about."

"Are you saying that kiss Joe laid on you in the park wasn't worth remembering?"

"Oh, that." Boy, was it getting warm. Piper reached for her glass of ice water and took a big gulp.

"Yes, that." Ana smiled. "When were you planning to fill us in?"

Everyone peppered her with questions. They were acting like she and Joe were a couple. Nothing could be further from the truth. She had to set them straight.

"There's nothing to fill you in on. Nothing's going on." When her friends started rolling their eyes and acting like they didn't believe her, she decided to lay it all out for them. "I'm serious. Every time I think there might be a chance for something more, he withdraws. It's like there's an imaginary line between us, and if I try to cross it, all of his defenses go up."

Ana swirled the straw around in her glass. "If I recall right, he lit out of Whistle Stop right before his graduation day. No one ever knew why. There were lots of rumors and opinions. I always thought if I had a father like his that I would have left long before graduation. His father always gave me the willies. There was just something off about that man."

Piper wanted to tell them what a monster Joe's father had been, but it wasn't her place. Joe had told her about his past in confidence. If he wanted anyone else to know, he'd tell them.

"Sounds like he has his fair share of baggage," Alexis said. "I know a lot about that. Between Cord and I, we could fill the cargo section of a jumbo jet with our baggage."

This piqued Piper's interest. "How did you move past it?"

"Well, as you've all probably figured out by now, I'm stubborn. When I realized how much Cord meant to me, I knew I had to fight to keep him in my life."

"Even if he kept pushing you away?" Piper didn't think she could take that much rejection.

"Ah, but is he continually pushing you away? Or is he pulling you close one moment before freaking out the next moment over the intensity of your connection? Sometimes it takes guys a while for their heads to catch up with their hearts." Alexis winked at her as though she'd just revealed the secret to men.

Ella leaned over. "What she's saying is, most men are afraid of the C-word, so they find every excuse to keep their distance."

"So if they're afraid of commitment, what changes their mind?" Piper realized she had oh-so-much to learn.

"Time," they all said at once.

Was that the answer? Was she pushing too hard, too fast for something to happen?

Considering her past and her broken engagement, she obviously had a lot to learn about men. She continued to ponder this as the conversation spiraled off onto the subject of Ella's dreamy island honeymoon.

By the time they were ready to call it a night, they were the last ones in the restaurant. It suited Piper just fine. She didn't have anyone waiting for her at home, not even so much as a dog.

Speaking of dogs, she wondered if Java had made it home and stayed there this time. Not that she planned to stop by Joe's on the way home to inquire. No way. No matter how much she missed him.

She was giving him time. But how much time would it take? She wasn't known for her patience.

CHAPTER NINETEEN

A PHONE CALL WOULD do.

But it was so impersonal.

And Joe longed to see Piper's face light up when he told her the news. He knew that he'd been too firm with her when she'd offered to help decorate his coffee shop. Why couldn't she understand that he wanted to do it on his own? Was there something wrong with that?

She'd gone so far as to switch her running time in the morning, so they'd missed each other. And now that the plans for the festival were finalized, there was no need for them to meet each day. It didn't help that his building was near completion, allowing him to work there—no need for his table at the Poppin' Fresh Bakery. He'd been out of excuses to see Piper—until now.

Once she heard his news, it would put that glowing smile back on her face. Convinced this was a good idea, he decided to put his plan into action before he talked himself out of it. He didn't even know if she was home. He checked his watch. It was past closing time for the bakery, so she might be at her apartment.

As he let himself in the back door of Piper's building, he realized that in all of the time he'd known her that he'd never been up to her home. Nothing like the present to change that circumstance. He had to admit that he was curious to see her place.

After seeing what she'd done with the bakery by turning it into a sunny garden area, he had no doubt that her apartment would have lots of personality. Would it be black and white modern? He didn't think so. Maybe a colorful chic décor? Or it could be more earthy tones, as in a country classic appearance?

He climbed the wooden steps that creaked just a bit with each step. At the top of the landing, he found not one, but three doors. It didn't take much guesswork to figure out that the bright red door with a sunflower wreath had to be Piper's. The other doors were just a basic gray that matched the trim.

He approached the colorful door, not exactly sure what he would say to her. Luckily, he was pretty good at thinking on his feet—most of the time. He clenched his hand and rapped on the door.

Moments passed, and he didn't hear anything. Then there was a shuffling sound. He knocked again, just to be sure that she'd heard him.

"Coming."

That was definitely Piper's voice, but suddenly he wondered if she was alone. Why hadn't he thought of that before? She might have company—male company. The thought didn't sit well, not at all. But he didn't have any claim over her. In fact, if someone else was interested in her, it would be a good thing. Wouldn't it?

At last, the door swung open. Her eyes widened. "Joe, what are you doing here?"

"Is this a bad time?" He glanced past her to see if there was anyone in her apartment. He didn't see anyone.

"Um, no. What did you need?"

Okay. She was acting odd. "Aren't you even going to invite me in? I promise I have good news."

She sighed and swung the door wide open. "Come on in."

He stepped inside and immediately found they were, in fact, alone. He knew that it shouldn't be such a relief to him, but it was. Because no matter how much he fought it, Piper meant a lot to him.

But could he trust her? So many people in his life had let him down. He just couldn't afford to let someone else do that to him. But Piper was different. She was kind and thoughtful. She listened to him and didn't judge him. Maybe this time could be different, if only he could convince her to give him another chance.

Piper closed the door. "What's the good news?"

He didn't want to jump straight into that discussion, not quite yet. "I like what you've done with the place."

"Thanks. I like lots of color."

"I noticed." The only bland color in the room was the white paint on the walls. The couch was a deep royal blue with colorful, flowered pillows. The print on the curtains was brilliant pink, orange, and purple flowers. The room breathed energy, which reminded him of Piper. "Maybe I'll have to get some decorating tips from you when I get around to redoing my apartment."

"Sure, um, no problem." She kept fidgeting with a bit of red material. "What did you want to tell me?"

What was going on? She'd never so blatantly tried to get rid of him before. His curiosity grew exponentially. Perhaps he'd been wrong and she was hiding someone in her bedroom. A frown pulled at his lips. "If I'm keeping you from something...or someone, I'll go."

"Sorry." She sent him a small smile. "There's no one here. It's just that, oh, never mind. Why don't you sit down?"

He perched on the edge of the couch as she curled up in the matching armchair. "I wanted to tell you that I spoke with my friend, and he's willing to donate his balloon and time for the festival."

A big smile lit up her face. "That's wonderful. It'll be a huge draw. I just know it. In fact, we'll have to get some new flyers printed up with the information."

"He's participated in festivals before, so he knows what all is involved, including paperwork and such."

"All the better. Make sure you thank your friend for me."

"You can thank him yourself at the festival. I'm sure you'll want to take a ride."

She paused. "You know what? I will definitely do that. Thanks for letting me know."

"I figure it was the least I could do after the way you took on the bunting. I have to admit that when you first mentioned it, I didn't see the importance. But now I think it'll give the festival more of a party atmosphere and hopefully loosen up people's wallets."

Piper glanced away and worried her adorable bottom lip.

When she didn't say a word, he suspected there was a problem. "Piper, what's the matter?"

"It...it's nothing."

Something told him that even if she needed help, her stubborn pride would keep her from asking him, so it was up to him to drag it out of her. "Piper, what is it?"

"Really, it's nothing for you to worry about."

"Now, I am worried. You might as well tell me, because I'm not leaving here until you do." He leaned back on the couch and folded his arms.

Why did he have to be so difficult?

Piper really didn't want to have to fess up that the quilting circle had turned her down when she'd asked about them doing the bunting. She knew it was her fault. She'd gotten caught up with the idea, and once she'd mentioned it to Joe, she'd dug her heels in about its importance. And now that the ladies were busy with other endeavors for the festival, Piper had been spending every evening tracing patterns and cutting out triangles to make her own bunting.

She glanced across at Joe, who appeared to have taken up permanent residence on her couch. Meanwhile, he was consuming precious time that she should be using to make more bunting. She'd already accepted that she wouldn't be able to make enough on her own. They'd just have to make do with what she could make in the evenings.

Joe sent her an expectant look.

Oh, what was the point in putting it off any longer? She leveled her shoulders and lifted her chin. "The quilting circle wasn't able to do the bunting."

"Oh."

"They were already obligated to complete a king-size quilt to be raffled off, as well as a few other things."

"And why does this have you looking so worried?"

"I...I'm not. I actually have everything under control."

His dark brows gathered. "What does that mean?"

"I'm making the bunting—"

"You're what? All by yourself?"

"Yes." She lifted her chin ever so slightly. Stubborn pride refused to let her admit that she'd taken on too much.

"But you said you were going to have a group of ladies do it. How can you manage it all by yourself?"

Piper's chin lowered. "I'm doing the best I can."

His gaze scanned the room, stopping on the old sewing machine she'd borrowed from her mother. He got to his feet and approached the table in the corner of the room. "This looks like a lot of work."

It was, especially after being on her feet all day at the bakery, but what choice did she have? She refused to fail. "Don't worry. I've got this. I'm sure you've got other things to do tonight—"

"I don't have any other plans." He continued to examine the stacks of colorful triangles and then fingered the white bias tape.

"Surely you must be busy. Aren't you planning to launch your opening to coincide with the festival?"

He nodded. "But I'm running ahead of schedule."

"That's great." She was truly happy for him, but how was she supposed to get him out of her apartment now so she could get back to work?

"How hard is this to make?"

"Not very. Most of the work involves cutting out the triangles."

He picked up her pattern. "So you trace this on the material and then cut?"

"Pretty much. But I line them up carefully so they share the same edge. That way, I don't waste any material and I have to cut less."

"Makes sense. I think maybe I could handle that."

"But why would you want to?"

He turned to her. "Because I want to help you. You aren't in this alone. Remember, we're a team?"

Her gaze met his. For a moment, she got lost in the intensity of his eyes. "Do you mean that?"

"I do. You should have come to me earlier. We would have figured it out together." His voice was deep and soothing.

For the first time in a long time, she didn't feel alone. Sure, she knew everyone in town, but it wasn't the same as having someone there for her, someone who cared what happened to her.

"Where do we start?" His question drew her out of her thoughts.

She glanced at the table, noticing the stacks of material all ready for her to start sewing. "How would you feel about tracing and cutting triangles?"

"Point out the material, and I'll get started."

She frowned, realizing that sharing the table could be problematic. It wasn't a big table by any stretch of the imagination. And she didn't have anywhere else to set up the sewing machine.

As though Joe could read her thoughts, he said, "How about I clear off the coffee table and work over there?"

She glanced at the table and back at him. "Are you sure you want to sit on the floor? I could...uh..."

"I'll be fine. You stay at the table and start assembling things. I'll do my best to cut some reasonable triangles."

She helped him get situated. When her romance novels and cooking magazines were cleared from the coffee table, he dropped down to the floor and used the couch as a backrest.

He smiled up at her, making her stomach flutter. "See? I told you this would work."

"Thank you. I owe you."

"You don't owe me a thing. I'm doing this because I want to."

She didn't believe him. "I highly doubt you've been longing to spend your evening tracing triangles and cutting them out."

"Don't you know by now that I'd do anything for you?"

Her heart leaped into her throat. What was he trying to tell her? She had no idea, but it sure sounded good to her.

"We better get started." His voice deepened. "Looks like we've got a lot to do."

She swallowed hard and hoped that her voice sounded normal when she spoke. "How about some food? I can look in the fridge and see what I have."

"No need. We'll just order pizza."

"Are you sure?" She felt like she should cook him something to repay him for helping her.

"I'm positive. What do you want on yours?"

"That's easy. Pepperoni and mushrooms." She paused, realizing that maybe she should have checked to see what he preferred on his pizza.

Before she could ask him, he said, "We'll get half and half."

This intrigued her. "What are you having on your half?"

"Veggies."

"Really?" The word was out of her mouth before she could stop it. When he gave her a puzzled look, she added, "It's just, most guys I know love lots of meat on theirs. Are you a vegetarian?"

"There's something I should tell you."

That certainly didn't sound good. "Tell me what?"

"The reason I no longer eat meat on my pizza, and lots of other things, is that when my father died of a sudden heart attack, my mother got worried about me. She insisted I go to the doctor. I didn't think anything was wrong, but I went anyway to put her mind at rest. I figured after all she'd gone through living with my father that she deserved to finally have some peace of mind."

Piper's heart went out to him. He was such a good guy to look out for his mother, even after all he'd gone through. "You're such a good son."

He shook his head. "I'm not. Or I wouldn't have left her behind with my father when I left home."

Piper reached out to him and squeezed his hand. "She understands."

There was a poignant pause. "Anyway, when I went to the doctor, I had the shock of my life. My blood pressure was up, and my cholesterol was through the roof. With my father's heart issue, the doctor warned me what my future could be like if I didn't change my ways."

The pieces started to fall into place. "That's why you go running every morning?"

He nodded. "I started after that wake-up call. And now I do it because I enjoy it."

"And that's why you didn't want to keep eating the bear claws?" She felt absolutely awful for trying to force them on him.

He nodded. "I thought you wanted me to eat them to change my mind about selling your pastries in my coffee shop. I'm sorry if I handled that poorly and hurt your feelings. It was never my intention."

She understood so much more about him now. "And your heart, is it okay?"

He nodded. "Stronger than ever now that I take care of it."

"That's good."

Now that he was letting his guard down with her in a way that he never had before, she couldn't help wondering where they went from here.

She had absolutely no clue, but she couldn't wait to find out.

CHAPTER TWENTY

IT WAS GETTING LATE...REAL late.

Yet, wild horses couldn't drag Joe away.

They'd spent the rest of the evening talking as they worked. Their conversation meandered from this to that. Nothing serious and some of it making them both laugh. The only serious parts were about the plans for the festival and the eventual revitalization of the town square. He honestly didn't care what they discussed. He just liked listening to Piper's sweet voice.

Now, as she paused the sewing machine to stretch and yawn, he knew he should go. He didn't want to, but she needed some rest. He gathered the bunting material and supplies into a neat pile in the middle of the coffee table.

When Piper didn't seem to notice his cleanup effort, he said, "Time to call it a night."

Piper paused the sewing machine. "Not yet. I want to get just a little more done."

He got to his feet, finding he had a few sore spots after sitting on the floor for hours. "You have an early morning coming up. You need your rest."

As though she hadn't heard a word, she started the sewing machine. He walked over to her and put his hands on her shoulders. He'd been wanting to touch her all evening. And now that he had, he wasn't sure he'd be able to let go.

Immediately, the machine came to a stop. Her hand reached up and slid over his, sending his pulse racing. She switched off the sewing machine and stood. He should have moved, but his feet wouldn't cooperate. When she turned to him, she was standing right in front of him, the perfect position for him to steal a kiss.

She tilted her chin up and stared deep into his eyes. "Thank you for this evening. You took a boring task and made it fun."

"I couldn't think of anywhere I'd rather be than right here with you." It was the honest truth. She made his heart hammer with need. He tried to fight it, but he already knew it was a losing battle. Surely she could see the desire in his eyes, and yet, she didn't turn away.

"I wanted to spend the evening with you, too."

His heart collided with his ribs. Was that some sort of invitation for more? Or was it just hopeful thinking on his part?

They stood there for countless seconds. He kept second-guessing himself. He didn't want to make any more mistakes where she was concerned. Should he kiss her? Was it what she was waiting for? He'd soon find out.

His arms wrapped around her waist, pulling her close. She gazed up at him with a spark of interest reflected in her eyes. He didn't need any further invitation. His mouth pressed to hers. To his surprise, her lips didn't move beneath his although her generous curves remained pressed to him.

His gut reaction was to show her how she turned him on, but his brain still worked enough to warn him not to move too fast and scare her off. With a concerted effort, he moved slowly and deliberately, coaxing her to let down her guard and let him in. She could trust him. He'd do his best not to hurt her again.

Her hands slipped up over his shoulders and wrapped around his neck as their kiss deepened. He wondered if she had any idea of all the crazy things she was doing to his body. His heart was pounding so hard he wouldn't be surprised if she could hear it.

What was it about her that got to him like no one else did? She made him want to believe in love again. With her in his arms, it was like she'd healed the cracks in his heart, making it whole once more.

He wanted more of her—all of her. But he knew he had no right to ask that of her. None at all.

But as she kissed him back with her hands moving up over his shoulders, she didn't seem to want to stop this either. Was that possible? Did she want to see where this would lead them?

He didn't know, but he sure hoped so.

The kiss went on and on, until he just couldn't take it anymore. He had to know if she wanted more. If not, he had to stop here.

With every bit of willpower, he pulled back ever so slightly and rested his forehead against hers. His breathing was deep and unsteady. His heart was pounding like crazy. "Piper, do you want me to go?"

Both of her hands wrapped around the back of his neck. Her fingernails scraped up over his scalp, sending a cascade of delicious sensations rushing down his spine. Instead of words, her lips pressed to his. A moan swelled deep in his throat. Did she know the way she heated the blood in his veins, making every part of his body needy? Or was that her intent?

Just as quickly as she'd met him kiss for kiss, she pulled back. With her fingers still threaded through his hair, she gazed up into his eyes. "Is that answer enough for you?"

He smiled and nodded. Talking was most definitely overrated.

He scooped her up in his arms and headed for the bedroom. He had the feeling neither one of them was going to get much sleep tonight. And it would be so worth it.

"Piper, did you hear me?"

With great effort, she dragged her gaze away from the window where Joe had just strolled by. "What did you say, Mom?"

Her mother glanced around as though to make sure no one was paying them the least bit of attention, and then she lowered her voice. "I was asking if you'd come up with some fantastic recipe for my cake. You know, if this goes well, you could possibly make the cake for your brother's inaugural party."

"Whoa, Mom. Are you jumping ahead? Mason hasn't even entered the mayoral race."

"He will. He's just waiting for a strategic moment."

"Oh, okay." Piper's gaze kept straying to the window, watching for Joe. They'd been having such an amazing time this past week. Who knew that making bunting could be so much fun?

Her mother expelled an exasperated sigh. "Is there a reason you're barely paying attention to me?"

There Joe was again. He was carrying boxes from the back of a pickup to his store. She was itching to investigate as an excuse to talk to him because they'd both agreed to keep this wondrous new relationship low-key. They weren't eager for people to jump to conclusions when neither of them was sure exactly what this thing was between them.

"Piper, honestly, where is your mind today?"

"Sorry. What were you saying?" She searched her memory. "Oh yes, the cake for the auction—"

"Shh..." Her mother glanced around at the couple of men who were at separate tables. Mr. Wilks was reading a newspaper, and the other gentleman was on his laptop. "This is supposed to be just between you and me."

Piper stifled a laugh. Her mother was all about appearances, and it just wouldn't do for the citizens of Whistle Stop to know that her mother could barely bake a box cake much less whip up a cake from scratch. And Piper wasn't about to tell her mother that she wasn't the only one to place a secret order for a cake for the auction.

"Quit worrying, Mom. I think your secret is safe."

"I hope so. Well, tell me. What did you come up with?"

Piper had actually given the cake situation some thought. "I have two choices for you. Both are seasonal cakes, since this is Autumn Fest. How about a pumpkin cake with caramel cream cheese frosting?"

Her mother paused for a moment, as though considering the idea. "It's okay. What is my other choice?"

"An apple rum cake."

"Oh, now that sounds delightful—that is, if I ate sweets. But you know that I don't."

"Let me write this down so I don't forget." Piper looked around the front counter but couldn't locate a pen. She turned and searched the back counter.

"I see your jeans are getting loose. That's good." When she turned around, her mother was smiling triumphantly. "I knew those supplements would help you."

So did the daily runs each morning, as well as the Greek yogurt for breakfast, the salads for lunch, and the minuscule dinners. But according to her mother, her success was all due to the diet aid. Still, it was nice her mother had noticed. And it was certainly getting Joe's attention, too, which gave her the incentive to stick with the restrictive regime, even though she missed her cupcakes like crazy.

Mind over matter. Mind over matter. And a total hottie for a reward.

"Mom, would you like the cake topped with some pecans and caramel?"

Her mother hesitated. "I suppose so. It's a lot of calories, but not everyone worries about those things."

Thank goodness. Even though Piper was dieting, she was nowhere near as serious about it as her mother. Which made Piper a little sad for her mother, as she didn't understand the concept of moderation.

There went Joe past the window again. What was that man up to?

"Piper, are you listening to me?"

"Um, sure." There he went back past the bakery.

Her mother turned to follow her line of vision. "Oh, so that's who has you so distracted. Honestly, Piper, do you think a barista will make you happy?"

Piper focused her attention back on her mother. "He's more than a barista. He owns the place. And, yes, I think he could make the right lady very happy."

Very happy indeed. But was she the right lady? Was she brave enough to put her heart back on the line?

This was the way every morning should be.

Joe held the door for Piper to exit Sam's Hitchin' Post, where they'd just grabbed a couple of energy drinks. This had been one of Joe's favorite stops as a kid, as Sam used to always slip him a lollipop. And not just any old lollipop, but the kind with the bubble gum in the center. The memory had a smile pulling at Joe's lips.

Piper glanced at him as she passed by him. "You're smiling. What gives?"

He let go of the door and joined her on the sidewalk. "I don't know what you're talking about."

"Uh-huh. Why do you have such a hard time admitting that you're happy?"

"I do not." Did he? He'd never really thought about it.

She nodded. "You were smiling the whole time you were in the store. I take it that it holds some good memories for you?"

There was no reason to deny it. "Yes, it does. We used to come into town every Saturday morning to shop. And my favorite stop was always Sam's."

"Did it have anything to do with this?" She held out a lollipop.

"How did you know?" Joe accepted the candy and tore off the red wrapper. He stuck it in his mouth, surprised to find that it tasted just as good as he remembered. So maybe he did have some good childhood memories.

"I didn't know. It was Sam who insisted I give it to you."

Joe glanced at her. "Thanks."

"You're welcome. But why are you thanking me?"

"For helping me remember the good parts of my childhood."

She smiled and nodded. "What other good memories do you have?"

"When I was real young, my mother would take me to visit my aunt. My father would drive us into town, and we'd take the train."

"Lucky you. I always wanted to ride on it, but my mother hated the train."

"Not my mother. She was always in such a good mood when we went on it. Looking back now, I'm sure it was because she was getting away from my father. But as a little kid, I didn't put those sorts of things together. I just knew that train trips made us both happy."

"Would you go away for long?"

He shook his head. "Not long enough. Sometimes, I wished we could just keep going on that train and find another life, but my mother said my father would miss us too much. I wonder if she truly believed that, or if she was just too afraid to leave him."

"At least she's happy now."

"I guess that's something. It's just all of those wasted years—"

"Don't dwell on it. You can't change the past. Think about the good times, like your visits to your aunt."

"Too bad there weren't more of them. My mother was always uptight on the way home. So I'd entertain myself with a coloring book or some such booklet that the train attendant would hand out to kids. I used to daydream about one day being a conductor."

"Really?" Piper studied him for a moment.

"What? I could have done it."

"I'm sure you could have. I'm just imagining you with a conductor's hat. Yep, you'd still be just as cute."

He glanced away, not used to such compliments. "What can I say? I was just a little kid."

"I think it was a great dream. You know, it's not too late to become a conductor. And when they reopen the depot here in town, you can work close to home."

He shook his head. "I've got a new dream."

"And what's that?"

"Starting a string of coffee shops. I had three of them in Albuquerque, but Denise got them in the divorce."

"So Fill-It-Up Joe will be your flagship store?"

"Yes. I have everything invested in it. If it goes under, so do I." He had absolutely no idea what he'd do if the business failed. Maybe he would have to reconsider the idea of becoming a railroad conductor after all.

"You'll be a huge success."

"How do you know?"

She stopped and turned to him. "Look at all of the challenges you've overcome in your life, and you are standing here stronger than ever. If you set your mind to opening a chain of coffee shops, you'll do it. I just know it."

Her faith in him meant a lot. "Thank you."

"Any time you need a pep talk, I'm your girl."

They started to walk again. When they paused at the intersection, Piper turned as if waiting to cross the street as they did each morning. But today he wasn't ready for this conversation to end. It was really nice, and the company wasn't so bad either.

"Do you have to go back yet?" He hoped this one time she would relent and return to work just a little bit later than normal.

She paused and looked at him. "What do you have in mind?"

He shrugged. "Nothing in particular. I'm just enjoying the company, and I'm not ready to see it end just yet."

"Okay. But it can't be long."

He crossed his heart. "I promise."

She turned his way, and they continued up the quiet street. He longed to reach out and take her hand in his, but he resisted. They'd agreed they would not display their relationship in public. Not yet.

The funny thing was that keeping their relationship under wraps was more her idea than his. But he couldn't blame her. Her last breakup set tongues a-wagging for months. If they didn't work out, he didn't want to hurt her like that, so he played along with her request.

At this point, he would do anything to make her happy.

CHAPTER TWENTY-ONE

IN THE WEEK LEADING up to the festival, Joe had never been so happy in his life. Every morning when he woke up, he wondered if it was all some sort of dream. Then he'd show up at the town square, where Piper would meet him with a smile and a quick kiss. That definitely wasn't a dream—it was better.

With nothing left to do at the coffeehouse until a couple of rush orders arrived, he'd decided to volunteer to build the game booths and benches. The physical effort in hauling wood, cutting it, and nailing it together helped alleviate some of his anxiety over the launch of his business. Everything was going to be fine. He reasoned that if he told himself that often enough, he'd begin to believe it.

Joe was hammering a two-by-four for a game booth when he heard his name being called. He glanced up to find his friend Holden headed in his direction.

"Hey, man, I see they've put you to work." Holden slapped a hand on the wood frame as though to test its sturdiness. "Wish I could help, but until I can get a couple more ranch hands, I'm swamped."

"So then what brings you to town? Surely you couldn't be so lonely you came to watch me swing a hammer."

"Do you really think I'd actually miss that ugly mug of yours?" Holden laughed. "Not a chance. I needed some supplies."

"And you need something else or you wouldn't be talking to me. Do I even need to ask if you're in search of some free labor?" Joe grabbed another nail and hammered it into the board.

Holden lifted his Stetson and rubbed a hand over his forehead. "The thing is, I really need help getting the herd moved to higher ground. But never mind, you're busy here."

The truth was, they already had enough volunteers to complete everything in time for the fundraiser. Mrs. Sanchez had made certain of it. He'd volunteered just to keep himself busy and away from the temptation of talking to Piper all morning when she had work to do. He'd already monopolized enough of her time both night and day—perhaps too much so.

He needed some time away to clear his head. Whether he'd planned it or not, this thing with Piper was getting serious. It wasn't fair to her to lead her on if his feelings weren't real.

He glanced over to where she was helping a customer carry their order to their car. Piper had on those slim-fitting jeans that nestled against her hips, right where his hands went when he was pulling her close for a kiss.

As though she sensed he was staring at her, she turned her head. When their gazes met, his heart thumped. He wanted nothing more than to go to her, but he resisted.

That was a fine example of his dilemma. Was it purely a physical attraction? Or was it something much deeper?

He had to get this figured out.

"I don't have anything here to hold me back." Joe returned his hammer to his toolbox.

"Are you sure about that?"

Joe glanced up. "What's that supposed to mean?"

"I see the baker lady over there. She keeps glancing your way."

Without thinking, Joe looked over his shoulder. The tiny red T-shirt that emphasized her chest made her stand out like a bright flag, reminding him of what he was missing. Her laughter. Her teasing. Everything about her.

"She's not looking my way."

"Uh-huh." Holden cleared his throat as though to smother a chuckle. "You sure she won't miss you? Or is it the other way around?"

"It's neither," he said quickly, maybe a little too quickly, as Holden eyed him doubtfully. "It's not like we're a couple or anything. We're friends." But that didn't sound right even to his own ears.

"Sure sounds like that little lady over yonder has her claws in you."

Joe stood up to his full height, which thankfully was just a bit taller than Holden. His fists settled at his waist as he glared at his friend. "If you want help today, you best lay off. There's nothing between me and Piper, at least nothing to concern you. So let the subject drop."

Holden held up his hands. "Hey, I don't know a thing about women. It just seemed like..."

Joe scowled at him, not wanting him to finish that statement, because between sweet-as-pie kisses, morning runs, and nights holding her in his arms, they'd bonded. He'd let down his guard and trusted her more than any other person. He'd thought that maybe, just maybe, they might have something. But how did he know if all of this was real?

His head started to pound. "Let's go before I change my mind."

With nothing requiring his attention here in Whistle Stop, he didn't have an excuse to turn away Holden's request for help. After all, some distance would help him get his head screwed on straight where Piper was concerned.

He hoped.

Joe wanted to go to the Poppin' Fresh and give Piper a proper good-bye. But with Holden already giving him a hard time about her, Joe settled for a text message as he grabbed some clothes to take with him.

Holden needs help at the ranch. Will be gone a few days. If anything comes up, call me.

The day was done.

Piper flipped over the closed sign on the door and turned the lock. On her way back to the kitchen, she switched off the overhead lights, leaving only the glow of the lights in the display case.

With the bakery closed for the evening, Piper took solace in the silence of the store. Though she loved the residents of Whistle Stop, sometimes she enjoyed the utter silence of being alone. She'd never admit it to anyone, but sometimes she grew tired of smiling—today was one of those days.

She walked over to the desk off to the side of the kitchen and picked up a stack of new orders coming in from neighboring towns. The wedding cake for Laney and David had been the catalyst to this new rush of business. Her dream was coming true.

She thumbed through the pages, finding a number of wedding cake orders. A smile tugged at her lips. Luckily, the couples had ordered months in advance. Later, she'd go through and make sure she had enough time to accommodate them all. But for now, she released the orders, letting them flutter down onto the desktop.

Her problem was, she missed Joe.

Since when did she get so used to spending all of her free time with him? She couldn't let herself get reliant on him. It wasn't like there was a commitment between them. He still had his own life. And she had hers. Plain and simple.

Then why was she bored and restless?

After pacing back and forth, she decided to go for a walk around town. Hopefully, the fresh air and exercise would burn off her frustrations. Otherwise, this could end up being a very long night.

After locking up, she set off at a brisk pace. This evening's outing had nothing to do with exercise or diet. The more she thought about Joe, the more she realized just how crazy she was about him.

She lapped the town faster than she wanted. The walking just wasn't cutting it. As she walked around the town square back to Poppin' Fresh, she passed in front of the coffee shop. Even though it was dusk, no lights were on inside.

With Joe being out at the ranch with his buddy Holden, she couldn't resist pressing her nose to the coffeehouse's window and peering through the crack between the large sheets of white paper. Why in the world did he insist on keeping the big reveal a secret from everyone—including her?

It was too dark for her to make out anything. *Drat.* Then she recalled his sketches with the stark, empty storefront. Surely Joe didn't think the coffee alone would draw in the people. This was a small town. People liked to congregate, catch up on the latest gossip, and discuss the upcoming football game. Where exactly were they going to do that according to his sketch?

"Busted."

The voice made Piper jump and her heart lodge in her throat. With a hand pressed to her pounding chest, she turned. Her brother stood there, grinning as though he'd caught her sneaking the last store-bought cookie from the jar their mother kept above the sink. "Mason, do you have to sneak up on people?"

"I wasn't sneaking, I was walking. You're the one who appears to be up to no good."

"I am not." Heat rushed to her cheeks. Why did her brother still have a way of needling her?

He arched a brow. "Do you always go around town pressing your nose to windows?"

"I was not. I was…I was, oh, never mind." She wasn't even going to attempt to explain her complicated relationship with Joe. It was time to turn the tables on Mason. "So, I haven't seen you much lately."

"I've been out of town looking into, um…setting up a satellite office."

Her brother was a CPA with a growing list of clients, but she had no idea he'd gotten this successful. "Things are going that well for you?"

"It's been a lot of work, but it's starting to pay off."

"Do you really think now's the time to pursue political aspirations?"

Mason glanced away. "I don't know what you're talking about."

"Don't act so innocent. Did you honestly expect Mom to keep your secret?" Their mother couldn't keep a secret if her life depended on it. And knowing this, why her brother would ever confide in her was beyond Piper's imagination.

His brows drew together. "But I didn't tell her anything. Certainly not anything I wouldn't mind the rest of the town knowing. What have you heard?"

"That you're running for mayor in the spring." His mouth gaped before he pressed his lips together, giving Piper a chance to continue. "I take it you didn't tell her that."

He shook his head. "Are you kidding? I haven't even told Bella yet—"

"You didn't? Are you serious? You really need to talk this over with your fiancée."

He shrugged. "I...I haven't gotten to it yet."

Piper crossed her arms and eyed up her big brother, who in turn was busy studying the sidewalk with great interest. "Don't you think you're taking on too much, between your expanding business and your upcoming wedding? I don't know how Bella deals with your workaholic tendencies."

He kicked at a pebble. "She doesn't like it."

She couldn't blame Bella. Piper knew how focused her brother could be. He was a lot like their father, taking on more than he could handle. "Don't do this."

His gaze met hers. "Do what?"

"Get caught up in an election."

"You don't understand. The town needs me. It's on the verge of a rebirth."

Frustration bubbled in her veins. "And you're the only person who has what it takes to turn Whistle Stop around?"

"Yes."

"No, you aren't." She shook her head. "Wait. Since when are you interested in politics?"

"I...I always have been—"

"No, you haven't. Remember who you're talking to. I'm your sister. I know you better than most people. You've never once taken a big interest in elections."

"Okay. Fine. But this has to stay between you and me." When she nodded, he sighed. "I need to put Whistle Stop back on the map. My business is dying."

That was news to her. "I thought you had all of these new accounts from surrounding areas. I thought that's what all of the traveling was about."

Mason rubbed the back of his neck. "That's what I want people to think. I don't want anyone to know about the bind I'm in. Nothing chases away clients like news of a sinking ship."

"Oh, Mason. I'm sorry." Piper reached out to hug him, but he backed away.

"I didn't tell you this to gain your sympathy. I need your help to keep Mom from spreading the news about my candidacy until I make my official announcement. You know how this town can be...stuck in its ways."

"That's true. But they're trying to change things."

"I can't wait around for Mayor Ortiz to get his act together, if he ever does."

She wasn't particularly fond of the mayor. He'd almost been her father-in-law, but he'd had absolutely nothing to do with her failed engagement. And if she were honest with herself, the reason her relationship had crumbled was that she and David had never truly belonged together. He was the man her mother wanted her to be with, not who Piper wanted to be with.

She had a feeling her brother was about to make his own grave mistake. Maybe it wasn't too late to reason with him. "The mayor, he's doing his best. Just give him and the town council some time."

"I can't. It's taking too long."

"You can't blame them for the wildfire on Roca Mountain."

"I don't. But someone has to do something to pick up the pace. Businesses are closing their doors, and residents are moving away."

"Just stop and think this over. Are you sure your relationship with Bella can handle the strain of you running for mayor on top of everything else?"

"I don't know." He ran a hand over his clean-shaven jaw.

"Promise me you'll think about it some more before you do something you'll come to regret."

Worry reflected in Mason's eyes. "But I have to do something, or everything I've been working toward will be ruined."

Her heart went out to him. "I'll give it some thought and see if I can come up with anything."

"Thanks. But the biggest help you can give me is keeping Mom under wraps."

"I'll try."

"I've got to go." He paused and glanced at her. "I know we got to talking about me, but when I came upon you, you looked like you had something serious on your mind. Anything you want to talk about?"

Piper shook her head. Her brother already had enough worries to contend with. "I just had an idea, and I was trying to decide on its merits."

Mason's gaze moved to the coffeehouse. "Wouldn't have anything to do with your competition, would it?"

She shrugged. "He's not really my competition."

Her brother's face lit up with interest. "Is there something I should know?"

"Seriously, don't you have enough of your own issues without having to stick your nose into in my life?"

"It's a big brother's prerogative."

She shook her head. "You're forgetting that I'm all grown up now. I've got everything under control."

"You keep telling yourself that. I've got to go." Mason headed toward his office.

She turned back to the coffeehouse and frowned. She didn't want Joe's coffee shop to end up being one of those businesses that her brother had mentioned were closing their doors. She worried her bottom lip.

She couldn't help but feel Joe was making a serious miscalculation. If he wanted a thriving business, he had to make his customers feel welcome. She didn't want to see him fail before he even opened his doors. His life already hadn't been easy. And she really wanted him to stay in Whistle Stop—permanently.

In that moment, she realized why his business being a smashing success was so important to her.

She loved Joe.

And it wasn't like anything she'd ever felt before. He cared about her just as she was. He wasn't always trying to change her, like David had. Joe didn't criticize her. Instead, he pitched in and helped her.

Now it was her turn to help him.

The more she thought about staging the front of the coffee shop, the more excited she got. If Joe could see with his own eyes what she had in mind...if he could walk around and have a seat...if he could just experience the atmosphere, he'd see that her idea had merit.

Determining she was on to something, her mind filled with the ideas she'd tried telling Joe about previously, back when he'd shut her down. She brushed aside the sting of how he'd excluded her and her suggestions. Things between them had come a long way since then. Besides, if he didn't like it, the plain, stark space could easily be restored.

She rushed up the back stairs of her building. She couldn't wait to see the surprise on Joe's face when he saw how comfy and welcoming she could make the place. And she knew just how to accomplish it.

In the attic, she had a collection of old furniture that was still in excellent condition. They were pieces she'd saved from the beauty salon that once occupied her bakery's storefront. Maybe if she could give Joe an idea of what he could do with the space without spending much money, which she knew all too well was very important to him, he'd see her idea had merit.

Satisfied she had enough furniture to make this plan work, she rushed over to Joe's place. The back door was locked. He'd obviously spent long enough in the city that he'd learned to lock the place up tight as a drum.

Frustration weighed heavy on her. How was she supposed to help him now? Just about to give up, she gave the building one final glance when she spotted a window on the first floor that was open a crack. She rushed over to give it a push, opening it farther. There wasn't a lot of room, but it looked just big enough for her to shimmy through.

But first, she had to find something to climb on. She glanced all around the alleyway, but the garbage had just been picked up that morning. So, when all else fails, improvise. She ran inside the bakery and quickly spotted a step stool.

With the stool tucked securely under her arm, she rushed back to his place. She smiled. This was going to be the best surprise of all. Just wait until Joe saw the coffee shop. He'd regret turning down her help before.

He was supposed to return sometime that evening. She hoped it was sooner rather than later. The truth was, she missed their talks, the sound of his voice, the way his eyes crinkled at the corners when he smiled.

She missed everything about him.

She wanted him to be a permanent part of her life, and this was the only way she could think of to show him just how much he meant to her. A shiver of excitement rippled through her stomach as she pictured the surprise on Joe's face when he spotted her handiwork.

CHAPTER TWENTY-TWO

A YAWN CROSSED HIS lips.

Joe kept one hand on the truck's steering wheel as he stretched. Exhaustion coursed through his body. Maybe he should have listened to Holden and stayed another night. After all, he'd been up before the sun and had worked all day. But he couldn't get Piper off his mind.

He missed her. A lot.

The time away had given him the clarity he'd been seeking. He'd sorted out his feelings for her. It'd been so much easier than he'd ever imagined.

He loved Piper. Heart and soul.

Now he was wrestling with whether to reveal his feelings right away or give it some time. What if she didn't feel the same? What would he do then? Talk about making things awkward, considering their businesses were next door to each other.

Maybe it was just exhaustion muddling his thoughts. A good night's sleep would clarify things. Tomorrow he'd have the answers.

When he entered the edge of town, everything was quiet. Whistle Stop was asleep. He had to admit that this was one of those times when he remembered what he loved about this place and why he'd finally returned after all of those years away—the peaceful serenity. There was just something about this town that put him at ease. Though ghosts of the past still lurked in the shadows, the beauty of the present far outweighed the horrors of the past.

Right now, he was savoring the thought of collapsing on his king-size bed. He was so tired that he wasn't even sure he was going to take off his clothes. He might just fall face first onto his pillow and slip into a deep sleep.

He eased into the town square. As expected, not a soul was stirring. He considered parking in front of the coffee shop. It was then that he noticed something. A flickering light in the coffee shop. How was that possible?

He might be tired—okay, exhausted—but his memory was intact. He'd made sure to turn everything off, both upstairs in his apartment and downstairs in the shop.

Was it a burglar?

In Whistle Stop? Nah.

There was nothing in his coffee shop worth stealing.

Joe swung his pickup off to the side of the road and hopped out. As his feet moved swiftly over the asphalt, a sick feeling started to churn in the pit of his stomach. Something wasn't right here. Was that smoke? He inhaled more deeply. Something most definitely wasn't right.

When he neared the covered windows of Fill-It-Up Joe, he knew where the light was coming from. His chest tightened. The building was on fire.

The automatic fire alarm was one of those details he had yet to mark off on his to-do list. He grabbed his cell phone and dialed 911. His gaze zeroed in on the flames licking at the windows. *This can't be happening. It has to be a nightmare.*

When his attention moved to the Poppin' Fresh Bakery, his frantic thoughts turned to Piper. His gaze lifted to the second floor. She'd be upstairs, sound asleep. With their buildings connected, it wouldn't be a stretch to imagine the fire jumping over to her side.

He had to get her to safety. After giving the operator the necessary information, he disconnected the phone call just as he heard the alarm at the fire station blow, piercing the silence of the night with its eerie screech. Joe took off running to the Poppin' Fresh. He grasped the metal handle of the front door, relieved to find it was still cool to the touch. But frustration pumped through his veins upon finding the door locked. He banged on the wood frame with both fists. "Piper! Piper, wake up!"

The siren continued to pierce the night with its call to action. He stared up at the second floor. There were still no lights. Had she heard him?

With adrenaline fueling him, he set off at a sprint for the back of the building where a staircase led to her apartment. When he got there, he noticed flames beating against the windows of his side of the building, and smoke seeped around the back door of Piper's place.

There wasn't time to waste waiting for the firefighters. He had to get in there. The thought of Piper dying in this fire made his heart lurch.

He tried the doorknob. It was locked. Since when did she start locking her doors? Wasn't she the one who'd preached at him about not having to worry about crime in Whistle Stop? And if someone did bother to steal, they were obviously far worse off than them.

Luckily, he had on a jacket to offset the chill of the evening. He pulled his sleeve down over his hand and banged his elbow hard against the glass panel in the door. The thin pane gave way easily. Careful not to cut himself on the sharp pieces, he reached through and turned the dead bolt.

He swung the door open. "Piper!" Nothing. "Piper!"

The smoke wasn't heavy...at least not down in the kitchen. He had no idea what to expect on the second floor, but that didn't stop him from taking the steps two at a time in the pitch dark. He knew his way around after spending every evening in the past week or so at her place.

He burst through her front door. "Piper!" There was no sound. He turned, squinting into the dark. "Piper, speak to me."

In the darkness, he tripped over something on the floor. Piper did have a lot of stuff crammed into the apartment. Though his shin ached, he kept moving toward the bedroom.

He heard the distinct sound of a door squeaking open. "Joe? What are you doing here in the middle of the night?"

"Hurry! There's a fire."

"What? Where?"

"Come on." He reached for her, but she backed away. "Piper, we have to get out."

"I...I need my stuff."

He lunged forward, catching hold of her hand and pulling her toward him. "You have to come with me."

She spread her hands out in front of her as though searching for something. "But I have to get—"

"There isn't time. We have to go." The sirens of emergency vehicles grew closer. Gripping her hand tightly, he started down the steps. The smoke grew thicker, and he started to cough.

Piper hesitated, but he didn't let go of her, nor did he slow down. He'd heard of the dangers of inhaling smoke. Piper coughed repeatedly. There weren't any flames here, just smoke. Lots of smoke. His lungs and eyes burned.

At last, they reached the ground floor. In the dark, his hand fumbled around until his fingers wrapped around the doorknob. He threw the door open and rushed out into the fresh night air. Cough after cough racked his body. Joe had never realized until that moment what a blessing it was to be able to breathe clean air.

"Wait. I need to put on some clothes." Piper pulled free from his hold.

She doesn't have any clothes on?

He immediately turned to her, taking in her disheveled appearance. It appeared all she had on was an oversized T-shirt. Even her feet were bare. Any other time, he'd have been enticed by her appearance, but this definitely wasn't the time. "We need to get you something to wear."

"I've got it." She held up some jeans and shoes. "Just give me a moment."

While she slipped on her clothes, he glanced back at the building. Dark smoke poured out of every crevice. His stomach sank down to his cowboy boots. He just hoped help arrived in time.

"Okay, I got my jeans on. Just need my shoes." Piper gripped his arm as she slipped on a pair of tennis shoes. "Done. Let's go."

They moved to the front of the building where the glow of the fire was very obvious in his storefront. The thought of his dreams and hopes going up in flames made his stomach churn.

"I...I'm sorry." Piper's voice was soft at his side, but he heard her.

He pulled her close, drawing strength from the knowledge that she was safe. He hugged her close.

Emergency vehicles rolled to a stop with sirens blaring and red lights flashing, reflecting off the building and highlighting the surrounding trees. As the sirens silenced, men all suited up in yellow and black gear set to work, yanking a long line of hose from the fire engine. One man barked off orders as some of the other men grabbed oxygen tanks.

All around them there was a flurry of motion.

"Come on. We need to get out of the way." Joe grabbed Piper's arm as she stared at the horrific scene before them. He couldn't blame her. None of it was making any sense to him either.

"What are we going to do?" There was a note of shock in her voice.

"I have absolutely no idea."

He didn't even want to think about what would have happened had he decided to take Holden up on his offer and spent another night on his couch. Would Piper have woken up in time to get out safely? A chill raced over his skin.

"I'm so sorry." Piper's voice was soft and cracked with emotion.

"It's not your fault."

She gazed up at him with tears gathering in her eyes. "I...I..."

"Shh...it's okay. This wasn't anyone's fault."

Or was it? Maybe he'd been in such a rush to leave for Holden's ranch that he'd left something on. Though he highly doubted it. There had to be another explanation. But what?

He raked a hand through his hair. There'd be enough time for answers later. All he knew was that Piper was not to blame. Heck, she'd been sound asleep next door. She easily could have died. The thought sent ice-cold fingers of apprehension inching up his spine.

"Don't worry. Everything will be all right." He didn't know exactly whom he meant those words for, himself or her. And he didn't know if he believed them. But the ashen appearance of Piper's face had him worried. It could be from smoke inhalation or shock. "Do you need a paramedic?"

She shook her head. "I...I'm fine."

"You're sure?"

She nodded. Her gaze moved back to the smoke billowing from their building.

He didn't exactly believe her. But who could blame her for looking so poorly when both of their worlds were wrapped in a ball of flames and smoke. In this very moment, it was hard to believe that anything would ever be all right again. "I just don't understand. How did this happen?"

"I'm so sorry." A tear splashed onto Piper's cheek.

"You don't have to keep saying that. You had nothing to do with the fire." Seeing her genuine distress, he didn't take time to think, he just acted, pulling her close. With her body pressed to his, he leaned his chin against her head. "I don't know what I would have done if something had happened to you."

His hand stroked her silky hair, and he breathed in the strawberry scent mingled with the foul odor of smoke. He gripped her tighter, not wanting to think about how close he'd come to losing her. He couldn't imagine his life without her in it.

She might drive him up a wall with her stubbornness, but she also made him smile like no other. She made him feel like anything was possible. Even overcoming his past and learning to trust again. He'd never had a person affect him so deeply. Maybe she was exactly what he needed—she was teaching him to live again.

Piper pulled back and swiped at her eyes. "What are we going to do?"

"Don't worry. We have plenty of time to figure it out."

She turned to the building. "But...but everything's ruined now."

He wrapped his arm protectively around Piper's shoulders, wanting to give her what little comfort he could. He glanced down at her, noticing her T-shirt was thin. He ran a hand over her arm, noticing her skin was chilled from the night air. He doubted she noticed as she stood transfixed, staring at the blaze as smoke now started to pour out of her storefront too. This nightmare just kept getting worse.

He shrugged off his jacket and wrapped it around her shoulders. She glanced up at him with unspoken questions in her eyes. "Take it. You need it."

"But I'm not cold."

"You will be." Once the shock wore off and the stark reality of the situation settled in. "I have to go see what I can do to help."

She reached out, grabbing his arm. "Don't leave me."

The fear in her voice dug at him, but he had to find out how much damage had been done. It was his fault that Piper's business was in jeopardy. He placed his hand over hers. "You'll be safe. I promise." He glanced around for someone to stay with Piper. "I won't let anything happen to you."

Mrs. Sanchez hustled up to them in her fuzzy pink robe. "Lord have mercy, are you two okay?"

Piper didn't speak. She was once again focused on the fire.

"I need to go talk to the firefighters." Joe couldn't just stand here and do nothing while everything he'd worked so hard to rebuild went up in flames. He glanced over at Mrs. Sanchez. "Can you keep an eye on her?"

"Sure, I can." Mrs. Sanchez wrapped a protective arm around Piper. "But you should stay here, too. They'll talk to you as soon as they can."

Joe glanced around as more and more of Whistle Stop's residents gathered in the town square. The worry written all over their faces mirrored just a fraction of the turmoil churning within him. How did this happen? How did his dream go up in a puff of smoke?

He moved to stand in front of Piper, hoping to gain her full attention. "It'll be okay. I promise you won't lose your bakery. We'll rebuild it if we have to."

She gazed at him as though in some sort of trance. It wasn't until she nodded that he knew she'd heard him. Her lack of words worried him, but under the circumstances, he couldn't blame her. He didn't think either of them were okay, or would be until this nightmare was over.

He reached out to her, stroking the back of his hand over her soft cheek before leaning forward and placing a kiss on her forehead. "Wait for me."

Again, she nodded.

Hoping for good news about the Poppin' Fresh Bakery, Joe headed for a group of firefighters. *Please don't let it be as bad as it looks.*

CHAPTER TWENTY-THREE

NUMBNESS SPREAD THROUGHOUT HER.

Piper stood still as Joe strode away. She had no idea how he was able to walk. Right now, her legs felt anything but sturdy. If she were to take a step, she was certain she'd land face first on the ground.

Her mind struggled to grasp the sight before her. Firefighters rushing here and there. A shower of water shooting up to the roof. Smoke pouring from every opening in the building.

This makes no sense.

What is happening?

She realized the surprise she'd planned for Joe had gone up in smoke—literally. And then a worse thought set in. Joe wouldn't stay in Whistle Stop after losing his business. And she couldn't imagine not having him in her life. She'd come to look forward to seeing him each and every day.

Ever since their first morning run together, she'd fallen for him. Or perhaps it had been before that. Each smile. Each touch. Each look. He'd beat down the wall she'd erected around her heart and had shown her what it was like to be truly loved.

In return, she loved him with every fiber of her being.

The very thought of him being erased from her life made the breath catch in her throat.

She was about to lose everything. Everything!

A sob swelled in the back of her throat.

The sight in front of her blurred.

Including Joe.

Her body swayed.

"Whoa there. Let's sit you down." Mrs. Sanchez guided her over to one of the few park benches that was safe enough to sit on. "I know this is hard, but you aren't alone."

Piper struggled to swallow down her anguish. She sent up a silent prayer that not everything would be lost. She didn't ask it for herself—she asked it for Joe. God could have her bakery, but she prayed he'd spare Joe's coffee shop, his dream. He just couldn't lose everything after all the misery life had already thrown at him. No one deserved what Joe had lived through.

"Piper! Piper!" came frantic voices in the night air.

She sucked in a deep breath, hoping it would settle her nerves. The truth was, she didn't think anything would settle them, not even a triple-chocolate cupcake.

Ana was the first to reach her. "Thank goodness you're okay."

They hugged.

Then she heard her name called again.

Alexis rushed up to her. "Piper, I came as soon as I heard. Sweetie, what can I do?"

Piper sniffled. "Wake me up from this nightmare."

Sympathy shone in Alexis's eyes. "I wish I could." She glanced around. "Where's Joe?" Then a look of panic crossed her features. "He's not still in there, is he?"

Piper shook her head. "He rescued me. I was asleep. I didn't even know there was a fire until he showed up at my door."

"Thank goodness he woke up."

"I don't think he woke up. When I went to bed, he wasn't home from Holden's." An arched brow had her adding, "Holden's a friend of his."

Ella was the next to arrive. She glanced at the now-thinning smoke and then back at Piper. Instead of offering platitudes, she simply wrapped a supportive arm around her. "I'm here for you. Whatever you need."

Piper's gaze scanned the area. Where was Joe? She'd been able to make out his form in the lights from the vehicles and the big spotlight the firefighters used to illuminate the area. But it'd been a while now since she'd been able to locate him.

She had to believe that Tony, Moe, Cord, and the rest of the firefighters would make sure Joe didn't get himself into any trouble. Still, she found herself continuing to seek out his image. She wished he'd come back to her.

She'd never felt that comfort in anyone else's presence. There was just something special about him, something that went beyond the way he made her heart race. It was something much, much deeper.

And the truth was, that in all the time they'd spent together, she'd never worked up the courage to tell him how she felt. She didn't think she could bear him rejecting her love.

But by playing it safe, she risked him packing up and leaving Whistle Stop. She couldn't let that happen. The time had come for her to be honest with him.

If he knew she loved him, he'd want to stay and rebuild.

Talk about a nightmare.

As the last firetruck pulled away from the scene, Joe stood alone on the sidewalk, staring through a darkened window into his coffee shop. Though it was still too dark out to distinguish shapes and figures, he'd already had a preview of the devastating damage when the fire crew had gone through the building with their flashlights, making sure the fire was indeed out.

The fire marshal would be called first thing in the morning to determine the cause of the fire. Joe wasn't up on fire procedures, but something told him they suspected something besides old wiring had caused the blaze which had started in the coffee shop. His gut churned. Was it possible Whistle Stop had an arsonist?

The thought was so preposterous he wanted to outright reject the idea. Everyone knew everyone else in this small town. If someone was that off-balance, he'd have heard. People wouldn't just stand by and watch someone in obvious need risk their own life, not to mention jeopardize someone else's. No. There had to be some other reason for the fire chief to consider this a suspicious fire. He couldn't blame the man for having questions. He had a growing list of his own.

How could this have happened?

Was it accidental?

Or had someone set out to destroy him?

Joe blamed himself. He should have stayed here, and then none of this would have happened. He'd have been on top of everything. Why, oh, why had he left town?

In that moment, he felt a gentle hand brush over his back. Then another hand joined it and wrapped around his chest. It was Piper. She was hugging him, as though sensing he needed her strength.

He sighed.

He was wrong about one thing...

He hadn't lost everything after all.

The most important part of his life was holding him close. He loved Piper with all of his heart. The tension eased from his body.

He turned in her arms until they were chest to chest. Her face was pale, and her eyes were bloodshot, most likely a combination of irritation from the smoke, lack of sleep, and tears over their dreams being destroyed.

She pressed a hand to his chest. "What...what will you do now?"

In all honesty, he didn't know. But he didn't want her to worry about him. She had enough worries with everything she'd need to do to get her business up and running again.

"Don't you worry," he said. "I'll figure something out." He hated to see the pain in her eyes. He wanted desperately to smooth her worries. "Everything will work out. You'll see."

Her hesitant gaze moved to the building still dripping with water, sooty lines from the smoke trailing up the front. "I don't think it's going to be easy."

"Never said it would be easy. But I do think it's doable."

"Will...will you remain in Whistle Stop?" Her gaze searched his.

"I'm not going anywhere."

He'd really missed her the past few days—more than he'd imagined possible. There were so many times he'd wanted to bask in the glow of her smile, hear the lilt of her voice, watch her eyes light up with excitement. At last, he was ready to face the truth he'd been fighting for so long. It was abundantly obvious that he was in love with Piper.

The only good thing that had come out of this damn fire was that it'd made him realize life was full of uncertainty. He couldn't drag his feet. He had to seize the moment.

"Thank you for staying here with me." His voice was deep and rumbled with emotion that he was unable to contain.

"I am right where I belong."

His hand moved to her face. His thumb gently stroked her cheek. He couldn't imagine ever leaving her. At last, he was truly home. Wherever Piper was, it was his home.

His heart pounded as he searched for the words to tell her how he felt. And then, instead of words, he wanted to show her. He drew her closer, and she willingly obliged. When her soft curves pressed to him, need thrummed through his veins.

He stared deep into her eyes. He most definitely loved her. He'd never felt an emotion so strong, so delightful.

Loud footsteps sounded behind him. They came to a stop, and someone cleared their throat. He didn't want to release Piper. He just wanted to keep holding her, savoring this new amazing feeling.

"Joe, can I speak to you?" Tony Granger's voice came from behind them. "It's important."

Joe inwardly groaned in frustration. With great reluctance, he released Piper from his embrace, but he caught her hand in his, needing the physical connection. "We'll finish this later."

Her worried eyes met his as she nodded in understanding.

He turned to find Tony standing behind him in full uniform with the fire chief emblem on his helmet.

"The fire's out. It looks worse than it was. It's a good thing you came home when you did. You really should have smoke alarms—"

"I'm having a fire and burglary system installed, but it's not scheduled until next week."

Tony nodded in understanding. "As it is, we were able to knock down the fire without losing the whole building."

That was good, so why did he have the feeling there was still more bad news about to come his way? Joe braced himself for the worst.

Tony shifted his weight from one booted foot to the other. "The first floor is a mess. It's going to need a lot of work. But the other floor doesn't have nearly as much damage. Do you have insurance?"

Joe released a pent up breath. All was not lost. "I had to secure insurance coverage in order to get a loan."

"Good. That will help a lot."

Joe squeezed Piper's hand and then asked the question on everyone's mind. "What about the Poppin' Fresh Bakery? Is there much damage?"

Tony adjusted his fire helmet. "On that front, we have some good news. We were able to contain the fire, and other than some smoke and water damage, the bakery should be fine."

Joe breathed easier. "Thanks. We'll take any bit of good news we can get at this point."

"You'll need to keep an eye on the coffee shop for a bit just to make sure the fire doesn't catch again. Can you do that?"

Joe nodded. "I'd never be able to sleep now anyway."

"I'm really sorry this happened." Tony patted his shoulder before he walked away.

It wasn't until then that Tony's words started to sink in. More questions started to plague Joe. He held up a finger for Piper to wait. "I'll be right back."

"Go ahead. I...I'll be fine."

He rushed after Tony, knowing if he didn't get some details about what started the blaze, he'd never be able to shut his eyes, even when it was safe. Obviously it'd started in the coffeehouse, but that just wasn't enough to settle his mind. He needed something more.

This couldn't be real.

This whole night had to be a nightmare.

Piper gazed over at the building where the spotlight was still highlighting the smoke-stained bricks and broken windows. The acidic stench of smoke hung in the air. A fresh wave of sadness washed over her. She knew how much that business meant to Joe and now it was ruined. How had it all gone so wrong?

She glanced over at him talking with Tony. She was certain he was dragging answers out of Tony, answers about how the fire started. Her feet started moving in that direction. She had to know, had to understand how something this horrific could have happened.

"I can't give you a definitive answer." Tony glanced her way and then back at Joe. "You'll have to wait until tomorrow when the fire marshal goes over the scene."

"I just need your best guess." Joe's voice held a determined tone. "Based on your experience, I'm guessing you have a pretty good idea of what happened here. If it's my fault, I need to know it."

Tony gave him a long, hard stare. "If I had to hazard a guess, and it is only a guess until the fire marshal has a chance to issue an official report—"

"I understand. Just give me something to go on."

"Okay. This is just between us." When Joe nodded, Tony continued. "It appears an overloaded electrical outlet and old wiring triggered the fire. The fuses should have kicked off automatically, but for some reason the breaker wasn't tripped. I don't know why. There are a number of unanswered questions at this point."

The fine hairs on Piper's arms rose. This nightmare just seemed to get worse and worse.

"An overloaded outlet?" Joe's forehead creased as he thought it over. "But I wasn't home. Nothing should have been running."

"Are you sure? It's easy enough to forget things."

Joe shook his head. "I'm real careful about those things."

Piper listened in horror. She'd been in Joe's shop. She'd been the one to plug in a bunch of stuff. She'd been the one to destroy his business, his home. She moaned in agony.

Joe wrapped an arm about her waist. "Are you all right?"

She blinked repeatedly, trying to keep her emotions from spilling forth. She had to get this out, and she couldn't do that if she broke down now. Joe deserved the truth, the whole truth.

"It was me." Her voice crackled with emotion.

"What was you?" Joe gripped both of her upper arms as though worried she was going to topple over. "Piper, you're not making sense. What are you talking about?"

"I...I was there. I did it."

"You were where? Piper, start at the beginning."

"I wanted to surprise you. I...I thought if I could show you what you could do with the space, how you could make it more intimate for the customers, that you'd realize I was right." Piper sniffled and dashed the back of her hand over her eyes. "I wanted to surprise you. I thought I was helping—"

"Piper, what did you do?" Joe looked at her like he didn't even know her anymore.

"I...I had some extra furniture in my attic that wouldn't have cost you a thing to use to create a seating area for your customers."

"But what does any of that have to do with an overloaded outlet?"

He was going to hate her. And she deserved it. How had she destroyed absolutely everything?

"I wanted to light up the place so I plugged in a bunch of lamps. I wanted it all lit up for when you got home. Then I was hurrying and dropped a potted plant. I plugged the vacuum in the same outlet. I...I must have overloaded the circuit."

Joe staggered back from her as though she'd just stabbed him in the chest. She was pretty certain that at this precise moment he wouldn't see much difference between stabbing him and burning down his dream. There had to be some way to turn this around.

She pleaded with him with her eyes. "I didn't notice anything wrong when I left."

"That's because it would have started with the wiring in the walls." His eyes grew dark and unreadable. "Let me get this straight. You burned down my place because you didn't approve of my decorating?"

She worried her bottom lip as she fought to keep the tears in check. With her throat thick with smothered sobs, she shook her head. He had it all wrong.

His voice took on a menacing tone. "I already told you I wasn't interested in your help. Yet, the minute I leave town, you take it upon yourself to make decisions for me because you know better than I do what's right for my business?"

"It...it's not like that."

"You"—Joe pointed accusingly at her—"you just had to meddle, didn't you? It didn't matter what I said, what I wanted." His voice shook with anger. "Why in the world did I think things would be different with you?"

She opened her mouth, but no words would come to her. He was right on all counts.

"Calm down." Tony stepped between them. "We don't know anything for sure. And Piper told you she didn't notice anything wrong when she left. Why not let it go until the marshal's report comes in?"

Piper stepped around Tony. "Please, Joe. You have to believe me. I would never do anything deliberately to hurt you."

His eyes said he didn't believe her, not one single word. The warmth and caring that had been reflected in them just moments ago had disappeared. Now there was just a hard, cold look. And it was her fault. All her fault.

CHAPTER TWENTY-FOUR

How could he have been so wrong about Piper?

Joe staggered back from the woman he'd almost confessed to loving. Boy, would that have been a huge mistake. Now, as he stood there staring at her, a tear splashed onto her cheek, but he was too devastated for it to affect him. His mind and body were on overload.

He barely recognized her as the sweet thing who had baked him a bear claw each morning or listened to him bare his scarred soul to her. Before him stood a meddling stranger. Someone who'd stolen his future from him.

Grief and pain collided within him. "Why? Why would you do this?"

"I didn't mean to—"

"Was I not nice enough to you? Were you that worried about the competition?"

"No. No. It...it wasn't any of that."

He pressed his hands to his waist and blinked repeatedly. "I don't understand how someone who says they're my friend could do this."

"I'm sorry. I...I'll fix it—"

"No! You won't! I don't want your help. Every time I have something that's important to me, someone I'm supposed to be able to rely on, to trust, comes along and destroys it. And in the process, they destroy a little piece of me."

"I...I'm sorry." She blinked and swiped at her cheeks. "I would do anything to erase this whole night."

"I shouldn't blame you. I should blame myself. I trusted you more than anyone. I opened up to you about the most painful experiences in my life. And that's all on me. If I hadn't, none of this would have happened."

Piper staggered backward.

He glared at her. "Stay away from me. I don't ever want anything to do with you."

A sob tore from her throat. She held a hand to her mouth and took another step back.

Good. She was finally getting the message.

In one night, he'd lost his home, his business, and now the woman he'd thought he loved. How could he have been so foolish? He knew what happened when he trusted others—what always happened—he paid a steep price.

"We were all wrong for each other. Just go away." He turned his back to her.

Joe's body started to tremble. He folded his arms across his chest as his gaze took in the black soot stains trailing up his building. Everything was ruined.

"Here. You need this." A gentle female voice said before the woman draped a red blanket over his shaking shoulders.

He glanced over at the woman. Her warm smile and short, silver hair looked familiar, but he couldn't put a name to the face. His thoughts were a jumbled mess. Nothing was making sense.

"Can I get you anything else?" The older woman sent him a worried look. When he shook his head, she said, "I think I should call the paramedics and have them take a look at you. I think you might be suffering from shock."

Was that it? Was that why he'd been a monster to Piper?

"Come on." The woman gave a tug on his arm.

At last, he regained his speech. "Thanks. I...I'm fine."

She sent him a look that said he was about as far from fine as a person could get. And he couldn't argue with her. But he didn't think there was a thing the paramedics could do for him.

He continued to stand there. A tremor raced through his body as the shock and anger drained away. Adrenaline fled his veins, allowing exhaustion to take its place. The weight of grief and guilt settled on his shoulders, pushing him down, making it hard to keep standing.

His gaze sought out Piper, but she'd already disappeared. Good for her. She got away from him, because right now he didn't even recognize himself. He couldn't even recall half of the things he'd said to her. He knew whatever the words had been, they'd hurt her. The pained look in Piper's eyes was the one thing his memory retained.

His gut reaction was to go after her, to apologize for his overreaction.

But he couldn't do it. As hard as it was for both of them, it had to be this way. He'd been foolish to think he could have a relationship with Piper, with anyone. Past experience should have been lesson enough.

People changed, and in his experience, it was never for the best.

Then why did it feel like she'd walked away with his heart in her hands? And why did it feel as though he'd just pushed away his one chance to write his own happy ending?

"Do you have someplace to go?" The woman was still standing there, as though watching over him.

She obviously didn't trust him to his own devices. And he didn't blame her. He'd taken a horrible situation and made it unbearable. No one should be around him.

Realizing the woman was staring at him expectantly, he decided he better pull it together long enough to answer her before she called 911. "I...I can go to my mother's."

"You're Martha's boy, aren't you?"

He nodded.

"Can you walk there? Or should I find you a ride?"

His mother lived only a few blocks away. He'd walked there many times. "I'll make it."

"Lead the way."

"But the building, I need—"

"You need to go rest before you cause more damage. Someone else will watch it." She took his arm, and they started walking.

So she had heard how he'd spoken to Piper. He wanted to ask her what all he'd said in the heat of the moment, but he didn't dare. He wasn't sure he could cope with the guilt. He'd deal with it tomorrow. He'd deal with everything tomorrow. It surely couldn't be as bad as tonight. Could it?

"We're here." The woman's voice was calm and reassuring.

He glanced up to find they were standing on the porch of his mother's small bungalow. The porch light flicked on, and then his mother was standing there in her robe. She ushered them both inside.

The two women spoke in hushed tones as he headed to the small guest room where he'd stayed when he'd first moved back to town. He'd just lain down on the bed when his mother rushed into the room.

"Thank goodness Mrs. Noel was there to bring you home." His mother held out two pills and a glass of water. "Here, take these."

He didn't have it in him to argue. He'd done enough of that tonight to last a lifetime. He never ever wanted to raise his voice again. He never ever wanted to be responsible for putting such a pained look on someone else's face.

His mother turned off the light and closed the door.

The events of the night played in his mind, blurring together into a gnarled mess.

Then the blackness of the night mercifully sought him out.

CHAPTER TWENTY-FIVE

PIPER AWOKE TO THE smell of fresh-brewed coffee.

She glanced around, realizing the blinds had been pulled and the drapes drawn, making the room much darker than it really was outside. Oh my! There was sunshine sneaking through the cracks. She'd totally slept in. She jumped out of bed.

She looked down at the large, pink, flowered nightgown Mrs. Sanchez had lent her. She was ever so grateful for the woman's generosity, but right now Piper had to get to work. There were orders to fill. She rushed to throw on her jeans and T-shirt. The lingering scent of smoke on the clothing brought back the harrowing images from the prior night.

There was no work to get to. She'd be lucky if her bakery was salvageable after last night's blaze. Then she recalled her confrontation with Joe. The backs of her eyes stung.

No. She couldn't think about him now. She couldn't fall to pieces. There were things to be done. People needed to be notified, starting with Hannah and Alison. Piper glanced around for her phone, but then she realized in the rush to get out of the apartment last night that she hadn't thought to grab it.

Piper rushed from the bedroom and into the kitchen, where Mrs. Sanchez was sitting at the kitchen table with a pen in one hand and the phone in the other. She glanced up over the top of her glasses and held up a finger to indicate she would just be one more minute. Then she gestured to the coffeepot. That was a very welcome sight.

As Piper found her way around the kitchen, she glanced at the clock. It was nine a.m. Yikes! She must have been tired. She never slept this late. Ever. The fact she'd slept at all after everything that had happened was testimony to her exhaustion.

With a mug of steaming coffee, Piper took a seat at the table. She hoped to use the phone to speak with her employees. After which, she planned to head to the Poppin' Fresh to see what could be salvaged. Something told her Joe was already there, inspecting what remained of his coffee shop. He wouldn't be happy to see her again.

Mrs. Sanchez ended her call. "Sorry about that. There's lots to do today."

"There is?" Was there some sort of function she wasn't aware of? She searched her memory but came up empty.

"Of course there is." Mrs. Sanchez reached over and patted her hand. "Don't worry, dear. Everything will be all right."

"Could I use the phone? I need to call Hannah and Alison. And I...I left my phone in my apartment."

"Sure, you can use the phone. But there's no need to call either of them. They already know about the fire."

"They do?"

Mrs. Sanchez nodded. "While you've been getting some much-needed sleep, I've been on the phone.

Most of Whistle Stop knows about the fire, and everyone sends their love."

"I'm sorry." She seemed to be saying that a lot lately. "I didn't mean to sleep so late. I guess I was more wiped out than I thought. But it's not me that people should be concerned about. It's Joe. It was his place that went up in flames."

"Don't you worry about him. He'll be taken care of."

"He will?"

Mrs. Sanchez sent her a knowing smile. "Let me get you some breakfast, and then we'll head over there. Things always look better in the light of day."

Piper really wanted to believe her, but she didn't think there was anything that would make this situation better. "Thanks for everything, but I don't think I can eat a bite."

"But you have to eat something to keep up your strength. There's going to be a lot for you to deal with today. Now, name your pleasure: eggs, oatmeal, toast, bacon?"

None of it sounded good to her, but she had a sneaking suspicion she wouldn't be able to get away from the table without eating something.

As though Mrs. Sanchez sensed her hesitation, she added, "How about some poached eggs and toast? Those should be easy on your stomach."

"Sounds good. Have you spoken to my mother?"

"She phoned here this morning. She was worried, but I assured her you were fine. She said she would be around later."

Piper wasn't looking forward to that meeting, especially if her mother found out that Piper was responsible for the blaze. Her throat tightened, and she blinked repeatedly. Luckily, Mrs. Sanchez was busy making breakfast and didn't notice that she'd become worked up.

Piper swallowed hard. She didn't deserve to wallow in tears. Nor did she deserve how nice Mrs. Sanchez was being to her. Maybe she hadn't heard the whole story last night. That had to be it, otherwise she wouldn't be bending over backward to help her.

Now Piper needed to ask the one question that was eating at her the most. "Did you hear anything about Joe?"

Mrs. Sanchez turned up the heat on the stove. "As a matter of fact, I haven't heard anything about him. Perhaps he slept in, too. After all, that was a very traumatic night for both of you. I'm so sorry—"

"Don't be sorry." Piper couldn't stomach the sympathy when she deserved nothing more than condemnation. "I...I started the fire."

Mrs. Sanchez arched a dark brow. "I don't believe that."

"It's true. It...it wasn't intentional. But that doesn't excuse my actions." Piper stared down at the parquet tabletop, unable to face Mrs. Sanchez and see the disappointment in her eyes.

Mrs. Sanchez approached the table and sat down. "I wasn't going to say anything, but I heard what Joe said to you last night, and it was dreadful. He shouldn't have said those things—"

"Yes, he should have. He's right. I had no business being in his shop. I was doing exactly what I blame my mother for doing with me, meddling."

"You were trying to take care of someone you care for." The woman reached out a hand with gemstone rings on three of her fingers. She grasped Piper's hand and squeezed. "Listen to me. He didn't mean anything he said last night. He was in shock. He cares far too much about you to let this stand between you two. You make the perfect couple."

If only Piper could believe that, but she couldn't. He'd only spoken the truth. And now she must carry the burden.

She sniffed back the tears that were threatening to spill onto her cheeks. "Thank you for being so kind and understanding. I really don't deserve it. I don't deserve him."

"You'll see in time that things will look different." Mrs. Sanchez stood. "The water's boiling, so I need to get these eggs on. And we must get a move on. We don't want to be late."

"Late for what?"

"Don't you worry. You'll find out soon enough. Trust me. Things will look up for you soon."

Piper highly doubted it. Things looked awful. Terrible. Devastating.

That's how Piper pictured the scene in the town square. And if Joe was there, which he most likely would be, she didn't have a clue what she'd say to him. No idea at all. Sorry just wasn't enough.

Were they all there for her?

Tears sprang to Piper's eyes when she saw most of Whistle Stop's citizens standing on the sidewalk in front of the Poppin' Fresh Bakery. They carried mops, rags, buckets, and all sorts of cleaning supplies.

"What's everyone doing here?"

"They're here for you." Mrs. Sanchez patted her arm. "When I spoke to the fire officials this morning, they gave the all clear on the bakery and your apartment."

"They did?"

Mrs. Sanchez had a guarded look on her face. "It isn't all good news. There's water and smoke damage."

Piper wasn't sure what that meant, but she fully intended to find out as soon as possible. She scanned the mass of faces for one in particular—Joe's. But she didn't see him anywhere.

"I can't believe so many people showed up to help."

"As soon as they heard their favorite bakery was in trouble, they were more than eager to pitch in."

"But what about Joe? He's the one who really needs the help." Her gaze strayed to his coffee shop with the broken windows. Guilt weighed heavy on her shoulders. "They should be helping him."

"I promise that he'll get help when the time comes. But it's going to take a lot more than a mop and pail to fix up his shop."

"Oh." It was the only word she could muster as her gaze grew hazy with unshed tears.

"Now, now. Don't go getting all worked up. I told you everything will work out. It just might take some time. Cheer up, girl. These people are here because they care about you."

Piper's gaze moved back to the eager faces of people she'd known her whole life. "But I don't know how to thank them all."

"There's plenty of time for that later. Right now, there's work to be done. We'll have you back in business in no time."

Piper knew all too well that it wouldn't be that easy to reopen. There would be bureaucratic red tape to cut through. "I'll need to be inspected and—"

"Stop worrying. I'll be placing more phone calls while you oversee the cleaning process. We'll have you up and running before the Autumn Fest. Just you wait and see."

If anyone else had made that statement, she wouldn't have believed them. But she'd witnessed more than one or twice how Mrs. Sanchez was able to work miracles. She didn't know how or why she had someone so special in her life, but Piper was immensely grateful—even if she didn't feel deserving.

She turned to her friend and gave the woman a big hug. "Thank you so much for everything. You are an amazing woman."

Mrs. Sanchez hugged her back. After a moment, they pulled apart. The woman's eyes were red and puffy. "Now see what you went and did?"

Piper couldn't believe it, but a smile tugged at her lips. Just a little one, but it was a smile nonetheless. "Thought you were just telling me not to get misty."

"It's your fault. We better get moving before we both end up teary-eyed."

They'd started across the street when a well-dressed man stepped out of a gray sedan. "Excuse me. Are one of you Ms., uh"—he glanced down at the clipboard in his hand—"Ms. Noble?"

"I am," Piper said. "What can I do for you?"

"Your insurance agent called in the fire this morning. And it looks like I'm here just in time."

Her muscles stiffened. Please don't let there be another problem. "In time for what?"

"I need to document the damage in order to process the claim."

"The claim?"

He nodded. "It's all part of your policy. I'd say that I would send out a cleanup crew, but it looks like you have that all in hand."

"Will this take long?"

He shook his head. "I just need to take some pictures and document a few things. Then you're welcome to start cleaning up. However, if you want a professional crew, that can be arranged."

Piper looked around at the anxious faces of neighbors and friends. She'd never felt more love than she did at that moment. "I think we have it under control. Thank you." She was just about to go unlock the door when she thought to ask, "Do you know about the damage to the business next door?"

"No, I don't. Our company doesn't insure it."

She showed him inside, and true to his word, he made short work of getting the information he needed for his report. Then the building filled up with so many helpful people that Piper wondered if they'd exceed the fire code. But she highly doubted anyone would say a word, since the fire chief and assistant chief were among those helping to put the bakery and her apartment to rights.

Any other time, she might have felt invaded with all of these people in her personal space, seeing the dirty dishes in her sink and the laundry heaped up over the top of her laundry basket, but she was so overwhelmed by the outpouring of kindness that she just let it all wash over her. Now if only she could do the same for Joe.

CHAPTER TWENTY-SIX

WHERE DID HE EVEN begin?

Dressed in his clothes from the day before, Joe swallowed the last of the coffee his mother had poured for him. He didn't have time to waste. There were phone calls to make. Forms to fill out. But first, he had to see the building in the daylight.

The events of the fire came to him in bits and pieces. The parts he could recall were fuzzy and awful—more than that, they were horrid. If his mother hadn't slipped him some painkillers with a sleep aid, he might never have slept last night. He thanked his mother this morning. The sleep was exactly what he'd needed. It gave him clarity. And all he could see now was how poorly he'd treated Piper.

He turned to his mother. "I need to go see what's left of the place."

"Are you sure you don't want something to eat? It might do you good."

He shook his head. He had absolutely no appetite. He'd started out the back door when there was a knock at the front door. Who could that be? His mother didn't have many friends. It was sad but true.

Even with his father gone, his mother was still prone to keeping to herself.

He turned to his mother. "Are you expecting anyone?"

"No. No one."

"I'll get it." He strode to the front door and swung it open. A man he'd never seen before stood there. "Hi. Can I help you?"

The man's inquisitive gaze met his. "Are you Joseph Montoya?"

"Yes, I am. What can I do for you?"

The man introduced himself as the county fire marshal. His reason for the visit was to give Joe the findings of his report. He told Joe it wasn't customary to deliver these reports in person, but the fire chief, Tony Granger, was a personal friend. Tony thought that Joe needed to hear the results as soon as possible.

This information only piqued Joe's curiosity even more. "What did you find?"

"I saw from the permits you secured for the renovation that you hired an out-of-town electrician."

"Yes, he came at a great price, and I was trying to keep costs as low as possible. There's a lot of overhead when starting up a new business."

The marshal lifted his ball cap and rubbed his brow before settling the cap back on his head. "The problem is that, in order for the electrician to give you that great price, he cut corners. The job he did was substandard, and normally that would have been caught by the electrical inspector, but I see he wasn't scheduled to go over the coffee shop until tomorrow."

"Wait. What you're saying is that the fire could have been started by anyone plugging anything in at any time?"

The marshal nodded. "Afraid so. It was like a time bomb waiting to go off with just the right combination of usage."

"And the fuse box?"

The marshal shook his head. "The man used the wrong size breakers. That, along with the substandard wiring he did, made a real mess of things. If you decide to move forward with the project, you need to hire a good electrician to fix the wiring."

"So what you're saying is even I could've started that fire?"

The marshal nodded. "You're just lucky no one was hurt. If I were you, I'd find other ways to cut your expenses next time."

Joe thanked the man and shook his hand.

Guilt riddled Joe. On his walk to the town square, he went over and over the fire inspector's words. The ones that struck him the hardest indicated that he, Joe Montoya, was responsible for that blaze. It had nothing to do with Piper, and it had almost cost her life. The thought made his stomach lurch.

How could he have thought that offering a contract to a cut-rate electrician was a good idea? Piper was right. He was too worried about the bottom line. He needed to worry more about what he was getting for his money, whether it was for the festival or the coffeehouse.

His hands balled at his sides as he recalled how he'd readily blamed Piper for the fire. He didn't recall everything that had gone down last night, but the tears in her eyes stood out in his memory. He'd been so certain it was all her fault, and here the fire could have just as easily been started by him.

He came up the alleyway behind his building, but as he approached the door, he couldn't help but notice the buzz of activity at Piper's place. The sight of Whistle Stop's residents taking time out of their busy days to help her only compounded his guilt. Why did he have to be the one person to dump on her when she'd been scared of losing everything? Why couldn't he have been there to support her instead of blaming her? What was wrong with him? Did he have too much of his father in him?

Then Piper stepped outside. Her back was to him. He should move before she saw him. He wasn't ready to face her, not yet. But his feet wouldn't cooperate. As though she could sense him standing there, staring at her, she turned, and their gazes met.

His heart pounded in his chest. Was it possible to miss someone who was standing right there in front of you? Because right now, he felt more alone than he had in his whole life. And he'd give anything to have his best friend back.

But he couldn't tell what she was thinking. Her face was pale, her expression unreadable. He should go to her and beg her forgiveness, but he continued to hesitate. In the back of his mind, a little voice kept repeating, What if you say the wrong thing again?

He knew he was being foolish. He wasn't in shock. He wasn't reacting in the moment. This time, he would think before he spoke. And there was only one thing on his mind, and that was apologizing. He inhaled a deep, steadying breath and took a step toward her. *Nothing ventured, nothing gained.*

At that moment, Piper's mother stepped out of the bakery and drew Piper's attention. Immediately, he stopped. Talking to her in front of her mother would be a disaster waiting to happen. And they'd both had enough tragedy in the last twenty-four hours to last a good long time.

With great regret, he turned on his heels. He approached the yellow caution tape covering his back door. He wasn't in the mood to be cautious. He had to get inside. He had to see if there was any hope for his dream.

When Joe at last stood inside the charred, smoky remains of his coffee shop, he wasn't prepared for the sight facing him. It was worse than his nightmares. The coffee his mother had given him before he left the house churned in his stomach.

He squeezed his eyes shut, trying to block out the cringe-worthy images. This couldn't be happening. How in the world had his life turned upside down in a matter of twenty-four hours?

Everything that he'd cherished was now lost to him...

His new beginning.

His business.

The love of his life...

CHAPTER TWENTY-SEVEN

IT WAS AMAZING WHAT people could do when they pulled together.

Piper was touched beyond words at how the citizens of Whistle Stop had dropped everything to help her. Even her own mother had broken out a pair of yellow kitchen gloves to protect her manicured nails and helped scrub down the bakery. But, in the end, their kindness had only compounded her guilt over what she'd done to Joe.

She'd stolen away his dream. He'd lost everything he owned. And it was all her fault. She didn't deserve to have her life put back together, not after she'd torched Joe's dreams. It just wasn't right.

Horrified that her innocent gesture had resulted in such devastation, she didn't talk about it with anyone. She kept stuffing her guilt down inside her, until it made her sick to her stomach.

Even though the bakery was now clean and about to be inspected, she wasn't up to reopening right away. Still shaken by what she'd done to Joe, she'd handed the keys to the bakery over to Hannah and asked her to accompany the inspector. Piper was taking some time off—she had some big decisions to make.

And she'd known just where to go, the Brazen H Ranch. It was just far enough out of town that, other than Alexis and Cord, she wouldn't have to worry about running into people who might have heard about the fire.

Alexis had extended an invitation to visit and help plan the wedding, and that was exactly what Piper intended to do. With wedding dresses, party favors, and shoes to pick out, hopefully she wouldn't have time to think about her own problems—at least not for a while.

Now, sitting at Alexis's kitchen table, Piper glanced over at her friend as she put the last lunch dish in the dishwasher. "Are you sure Cord doesn't mind that I'm staying here?"

"I'm positive. He's already tired of hearing about the wedding. He's thrilled to have someone else listen to me."

Piper didn't believe her for one second. "Cord is crazy about you. I'm certain he's just as excited for this wedding as you are."

Alexis smiled. "I suppose so. I think he just grumbles and groans out of jest. But still, talking to a guy about dresses and colors, well, it just doesn't work so well. Especially when the guy is a cowboy who is more comfortable in jeans and a chambray shirt than a tux and bow tie."

"I get your point. But to be honest, I'm not exactly into high fashion either." Piper glanced down at her mint green and blue striped blouse and faded jeans. "I don't think I'm going to be much help."

"You're wonderful help." Alexis dried her hands and made her way across the expansive kitchen. "But that's enough about me. I want to know what you're doing here. And please don't tell me it's about the wedding. I can see the worry in your eyes. Is this about Joe?"

Leave it to Alexis to grab the bull by the horns. Piper nodded. "I feel awful."

"You have to know that he didn't mean anything he said to you that night. He was in shock, and he took his frustration out on the person closest to him."

"He was right to be angry. The fire was my fault."

"You were only trying to help him."

Piper ran her finger over the condensation on her glass of sweet tea. "The truth is, I was meddling. I thought I knew how to help him with his business, but he was so stubborn trying to do things his way that he never gave my ideas a chance. So I decided to show him what I had in mind. Why, oh, why did I have to think I was right?"

Alexis squeezed a wedge of lemon into her tea and gave it a stir. "What was your idea?"

Piper shook her head. "You don't want to hear about it. Obviously, it was a miserable failure. And now I have to make it up to him. Somehow."

"Slow down. You obviously need to talk with someone, and since you aren't quite ready to face Joe, let me fill in."

Piper sighed. What would it hurt to tell Alexis? She had a great head on her shoulders and she had experience in the romance department. Maybe she'd have some advice that Piper hadn't thought of so far. But in all honesty, Piper really did think that all hope was lost for her relationship with Joe.

She recalled the pain and anger in his eyes. There had been no room there for understanding and forgiveness. Nor did she expect there to be. She would probably have acted even worse than he had if the roles had been reversed and he'd destroyed her bakery.

Piper took a sip of tea, wetting her mouth. "I'd seen sketches of the coffeehouse that Joe had done up. It was a very basic layout without an area for people to mingle or hang out while enjoying their coffee. I thought he should create a homier atmosphere, but he disagreed. He wanted to stay within his budget, and he was certain his layout would work."

"People in Whistle Stop do like to chat—a lot. It was something I had to get used to after coming from New York City, where most of the time I didn't know a soul in a coffeehouse except the barista. And that was only because I mainlined caffeine while working at my father's company."

Piper leaned back in her chair. "Whistle Stop is a lot different than the big city. A lot more laid-back, and it moves at its own pace. That's what I was trying to explain to Joe. I know he was born here, but he was gone for a long time. I thought maybe he'd forgotten the ways of Whistle Stop."

"So you decided to show him?"

Piper nodded. "While he was out of town giving Holden a hand at his ranch, I had time on my hands." As she realized that she hadn't told anyone, including her close group of friends, about how close she'd gotten with Joe, the heat rose to her cheeks. "We'd, uh, been spending a lot of time together recently."

"And I'm assuming it wasn't all about the festival."

Piper worried her bottom lip. Memories of Joe's gentle touches and whispered sweet nothings in her ear made the hole in her heart ache even more. "No. He stopped by—"

"Hey, Lexi!" Cord's voice boomed through the house. Alexis waved away the interruption. "Don't mind him. I'm sure he misplaced something, but he'll find it. Now, what were you saying?"

Piper glanced toward the doorway, but she didn't see any sign of Cord. She turned back to Alexis. "Joe stopped by my apartment one evening. He wanted to tell me that he'd been able to get a friend of his to provide hot air balloon rides at the festival. He knew I was really excited about the idea. Anyway, he saw that I was making the bunting to dress up the game booths for the festival and—"

"Lexi, didn't you hear me?" Cord strode into the kitchen.

Both women turned toward him, and he got a worried look on his face. Piper glanced Alexis's way to find she was glaring at him. The man looked as though he'd just stepped on a land mine and wasn't sure which way to move, so he stayed still.

Alexis sighed. "What did you lose?"

His gaze moved from his fiancée to Piper and then back again. "Sorry. I didn't mean to interrupt."

"Well, now that you have, and just when we were getting to the good part, you might as well tell me what you need."

His brows furrowed together as though he was trying to decide if Alexis was serious. At last, he said, "Do you remember when I bought those new nuts and bolts?" When she nodded, he added, "Well, I can't find them anywhere. They were in that little bag, and I swear I slipped it in my jacket pocket, but they're not there now."

Alexis glanced her way. "Sorry. I'll be right back."

Piper didn't mind. In fact, she enjoyed watching Alexis and Cord together. They were cute. And no matter how gruff Alexis tried to act, Piper knew she really wasn't mad at Cord. In fact, she'd be willing to guess they were sneaking a kiss now. If only things were that way with her and Joe. At one point, she'd thought they might be happy like Alexis and Cord, but then she'd gone and messed it up. Now she was left only with regrets, which was nothing compared to what Joe had to deal with because of her hasty actions.

A few minutes later, Alexis rushed back into the kitchen. Her cheeks and lips were rosy. And a tell-tale smile pulled at her lips. "Sorry about that."

"No problem. Did you find everything?"

"Um...yes." The color in her cheeks deepened. "Now, what were you saying? Oh yes, we were talking about bunting."

Alexis might not be the only one blushing after this conversation. "Well, he found out the quilting club wasn't able to help me with the bunting and that I was doing it on my own each night—"

"Why didn't you say something? I would have helped. So would have the rest of the group."

"Because it was my fault. I'd promised Joe something that I didn't know if I could provide. Anyway, he offered to help."

"Ah, that was sweet. I know most guys aren't into craft projects, so that was big for him. I knew there was something I liked about that guy, besides his taste in women."

"Things had been amazing since that night. Until I got the terrible idea to stage his coffee shop."

"I...I don't think it was a terrible idea."

"But you think it was overstepping, and you'd be right. What was I thinking?"

"You were thinking that you wanted to help him. You just got excited, is all."

Piper wished that was the case, but she knew it was something else. "The fact is, I meddled in his life, even when he asked me not to." And then the horrifying truth hit her all over again. "I've turned into my mother."

"You've what?"

"My mother always thinks she knows what's best for me. She never listens to what I have to say. She is always right. And now I've done that with Joe. Oh no." She pressed a hand to her mouth.

How many times in life had she told herself she would be different than her mother when she grew up? She'd promised herself she wouldn't be so pushy and unbending. And now she'd done just that, and it had cost Joe dearly. She had to make it up to him.

Alexis reached out to her and gave her arm a squeeze. "It'll all be okay."

"No, it won't. I've ruined everything. His business. His dreams. Our chance for happiness."

"Whoa. Slow down. Take a breath."

Piper blinked repeatedly, trying to keep her emotions at bay. "I...I never meant to hurt him."

"He knows that—"

"No, he thinks I did it on purpose. He thinks I'm mad because he bought that storefront before I had a chance."

"Piper, stop. He was acting out of shock. I'm sure now that he's calmed down, he sees things differently. The important question is, do you love him?"

Her bruised and aching heart thumped out the answer, but stubborn pride refused to let her admit it. "What does that matter?"

"Just answer the question."

Piper sighed. "Yes."

"Does he love you?"

She'd thought she knew that answer forty-eight hours ago, but now she wasn't so sure. "I thought he did. But—"

"No buts. You have something to build on. I'm sure you'll find your way through this situation. Just have faith in your love. It's what Cord and I did. It's how we ended up together."

Piper wasn't so sure her relationship with Joe was as strong as Alexis and Cord's. Maybe it had been at one point, but not now. There was no getting around the fact that her actions had caused him to lose everything. There was only one way she could think of to try to make this up to him and, in the process, tell him how much she regretted what she'd done.

Tomorrow morning she'd head back to Whistle Stop and put the bakery up for sale. She didn't know how hard it'd be to sell in the current economic climate, but she would try. She would give the money from the sale to Joe. It was the best she could do.

CHAPTER TWENTY-EIGHT

THE SUN HAD JUST set the following evening when Joe stepped outside.

He'd spent the last few days cooped up on the phone with insurance adjusters and contractors. It would take a lot of work and quite a bit of time, but it was possible to rebuild Fill-It-Up Joe. In the process, he'd finally worked up the courage to face Piper and apologize for his horrible behavior.

Mrs. Sanchez had lent him a small efficiency apartment over her house in town. He'd been hesitant at first because he'd heard that Piper had been staying with her, but when Mrs. Sanchez clarified that Piper was now able to return to her apartment over the bakery, he'd accepted the generous offer.

He didn't know how everything had gone off the tracks. Maybe it was a sign that he didn't belong with Piper. Perhaps he didn't belong with anyone.

He neared the Poppin' Fresh bakery. It'd been closed since the fire. And he knew he wasn't the only person in town who missed the bakery. The sweet scents. The delicious pastries. And the tempting coffee.

It was then that he noticed something new in the window of the bakery. He came to a stop and stared.

A For Sale sign was taped to the middle of the window.
What in the world?
That sign hadn't been there earlier. He would have noticed it for sure. This must mean that Piper was home. And it was time they talked.

He glanced up at the second floor to see a soft glow coming from her apartment. He wondered if she was finishing the bunting for the game booths by herself. The thought saddened him. But he realized it was for the best. They were just too different.

Piper needed someone who could put her needs first, someone who wasn't so damaged, like he was. As he walked to the back of the building, the memories of the night of the fire came back to him. How could he have said those things to her when it was his fault the fire had started? The thought of what might have happened if he hadn't returned home that night shook him to the core.

He let himself in through the back door and then took the wooden steps two at a time to the second floor. If he didn't get this out right away, he was afraid he'd lose his nerve.

At last, he stood in front of her apartment door. He heard loud music through the door—country music. And then he heard Piper singing along. He imagined her dancing around and singing as she did her work. As he listened more closely, he realized it wasn't a bouncy tune. It was a song about a lost love. A frown pulled at his lips.

Before he could examine what that might mean, he rapped his knuckles on the door. The music stopped, followed by rushed footsteps.

The door swung open. Piper's eyes opened wide when she saw him standing there. "Joe, um...hi. Um...do you want to come in?"

"Thanks. I would. It won't take long."

Her hair was swept back in a messy ponytail, and her face looked washed free of all makeup. He never had thought she needed anything on her face. Piper had a natural glow that needed no enhancement. She was dressed in a pink tank top that dipped low in the front and hugged the swell of her breasts. He swallowed hard.

His gaze kept moving downward. He soon found a pair of pink boxers with navy blue crisscross stripes. The word HOT in big bold letters trailed down the side. Oh yes, it was definitely getting hot in here. Very warm indeed.

She stepped back and opened the door wide open. He passed by her, catching the slightest hint of her floral perfume, or was it her body lotion? She'd told him once, but he couldn't remember. Not that it would matter much after this. He doubted they'd see much of each other except to pass along the sidewalk.

As he moved farther into the room, he noticed that she did indeed have the sewing machine hooked up and the material for the bunting scattered about. Guilt assailed him. If he hadn't let everything get out of control, he would be here helping her instead of her having to do all of this work on her own.

He cleared his throat and turned to her. "Piper, I came here to apologize—"

"For what?" She closed the door. "I'm the one that's sorry. I was meddling and...and I really messed up." Her voice cracked with emotion. "I'm so sorry."

His chest tightened. He knew the level of guilt she'd been carrying around. "You were meddling, but that's not what started the fire. Not really."

Her chin lifted, and their gazes met. "I don't understand."

His chest tightened. He knew she would be so hurt, so angry all over again, when she realized that he'd falsely accused her of torching his place. "I tried to call you, but I kept getting your voice mail."

"I was out of town for a bit, visiting with friends. They don't have good reception at the ranch. What did you want?"

He knew she hadn't gone visiting for fun. She'd left town because of him, and that made him feel awful. He'd only wanted to make her happy, and instead, he'd made her miserable. And now he was going to compound things between them even more—not that there was any coming back from what had already happened between them.

He shifted his weight from one foot to the other. "I wanted to tell you that there has been an investigation, and they found that faulty wiring, not an overloaded outlet, was the cause of the fire."

She looked at him like she didn't understand the significance of this finding. How was he supposed to say the rest without her hating him even more?

"I was so focused on the bottom line that I...I took the lowest bid on the project. The electrician I hired, well, he took shortcuts. Dangerous shortcuts."

Piper stepped back as though the impact of his words had slammed into her. "Are you saying the fire...wasn't my fault?"

"Yes. The breaker should have been tripped and shut everything down. When I think of what could have happened, how you were in such danger..."

Her eyes darkened. "But you blamed me. In front of my friends, in front of the whole town."

"And I am so sorry. I know it's no excuse, but I wasn't thinking clearly." He raked his fingers through his hair. "I was—heck, I don't know what was going through my mind."

"Everyone thinks I caused the fire that destroyed your business. It's why I've..." As though she realized she'd said too much, she pressed her lips together.

"You what? Put the bakery up for sale?"

She nodded. "I...I was going to give you the money so that you could rebuild the coffee shop. I know how important it is to you."

"Well, you can take down the sign. I wouldn't have taken the money anyway. I know that the Poppin' Fresh means as much to you as the coffee shop does to me."

"I suppose so. At least we have that in common."

"We have a lot in common." Didn't they? Their love of running. Their draw to Whistle Stop. Coffee. Pastries. Pizza. Dogs. The list went on.

Piper crossed her arms as though warding him off. "It's good that things ended between us. We...we didn't belong together. You want to do things your way, and you don't want any input—from anyone."

He wanted to argue with her. He wanted to tell her that he could let down his guard with her, but he was having serious doubts that, after what happened, he could do that with anyone.

She moved to the door and pulled it open. "It's time for you to go."

Piper was right. He moved slowly toward the door. He hated that things between them had crashed and burned so badly. He wanted to make it up to her, but he knew she wouldn't let him do it.

As he passed by her, he paused. His gaze caught hers. "You're an amazing woman. Thanks for letting me share a little of your life."

The For Sale sign was removed.

The next day, Piper reopened for business. She honestly didn't want to do it, but she'd run out of chocolate mint ice cream. So it was either go back to work or head over to Sam's Hitchin' Post for another half-gallon of decadence.

Suddenly, she realized that she didn't want more—well, she did, but not because she was truly hungry for it. She didn't want to compromise all of the weight-loss progress she'd made in the past couple of months. Not because of her mother. And not because of Joe. This time, she wanted to maintain her fitness for herself, because it boosted not only her self-confidence, but it also gave her more energy. And she liked that. A lot.

Plus, the day after tomorrow was the Autumn Fest, and she had a lot of orders to fill. Lots of secret cakes to bake for the auction. Her mother had already called twice that day to make sure her order would be done in time. Piper had promised it would be.

She had so much to do that she'd skipped another day of running. She told herself it was only because she had so much work to do, but secretly she was worried about running into Joe. She didn't know what to say to him. In fact, every time she thought of him, tears welled up in her eyes. Just like now. She blinked away the moisture.

She'd put Hannah and Alison on counter duty so that she could hide back in the kitchen, away from the many, many questions she was certain were on customers' minds. She slid another specialty cake into the oven and set the timer. It was so good to be back to work, but there were reminders of Joe at every turn, from his usual table out front to the bear claws she used to make for him. She missed him so much. But she just couldn't live life on his terms, at arm's length. When she was in a relationship, she needed to feel as though they were equals—partners.

She glanced up at the large pink cupcake-shaped clock on the wall. Almost lunchtime. With a break due and the walls starting to close in, she decided some fresh air was in order.

Out front, the whole street was abuzz with men, women, and children setting up for the festival. She could already imagine the bunting that Joe had helped her make fluttering in the wind. She just couldn't face any of it. Not yet.

She slipped out the back door and headed in the opposite direction, hoping for a peaceful walk. The sun was shining brightly overhead. That was one of the things she loved about Whistle Stop—the countless sunny days. It was invigorating. Exactly what she needed to lift her up, even if her heart felt as though it'd been smashed into a million pieces. When would she ever get over Joe? Sometimes she thought she never would.

A rapid series of loud barks had her glancing around. Immediately, she spotted Java. But instead of Mr.

Wilks holding the leash, a young man Piper didn't recognize had it.

"Hey, boy." She smiled upon seeing the dog all excited.

The dog jerked on the leash, and the man who was holding it didn't have a good grip, because the next thing Piper knew, the dog was headed straight for her.

Java stopped next to her, and she immediately grabbed for the leash. When the stranger caught up to them, Piper said, "Hi. I'm Piper, a friend of Mr. Wilks. Are you walking Java for him?"

The young man, in faded jeans and a white T-shirt with the name of an animal shelter printed on the front in blue letters, shook his head. "I'm taking the dog to the shelter."

"But why? Mr. Wilks loves him."

"I don't know all of the details, but apparently the owner died, and there's no one to take the dog. So they called me in to take him away."

"Mr. Wilks died? But...but when?"

"I don't know, lady. I'm not from around here."

Piper immediately knelt down and hugged Java. A tear slipped down her cheek. Java licked her cheek as his tail swished back and forth.

She'd known Mr. Wilks her whole life. How had she missed this news? Had she been so totally engrossed in her own problems that she'd missed hearing about him being sick? Guilt assailed her. She had to do better. And the first thing she was going to do was find Java a home.

"Can I have him?" She glanced up at the young man.

"I don't know. I'm only doing what I'm told."

"Please. I'll make sure I find him a good home."

"But there's paperwork—"

"Do you have the paperwork with you?"

He nodded. "I don't know about this. I don't want to get into any trouble. Maybe I should call my boss."

"Go ahead. I'll wait. Huh, boy?" Java gave her another kiss, as though he knew she was going to take care of him.

A few minutes later, the call was completed, the paperwork was done, and she was walking Java back toward the Poppin' Fresh. As much as she loved the dog, she knew someone who loved Java even more. Joe.

"You have to help me out here," she said to Java as they walked down the sidewalk. "I need you to be on your very best behavior in front of Joe. We need to convince him to take you, at least for a day or two. If we can get him to do that, I think you'll have him wrapped around your paw and he'll keep you. What do you think?"

As though in total understanding, Java barked.

"Good boy."

In no time, they were standing outside the back of the coffee shop. The door was propped open, and there was the noise of hammers inside. That was good. The sooner the repairs were started, the sooner Joe would be in business.

She hesitated at the doorway. She didn't want to walk Java in there. Even though it appeared that a lot of the debris had been swept away, if the men were working, there was a chance of nails and broken glass and such that could hurt Java.

While she tried to decide what to do, a workman came out the door carrying a couple of buckets of debris. He glanced her way. "Do you need something?"

"Actually, I do. Is Joe Montoya inside?"

The man nodded. "Hang on, I'll be right back." The man headed over to a big dumpster and emptied the buckets. "Now what did you need?"

"Joe. Could you tell him that I need to speak with him?"

The scruffy guy moved to the doorway and bellowed, "Hey, Joe! Some lady out here wants to talk to you!"

Well, she could have done that much. Sheesh! Java sat patiently by her side. She stepped in front of him to keep him a surprise for just a moment.

Footsteps sounded, and then Joe appeared in the doorway. His hair was a bit mussed. He was wearing a blue T-shirt with muck on it, his jeans had paint stains, and he had on a pair of fawn-colored work boots. And he had never looked so cute. Under any other circumstances, she'd have snapped a picture to keep on her phone. Sadly, this was not the right circumstance.

"You needed to see me?" His gaze was cool and gave nothing away.

"Hi. I hope you don't mind that I stopped by."

His facial expression was a mask of indifference. "I'm rather busy. What did you need?"

She wished he would let down his guard just for a moment. "I hope things are going well."

"As well as can be expected. Structurally, the building is sound. We're working on the second floor. It needs the least amount of repair."

"That's good." He didn't smile, so she didn't know if she'd said the right thing or not. This conversation felt like an obstacle course, and she was doing her best not to fall face first into a puddle of mud.

Joe pressed his hands to his trim waist and at last met her gaze head on. "Piper, if you have something to say, I'd appreciate it if you'd just get it out there."

This just had to work. Joe needed someone in his life, someone he could trust and love. She crossed her fingers for luck. "I brought someone to see you."

She stepped aside. Neither Joe nor Java moved at first. They both stared at each other as though surprised to see one another.

Joe knelt down on one knee. "Hey, boy."

Java ran over to him, tail a-wagging. A few doggy kisses later, Joe was smiling. Piper's stomach tumbled at how handsome he was when he wasn't frowning. Boy, did she miss him.

Joe turned a questioning gaze her way. "How did you end up with him? Did he get loose again?"

Apparently, she wasn't the only one to be caught up in her own world. "It seems that Mr. Wilks passed away. I don't have any of the details. But since he doesn't have any family, well, they were getting ready to ship Java off to the shelter. I just couldn't let them do that."

Joe turned back to Java. "Hey, boy, I'm so sorry. You must feel all alone now. But don't worry, Piper will take good care of you."

Wait. What? This wasn't how it was supposed to go. Joe was supposed to be eager to take Java. They were a perfect fit. Maybe Joe just needed his eyes opened a bit.

She toyed with the end of the leash. "I was wondering if you could take care of him. I know I shouldn't ask, but Java is so comfortable with you." When Joe's brows rose, she hurried to add, "Just for a few days or so. I can't exactly take him into the bakery with me. And I have to work late to fill the orders for the festival. I'd really appreciate it. And I know Java would be happy."

Joe looked as though he was about to decline her request when Java let off with a string of excited barks.

"I think he likes the idea." Piper prayed Joe did, too, because she didn't have any idea how to take care of a dog, and she really did have a ton of work to do. Speaking of which, she needed to get back to the Poppin' Fresh.

A long pause ensued. "I suppose I could do it."

"Great." When she handed over the leash, their fingertips brushed, and a tingly sensation rushed up her arm. Oh, how she truly missed him. If only...

CHAPTER TWENTY-NINE

Let the festivities begin...

Joe wasn't really feeling festive...not at all.

The memorial service for Mr. Wilks had been the day before. Piper had attended, as well as most of Whistle Stop. Word around the square was that Mr. Wilks had felt fine right up until he'd had a massive heart attack. A neighbor had found him at home with his dog by his side.

It got Joe thinking about his life. If he kept pushing the people away who cared about him, he'd end up like Mr. Wilks. Old and alone. Was that really what he wanted?

His heart kept telling him that wasn't the path for him. The truth was, he missed Piper. He missed her a whole lot. And though Java was a great dog, his canine companion couldn't fill the spot that Piper held in Joe's heart.

Thoughts of her had haunted him night and day since the fire. He replayed the horrific scene over and over in his mind. The memories made him inwardly cringe. How could he have been so awful to her?

No wonder she wouldn't forgive him. Who could blame her? He deserved whatever she decided to throw his way. He glanced over at Java. So why had she given him the dog? Did it mean she didn't hate him? Or did it just mean she wasn't equipped to take care of the energetic pup?

He glanced around for a glimpse of her, but there was no sign of her. He and Java kept walking around the town square. As co-chair of the Autumn Fest, he was obligated to be here to make sure things ran smoothly. He didn't think there was a business in town that was open today, at least none that he'd noticed when he'd participated earlier in the 5K Fun Run and Walk.

It was during the run that he'd noticed Piper participating. Maybe she was taking some of her own advice and loosening up. If only he could find a way to prove to her that he could do the same, then maybe they'd have a fighting chance at making this thing between them work.

A local country band started to play. Not even the strums of the guitars or the upbeat rhythm of the drums could put some pep in Joe's step. He was relieved to hear they were singing something cheerful and none of the lyrics were about lost love. He didn't think he could take that right now.

"There you are." Mrs. Sanchez rushed up to him, huffing and puffing. "I've been searching everywhere for you."

"Me? Why? Is there a problem with the festival?" He hadn't noticed anything when he'd made his rounds.

She shook head. "Everything is running smoothly."

"Then what is it?"

"I wanted to remind you that you're due at the dunking booth in"—she glanced at her watch—"twenty minutes."

"I'm what?" Then he recalled how Piper had teased him that she'd signed him up for the dunking booth.

"Is there a problem?" Mrs. Sanchez sent him a worried look over the black rims of her reading glasses. "I have your name right here." She tapped her pen on the clipboard. "Please tell me you haven't changed your mind. Everyone is having so much fun over there, and I don't know if I can find a replacement in time."

He was about to explain there had been a mix-up, but then he realized this might very well be the ideal opportunity for him to show Piper that he could let go of his well-placed defenses. If she saw that he could let down his guard, maybe then she might give him another chance. What did he have to lose?

"I'll do it, but can you do me a favor?"

The woman's penciled brow lifted. "What do you have in mind?"

"Could you make sure Piper is near the dunking booth when I'm in there?"

The woman's eyes twinkled with delight. "I knew not to give up on you two. When people are right for each other, nothing can keep them apart. You can count on me. I love playing matchmaker."

That much he knew about Mrs. Sanchez. If it were up to her, she'd have the whole town married off by now. But she was doing her best, one couple at a time.

In this case, he just hoped it worked.

So close and yet so far away.

It seemed as though every time Piper turned around, there was Joe. At the race. At the bandstand.

At the high-striker game. Once or twice she'd thought she caught him staring at her and glanced away. But as soon as she looked back, he'd moved on. It must be part of her imagination. Surely he wasn't missing her, too. Was he?

Impossible. Because as close as he was, she'd never felt such a huge, gaping distance between them. The empty spot in her heart ached. If only there was a way to bridge the gap.

The one bright shining spot in all of it was the fact that Java was by his side, and they truly looked happy together. Was it wrong to be jealous of a dog? She sighed and gave herself a mental shake. Now she really was being melodramatic.

"Hey, sis."

Piper turned to find her younger sister, Katie, strolling up to her. She smiled, and as soon as her sister was next to her, she gave her a big hug. "You made it."

"You doubted that I would?" her sister asked innocently.

"You have to admit that you spend as little time in Whistle Stop as you can these days."

Katie shrugged innocently. "I'm just busy. You know how it is running a business."

"And how is the chocolate business? Have you found a new home for it?"

"Not yet, but I haven't given up." Katie glanced at her. "But enough about me. Wow, look at you. You are looking great."

"Thanks," Piper said proudly. "At last, I'm doing the weight-loss thing for me and not everyone else. I feel great, and I have so much more energy."

"You might have to share your secret."

"That's easy." Piper told her about her exercise routine and her low-carb diet. "Everybody is different. You just have to experiment until you find what works for you. But between you and me, I think you look great just the way you are."

"Aww...thanks. But, you know, now that our brother has officially announced that he's running for mayor, a girl must look her best in front of the cameras."

They both laughed, because this was, after all, Whistle Stop, not some big city. No one would pay them any more attention than they already did.

"I still can't believe he's going ahead with this plan." Piper was really worried that he was taking on too much at once. "I warned him that with his business and the upcoming wedding, it might be too much, but you know that he never pays attention to me. I'm just the nosy little sister."

"You might be right. I passed Bella on the way over here, and she didn't look happy. She was smiling, but it was one of those forced smiles. I sure hope Mason knows what he's doing."

"You and me both." Piper glanced around and decided she should check in on the cake auction. She was curious to see how many cakes were up for sale. "Why don't we head over to—"

"Piper! Yoo-hoo! Piper!" Mrs. Sanchez's voice filled the air.

Piper hesitated. She really didn't want to work today. After all of the planning and whatnot, it was time to enjoy the fruits of her labor. And, besides, it wasn't often that her little sister paid her a visit—definitely not often enough.

Knowing she couldn't be rude to the kindhearted woman who'd done so many generous things for her, she turned. "Hi, Mrs. Sanchez. Isn't the festival turning out to be a huge success?"

The woman's face was a bit rosy, and she fanned herself. "I've certainly been getting my share of exercise today. At this rate, I should have signed up for that fun walk this morning."

"Maybe you can next time."

Mrs. Sanchez nodded. "I thought you'd want to accompany me to check on the donations."

Piper glanced at her sister. "Want to join us?"

"Sure."

Together they moseyed over to the donation center where they collected and counted all of the proceeds. A big placard behind them displayed the total amount they needed to revitalize the town square and the train depot. On the placard was a thermometer that was updated hourly with the percent collected.

"Oh, look, we're closing in on fifty percent." Mrs. Sanchez beamed.

"And we still have hours to go before the festival winds down. I think we're going to make it."

"I do, too," Katie piped in.

"And they're just about to update it." Mrs. Sanchez walked over to speak with one of the festival volunteers.

Meanwhile, something, or rather someone, caught her eye. Joe. And he was in the dunking booth. Oh no! She'd forgotten to take his name off the list of volunteers. Talk about taking a bad situation and making it worse. He was really going to hate her after this.

"What has you so distracted?" Katie asked.

"Um, nothing." Piper glanced away, but she just had to have another look at Joe sitting there in the dunking booth with a smile on his face. Really?

"Must be something."

Piper blinked just to be sure she wasn't imagining the whole scene. But he was still there. How could that be? He'd been so opposed to the idea of the dunking tank. Was it possible Joe was changing?

And then he started heckling the ball thrower. "Oh, come on. Surely you can do better than that. My mother can do better than that."

"Who is that?" Katie asked.

Piper continued staring at the scene unfolding in front of her. "It's Joe."

"Not him. I remember him from the town meeting. The other guy. The one throwing the balls. I don't remember seeing him before."

With concerted effort, Piper moved her gaze away from Joe. "That's Joe's friend. His name's Holden Wainwright. He's new to the area."

"Oh."

There was something to that very short answer. Maybe Piper wasn't the only one with her eye on a guy. "Why, Katie, do I detect a note of interest in your voice?"

"What? Um...no. I'm too busy to get involved with anyone."

Her little sister moved in mysterious ways. Piper had a feeling she was keeping a big secret, and that's why she'd moved to the big city. But until Katie was ready to talk, there wasn't anything Piper could do to help. "Maybe Holden is just what I need to convince you to move back here."

"Don't even think about it. I can't move home." Katie turned away from Holden. "But you sure seem to be interested in Joe. You can hardly tear your eyes off him. Guess you two did a little more than plan this event together. A few late nights, huh?"

"You're imagining things."

"Really? Then how come every time you look away, he's staring at you?"

"Really?" Piper immediately turned back to the dunking booth, hoping to catch him staring. It didn't work. He was busy heckling the next paying patron.

Katie smiled and sent her an I-got-you look. "You've got it real bad."

It was true. And Piper had no clue what to do about it.

CHAPTER THIRTY

THE LATE AFTERNOON SUN gave the town square a warm golden glow.

Piper stood off to the side of the large crowd at the cake auction. Katie had left already, leaving Piper to meander about on her own. All the while, she continued to try to reconcile what Joe participating in the dunking booth had meant. It had been more than just doing his duty. He'd been smiling, laughing, and good-naturedly taunting the ball throwers, making the huge audience erupt in laughter. Had she been wrong about him? Was he capable of letting go and rolling with the punches?

Her mother's cake was auctioned off, and it sold for the highest price so far. Piper got a smile out of how her mother beamed, as though she'd actually cracked the eggs and mixed the batter herself. For her mother, it was all about appearance. Piper doubted she'd ever change. Now if only her mother would accept her as she was.

Mrs. Sanchez was in charge of the auction. She was great at twisting people's arms so they'd pay more than they'd intended. Now, she held up a pitiful lopsided chocolate cake. "And this was donated by Whistle Stop's newest eligible bachelor, Joe Montoya.

Did you hear that, all of you single ladies? Here's a hot guy who is good with his hands." She winked at Joe. "Oh, and he bakes, too."

Piper's body tensed as the single, beautiful women turned interested glances his way. She knew without a doubt that he'd be walking away from this auction with nothing less than a handful of phone numbers, but more than likely he'd have some beauty on his arm. Something stirred in the pit of her stomach. The more she thought of him with his arm around someone else, the more the uneasiness stirred.

Mrs. Sanchez continued to work up the crowd. "Come on, ladies, let's show Joe our appreciation for going out of his way to help the auction with this amazing cake."

Hoots and hollers erupted in the crowd.

"She might not be saying that if she tasted it," Joe whispered in Piper's ear.

She nearly jumped out of her skin. While she'd been checking out the competition, he'd moved to stand next to her. Piper searched for a response, but her mind was buzzing with a million thoughts at once, the main question being: What was he doing standing with her?

She swallowed hard. "I...I'm sure it's good."

"Don't tell anyone, but it's out of a box."

Something wet pressed to Piper's hand. She immediately glanced down, finding the chocolate Lab sitting next to Joe.

"Well, hello." She knelt down to pet Java. "You look very happy."

"He ought to be. I think he's about to eat me out of house and home. Luckily, Mrs. Sanchez doesn't mind a four-legged houseguest."

"She's always so generous."

Joe patted the dog's head. "I suppose you're going to want Java back when the festival is over."

"I don't know about that. Looks like you two were meant to be together."

Joe asked the dog if he wanted to stay with him, and the dog barked before licking his hand.

"Guess that's your answer." Piper smiled, knowing that Java would have a wonderful home with Joe. She glanced back at the podium. "I think the bidding on your cake has started."

Piper was truly impressed that he'd taken the time to bake a cake. She couldn't help herself. She placed a bid. In the very next breath, some blonde outbid her, followed by some other eager young ladies.

Not about to be outdone, Piper raised her hand to bid again, but Joe pulled her hand down as the bidding ensued between three very eager women.

When Piper frowned at him, he said, "Let them have the cake. It's probably not very good anyway. However, if you're in the market for a very foolish man who's madly in love with you, I hear he can be bought at a very reasonable price."

Her heart leaped into her throat. Her gaze searched his eyes, looking for the truth. "What...what are you saying?"

"I'm saying if you'd like to bid on this novice baker, I can be had for a good price." His eyes twinkled with amusement. He was flirting with her.

She swallowed hard, searching for the appropriate response. "Really? And how much is this novice baker?"

"Hmm...let's see. Why don't we start with a couple of kisses and see where things go from there? But first, there's something I'd like to propose."

Oh no. The smile slipped from her face. "What would that be?"

"Well, you know how I'm rebuilding the coffee shop?" When she nodded, he continued. "I was wondering how you'd feel about putting in a connecting door linking your bakery with my coffee shop."

"Really?"

He nodded. "I thought it'd make things so much easier for us to go back and forth."

Her heart raced. "And...and why would we do that?"

He turned to her and pulled her close. "Because if you hadn't noticed, I'm absolutely crazy about you. I know I didn't handle things well, but I love you."

Happy tears welled up in her eyes. "I love you, too."

His head dipped as he caught her lips with his. Being in his arms was like coming home. Nothing had ever felt so right.

Applause jarred them out of their little world.

He whispered in her ear, "How about we take this someplace more private?"

"Not yet."

Joe frowned at her. "What else could be more important? After all, the festival is a smashing success. They don't need us any longer."

"You're forgetting something important."

"Nothing could be more important than this." He leaned forward and kissed her again.

She pressed a hand to his firm chest. "As good as that is, and it is very good indeed, there's something else more pressing."

Joe shrugged. "Well, I have no idea what you're talking about."

"The hot air balloon. You promised me a ride."

At last, he smiled again. "And so I did." He held his hand out to her. "One hot air balloon ride coming up. And then can we do more of the kissing and stuff?"

She smiled and shook her head. "Don't worry, there will be plenty of time for more kissing and stuff."

"Oh good."

They'd started toward the balloon when her mother stepped in their way. "Piper, you did an excellent job with the festival. Everyone is very impressed."

"Thank you, Mom. But I couldn't have done it without Joe."

Her mother turned to him. "Thank you, too." Just as quickly, she turned back to Piper. "And you look fantastic. I'm so glad those supplements are helping you lose weight. See? You should have listened to me sooner."

There was no way Piper was going to stand by and let her mother take credit for the hard work she'd put into getting fit. "Mom, I lost the weight in spite of you, not because of you. So going forward, any discussion about my weight is off-limits. Oh, and one more thing. You might want to be nicer to Joe since he's going to be a permanent part of my life."

Her mother gaped at them as Piper took Joe's hand and started to walk away. But Joe didn't budge. When she turned back, he was still staring at her mother.

"You should also know that I would love your daughter no matter what she weighs. She's beautiful inside and out. You'd see that if you weren't so worried about appearances. Your daughter is very special just the way she is. And I'm honored she wants to share her life with me."

Piper couldn't believe she'd almost let the man of her dreams get away.

She'd never ever make that mistake again.

Return to Whistle Stop with **A Moment on Cherish** as business owner Bella Nez and mayoral candidate Mason Noble strike a deal that will change their lives forever. You can learn more here:

https://www.jenniferfaye.com/books/a-moment-to-cherish/

Afterword

Thanks so much for reading Piper and Joe's story. I hope their journey made your heart smile. If you did enjoy the book, please consider…
- Help spreading the word about A Moment on the Lips by writing a review.
- Subscribe to my newsletter in order to receive information about my next release as well as find out about giveaways and special sales.
- You can like my author page on Facebook or follow me on Twitter.

I hope you'll visit Whistle Stop again and continue reading adventures of its residents. Coming next is Bella and Mason's story in A Moment to Cherish.

Thanks again for your support! It is HUGELY appreciated.
Happy reading,
Jennifer

About Author

Award-winning author, Jennifer Faye pens fun, heartwarming contemporary romances with rugged cowboys, sexy billionaires and enchanting royalty. With more than a million books sold, she is internationally published with books translated into more than a dozen languages. She is a two-time winner of the RT Book Reviews Reviewers' Choice Award, the CataRomance Reviewers' Choice Award, named a TOP PICK author, and been nominated for numerous other awards.

Now living her dream, she resides with her very patient husband and two spoiled cats. When she's not plotting out her next romance, you can find her curled up with a mug of tea and a book. You can learn more about Jennifer at www.JenniferFaye.com

Subscribe to Jennifer's newsletter for news about upcoming releases, bonus content and other special offers.

You can also join her on Twitter, Facebook, or Goodreads.

Also By

Other titles available by Jennifer Faye include:

THE BELL FAMILY OF BLUESTAR ISLAND:

Love Blooms

Harvest Dance

A Lighthouse Café Christmas

Rising Star

Summer by the Beach
Brass Anchor Inn

SEABREEZE WEDDING CHAPEL:

The Bride's Dream Wedding

The Bride's Pink Shoes
The Bride's Christmas Dress

WHISTLE STOP ROMANCE SERIES:

A Moment to Love

A Moment to Dance

A Moment on the Lips

A Moment to Cherish

A Moment at Christmas

TANGLED CHARMS:

Sprinkled with Love

A Mistletoe Kiss

GREEK PARADISE ESCAPE:

Greek Heir to Claim Her Heart

It Started with a Royal Kiss

Second Chance with the Bridesmaid

WEDDING BELLS IN LAKE COMO:

Bound by a Ring & a Secret

Falling for Her Convenient Groom

ONCE UPON A FAIRYTALE:

Beauty & Her Boss

Miss White & the Seventh Heir

Fairytale Christmas with the Millionaire

THE BARTOLINI LEGACY:

The Prince and the Wedding Planner

The CEO, the Puppy & Me

The Italian's Unexpected Heir

GREEK ISLAND BRIDES:

Carrying the Greek Tycoon's Baby

Claiming the Drakos Heir

Wearing the Greek Millionaire's Ring

Click here to find all of Jennifer's titles and buy links.

Made in United States
Troutdale, OR
04/17/2024

19240435R00179